EARLY MORNING MURDER

"Felix," Daisy called after the dog. He *never* did this. He usually waited for her or Jonas and followed commands. He never ran off.

Today was obviously different.

She called for him again, but he was on a mission. Daisy didn't like that idea at all. Hopefully he'd spotted a rabbit or a squirrel. Hopefully he'd spotted—

Felix had stopped about twenty yards ahead of Daisy. She saw something on the single-vehicle fire road. The splash of color was red. Felix whined, hunkered down, his paws stretched out in front of him. He barked several times before Daisy reached him.

When she did, she gasped and fell to her knees. Lydia was sprawled there . . . her red pom-pom hat on the stones a few feet away . . .

Books by Karen Rose Smith

Caprice De Luca Mysteries
STAGED TO DEATH
DEADLY DÉCOR
GILT BY ASSOCIATION
DRAPE EXPECTATIONS
SILENCE OF THE LAMPS
SHADES OF WRATH
SLAY BELLS RING
CUT TO THE CHAISE

Daisy's Tea Garden Mysteries
MURDER WITH LEMON TEA CAKES
MURDER WITH CINAMMON SCONES
MURDER WITH CUCUMBER SANDWICHES
MURDER WITH CHERRY TARTS
MURDER WITH CLOTTED CREAM
MURDER WITH OOLONG TEA
MURDER WITH ORANGE PEKOE TEA
MURDER WITH DARJEELING TEA
MURDER WITH EARL GREY TEA

Published by Kensington Publishing Corp.

Murder with Earl Grey Tea

KAREN ROSE SMITH

Kensington Publishing Corp.
www.kensingtonbooks.com

KENSINGTON BOOKS are published by

Kensington Publishing Corp.
119 West 40th Street
New York, NY 10018

All Kensington titles, imprints, and distributed lines are available at special quantity discounts for bulk purchases for sales promotion, premiums, fund-raising, educational, or institutional use.

Special book excerpts or customized printings can also be created to fit specific needs. For details, write or phone the office of the Kensington Sales Manager: Attn.: Sales Department. Kensington Publishing Corp., 119 West 40th Street, New York, NY 10018. Phone: 1-800-221-2647.

The K and Teapot logo is a trademark of Kensington Publishing Corp.

First Printing: June 2023
ISBN: 978-1-4967-3846-2

ISBN: 978-1-4967-3847-9 (ebook)

10 9 8 7 6 5 4 3 2 1

Printed in the United States of America

To all sisters . . . and friends who are like sisters.

ACKNOWLEDGMENTS

I would like to thank Officer Greg Berry, my law enforcement consultant, who so patiently answers all my questions. His input is invaluable.

CHAPTER ONE

"**D**o you want your mom and dad to be surprised?"

Daisy Swanson glanced at her Aunt Iris and her mischievous expression. Her aunt's short, ash-brown curls practically bounced around her face with her enthusiasm for planning an anniversary dinner for Daisy's mom and dad.

"You know Mom doesn't like last-minute surprises," Daisy reminded her aunt, who had been a cherished confidante since her childhood.

Lydia Aldenkamp, manager of The Farm Barn, where Daisy and her aunt were planning the dinner, glanced at her notes with the menu they'd developed. She suggested, "I can easily print out the menu with The Farm Barn logo, the date, and the time. Then you can present it to Rose and Sean a few days before. It would be more of a present than an unexpected surprise."

"That's a fine idea," Iris agreed. "Rose shouldn't be too bent out of shape by that. And at that stage, she can't control the plans we've made."

Daisy pushed her blond shoulder-length hair away from her face as she smiled and swiveled her attention back to her aunt. Her Aunt Iris and her mom got along like many sisters—they were sometimes at odds and sometimes on the same page.

"I think Mom and Dad will be pleased," Daisy agreed. "This time of the year when winter business is slow, the garden center isn't open on a Sunday."

"I love Gallagher's Garden Corner," Lydia said with sincerity in her voice. "Your parents always give us the perfect landscaping advice. I'm pleased to plan this dinner for them."

Daisy studied Lydia as she expressed her appreciation for Daisy's parents. The woman's Amish upbringing often flavored the way she dressed and presented herself. On this Pennsylvania February day, she'd worn a high-neck blue gingham blouse with a navy skirt. She also wore her burnished brown hair in a bun as she would have under a *kapp*, a required head covering for plain women. Lydia had left her Amish community behind during her *rumspringa*—the teenage running-around period after which Amish youth decided if they would commit to their faith.

Now Lydia closed her notebook and focused on Daisy's hand on the table. She pointed to Daisy's ring finger. "Every time I see your engagement ring, I think about how Jonas chose the perfect one for you. I do love antique settings."

The ring was vintage with old European cut diamonds set in platinum. However, what had drawn Jonas to the ring for Daisy were the two sapphires, one on either side of the center round diamond. He said those sapphires were the color of Daisy's eyes.

While Daisy remembered how romantic Jonas's compliment had been, Lydia's gaze quickly swerved to the gold band on her own finger. "When Neil asked me to marry him, and I left my home, we didn't even consider an engagement. We just got married."

Daisy and Lydia had been friends since last fall, when Daisy had planned a surprise birthday party at The Farm Barn for the man she'd been seriously dating, Jonas Groft. The Farm Barn was a farm-to-table restaurant and reception venue that had been perfect for the celebration. For the past few months, she and Lydia had taken early morning hikes on the restaurant's property. Lydia had revealed to Daisy that she'd left her childhood home at nineteen to marry Neil Aldenkamp, an *Englischer*. They'd now been married for fifteen years. Lydia had also confided that after several miscarriages, she'd finally carried her baby to term. Little Frannie was now three and absolutely adorable.

Lydia said with a sigh, "You and Jonas have taken your time joining your lives. Sometimes I wish Neil and I had done that."

Daisy, Lydia, and Iris were sitting at a table to the rear of The Farm Barn's kitchen near the walk-in refrigerator and freezer. Suddenly the back door to the kitchen swung open, and a woman about Lydia's age, who resembled her so perfectly that a stranger could hardly tell them apart, rushed inside. She looked harried.

For a moment, Daisy wondered if Lydia's twin sister Leah had come to pick up Frannie so Lydia could continue with managerial plans of the restaurant for the rest of the day. However, Daisy recalled that earlier, Lydia had mentioned that her husband Neil had driven Frannie to preschool.

On one of their many hikes, Lydia had told Daisy that she and Leah had stayed connected over the years in spite of leaving her Amish life. Daisy surmised that their twinship was a huge factor in that connection. Lydia wasn't officially shunned by her district because she hadn't been baptized into the Amish faith before she left. Still, her parents *had* shunned her. That had to hurt immensely.

Leah was dressed in a royal blue Amish dress with a black apron. Her *kapp* was set on brown hair, a little lighter than Lydia's. She'd looked upset when she'd come in, but now she tried to smile at Iris and Daisy.

Lydia stood and crossed to Leah. In a low voice, she said, "I can't talk right now. I have an appointment."

Nevertheless, whatever Leah wanted to talk about seemed more important than Daisy's and Iris's consultation with Lydia. Leah motioned to the door, as if asking if they could go outside. There was definitely tension between the two women.

Lydia turned back to Iris and Daisy. "I'm sorry. I need to speak to my sister. I'll only be a few minutes."

"Do you want my coat?" Daisy asked, offering her the fleece cat-patterned jacket that hung on the back of her chair. "It's only thirty-two degrees out there." February in Pennsylvania was usually cold, below freezing at night.

Lydia shook her head. "This won't take long. I know what Leah wants."

After Lydia stepped outside, Iris noted, "Leah didn't have a coat on, either, and she probably traveled here in her horse and buggy."

Daisy considered her friend Rachel Fisher's buggy. "Some of the buggies do have gas heaters, and there's usually a blanket. Maybe Leah wrapped a blanket around herself while she drove."

"I wonder if this is an emergency," Iris mused. "She seemed upset."

Glancing toward the closed kitchen door, Daisy said, "I don't know much about Leah. I do know she and Titus Yoder have a working farm. They've tried to have children but no luck yet. Lydia feels for her and understands what she's going through. Their discussions could be about business. The Farm Barn buys produce and eggs from the Yoder farm. But Neil also purchases eggs from their chicken supplier. I don't think Leah can provide enough of them."

Iris thought about the situation and decided, "It has to be hard for the two of them. I've read about how close twins can be. With one dedicated to the Amish faith and the other part of the English world, just how connected can they stay?"

That was a question to consider. Daisy's family was so crucial to the way she looked at life. She depended on them and would do anything for them. "It's hard to believe Lydia's parents haven't spoken to her since she left the community. I could never do that to a member of my family, let alone a child."

Iris was nodding before Daisy finished her thought. "I feel the same way, but the restrictions of Amish faith make the situation what it is, I suppose."

The back door to the kitchen swooshed open again. Lydia was half in and half out, with her sister pulling on her arm.

"We have to talk about this more," Leah pleaded.

"There's no point, Sister." Lydia's voice was firm. "Now go home. Neil will bring Frannie to you after preschool. She will cheer you up, ya?"

Leah seemed to respond with a weak, teary smile. She let go of her sister's arm and stepped away from the door.

Lydia closed it, returned to the table, blew out a breath, and sank into the folding chair. She murmured, "Mixing business with family connections always creates problems."

She didn't go on, and Daisy didn't know what her friend meant.

Lydia didn't explain, but returned to the details of Daisy's parents' anniversary dinner, as if they hadn't been interrupted.

After Daisy and Iris parked in the back lot behind Daisy's Tea Garden and entered through the Victorian's rear door, Daisy immediately saw that their kitchen bustled with activity. Tessa Miller, Daisy's best friend and kitchen manager, was slipping a tray of cinnamon scones into the oven. Eva Conner, Daisy's girl Friday, was brewing Earl Grey tea, which was the special for the month.

"Many customers this morning?" Iris asked as she unzipped her down puffer coat. "There were a few snowflakes out there, so it's probably going to be slow."

Tessa and Eva exchanged a glance, and Daisy wondered what that was about. She soon found out.

"Foster was serving two interesting customers," Eva said, with an impish smile.

"There are a few others," Tessa told them, "but those two . . ." She shook her head and tried to suppress a grin.

Foster Cranshaw was Daisy's son-in-law and proficient in his duties at the tea garden.

"I'll check," Daisy said, "as soon as I hang my coat in my office and wash up."

Eva let out a small giggle. "I think Iris is going to want to visit these two. They're at separate tables."

Now Daisy suspected she and Iris both had their curiosity piqued. They went to the hall and peered into the tearoom.

Marshall Thompson, a lawyer who had helped Daisy in more than one of the murder investigations she'd become involved with, sat at a table for two near the front window of the main tearoom. He had an office a few streets north of downtown on Cherry Tree Road. He could walk to the tea garden and often did. He cut an impressive figure, at six feet two with thick snow-white hair, and was wearing a blue pinstriped suit with a crisp white shirt and navy striped tie. Since fall, he'd invited Daisy's Aunt Iris to accompany him to plays at Willow Creek's Little Theater and to expensive restaurants in York and Lancaster. He didn't look happy at the present moment, though, as he took a forkful of a cherry tart and glared at the man two tables away. Marshall continued to glower as he set down his fork, picked up his teacup, and took a sip of tea. Daisy knew Earl Grey was one of his favorites.

Foster was standing beside the table where the focus of Marshall's concentration sat. Detective Morris Rappaport took a bite of what Daisy suspected was an apple muffin. He'd lost about twenty pounds since he'd started a healthier diet and bought a fitness tracker to count his steps.

The detective was in his late fifties. The lines on his face spoke of a difficult profession and years of being on the front lines of law enforcement. He had blond-gray hair and often used reading glasses. The tea at his place setting was iced. It had taken a while for Daisy to convince him to try any tea at all. He was the type of man who didn't particularly want to drink from a teacup. This morning, he looked spiffier than usual, with a brown wool sports jacket, tan slacks, and a cream oxford shirt, no tie. Unlike Marshall, he didn't often make plans ahead of time with her aunt. He would stop in at the end of a day and ask if Iris wanted to go to dinner at Sarah Jane's, the town diner. He'd invited her to bowl with him, too, and they'd seemed to have fun.

Iris whispered into Daisy's ear, "I'd better shed my coat and get out there."

Tamlyn Pittenger, a full-time employee, was at the sales counter, and Foster seemed to have service under control.

Daisy produced a hair tie from her coat pocket. She kept them here, there, and everywhere in case she needed to pull her shoulder-length blond hair into a ponytail.

"I'll wash up and start the potato and leek soup," she said to her aunt. "I think our lunchtime customers will appreciate it on a cold day like this. You take your time with Morris and Marshall and do what you have to do to keep peace."

To Daisy's dismay, Iris looked more upset than happy that she had two suitors sitting in their tearoom. Willow Creek was a semi-busy tourist town set in the midst of Amish country near Lancaster, Pennsylvania. Daisy and her aunt owned and managed Daisy's Tea Garden together. Their guests, or customers, often knew each other, gossiped about town functions, and chatted about their personal lives. It was normally a happy, nonconfrontational, cozy spot to have tea, baked goods, soups, and salads.

Before Daisy and Iris had bought the Victorian, a bakery had existed on the first floor. They'd renovated and rented the upstairs to Tessa. When they'd established Daisy's Tea Garden, they'd considered the fact that they wanted men to feel comfortable here as well as women. They had wanted to draw from professional offices in Willow Creek and Lancaster, too. The main tearoom, where customers could be served or buy goodies and go, was arranged with oak glass-topped tables and mismatched antique oak chairs. A yellow bud vase adorned each table and, in the winter, Daisy kept them supplied with dried herbs. The walls in the room where Morris and Marshall were seated had been painted the palest green to promote calm. Daisy didn't feel the room was promoting much calm between these two men today. She guessed one should have been seated where he was, and the other man should have been offered a table in the more private spillover tearoom. On specified days, she and Iris scheduled reservations there for afternoon tea, which included multiple courses.

As Daisy considered it now, she realized that the spillover space reflected unique qualities of the Victorian because of its bay window, window seat, crown molding, and diamond-cut glass. That room had walls of the palest yellow. The tables were white, and the chairs wore seat cushions in blue, green, and yellow pinstripes. But even that pleasant atmosphere might not have helped the present two disgruntled suitors' situation.

Iris straightened her shoulders and started to remove her jacket. "Maybe they'll finish eating and leave quickly."

"That's not the purpose of the tea garden," Daisy teased.

"Our tea and treats aren't going to calm those two. Morris always asks me when I've been out with Marshall."

"Does Marshall ask about Morris?" Daisy questioned.

"Sometimes," Iris said.

They walked to her office to hang up their coats and don their aprons. Daisy's women servers wore yellow aprons with the daisy emblem for Daisy's Tea Garden stamped on the front. Foster wore black slacks with a white oxford shirt.

After preparing for their morning tea garden duties, Iris headed for the tearoom and Daisy for the kitchen. When Tessa saw her, she gave her a bright smile and motioned to the peeled potatoes in the colander. "All ready for you."

Tessa was around Daisy's age. Today she wore her caramel-colored hair in a braid. In her spare time, she painted, and her kitchen wardrobe reflected her artistic streak. She liked to wear colorful smocks in lieu of the usual chef's coat. This morning, she wore a turquoise smock with little white snowflakes dancing all over it.

"I'm baking corn cake today," Tessa said. "I thought it would go well with the soup."

Daisy had devised a recipe unlike the usual cornbread. She used kernel corn in a light cake batter. It had been popular this winter with her soups.

"I soaked the leeks," Eva said. "They're all ready for you." Eva had celebrated her forty-eighth birthday. Sometimes she was the backbone of the kitchen, making sure the teapots were washed, the china sparkling clean, and ingredients measured and prepared for when Tessa, Iris, or Daisy needed them.

"Do you think we should have a talk with Iris when she finishes with those two in there?" Eva asked, concerned.

Tessa shrugged. "You mean like an intervention?"

"Those two men want the same thing," Eva reminded them. "They want Iris's undivided attention."

Daisy crossed to the walk-in, found the leeks, and pulled out the plastic container. She carried it to the counter where the potatoes were waiting.

"Iris has been juggling them both pretty well up until now."

Eva had prepared all of the ingredients for the soup, so it was easy for Daisy to gather them, then add salt and pepper. She'd keep tasting the soup to make sure it was up to her standards. By the time the lunch crowd arrived, it would have been simmering for a while, mixing the flavors into a delicious blend.

Daisy had just finished washing up when Iris returned to the kitchen.

"You look a tad frazzled," Tessa noted honestly, never one to hold back.

"One wouldn't leave before the other." Exasperation was evident in Iris's voice. "It's ridiculous. They both asked me out for this weekend, Morris on Saturday and Marshall on Sunday."

"Did you accept their invitations?" Eva asked.

"No," Iris said with a bit of vehemence. "I need to think about this. I need to think about them both."

"Wise move," Tessa said. "You have to make a decision soon."

"Maybe you should make a pros and cons list," Eva suggested. "Two columns, one for Morris and one for Marshall. Wouldn't that make sense?"

Iris rubbed her hand across her forehead, ruffling her bangs. "I suppose it might. But then there are those indefinable qualities that each of them has that you can't put down on paper. Morris's sense of right and wrong is absolute. He has courage, but he hasn't opened up much about his past and why he came to Willow Creek."

Daisy assembled ingredients to make corn

chowder while Iris talked. "Has Marshall spoken to you about his past?"

"Some. I know how much he loves his niece. I know after his wife died, he missed her terribly. Morris has a lot more question marks than Marshall does."

"You might not have an answer after this weekend," Tessa advised her. "But remember, rejection doesn't come easy to men. Once you make a decision, you might have lost the other one. So don't rush just because you want the situation resolved."

Daisy thought that was mighty good advice.

Daisy sat on the sofa with Jonas that evening in her home, a building that had been renovated from an old barn. He'd moved in with her shortly after they'd gotten engaged. Earlier this evening, Jonas had laid a fire in the floor-to-ceiling stone fireplace that was a focal point on the east wall in the dining area.

Pulling her bare feet from the braided blue and rust rug that had been woven by a local Amish woman, Daisy tucked them under her on the upholstered couch. Marjoram, her tortoiseshell feline with unmistakably unique markings—one side of her face was mottled like a tortoiseshell in tan, brown, and black, and the other side was completely dark brown—sat on the back of the sofa. Pepper, her black tuxedo cat, was tucked next to Jonas's leg on the sofa cushion, her head on her paws. Felix, the cream English golden retriever Jonas had adopted, lay along the coffee table, his liquid brown eyes focusing on them every once in a while, as if he were listening to their conversation. Daisy had been relating to Jonas what had happened with Iris at the tea garden.

"It was funny in a way," she said with a smile. "But Iris is torn, and I feel sorry for Morris and for Marshall."

"You can relate because you had to decide whether to date me or Cade Bankert?" Jonas asked with a playfulness in his expression.

She loved looking at Jonas . . . as well as loving him. He was in his early forties. A few strands of silver laced his thick black hair at his temples. A scar down the side of his cheek reminded her of his former profession as a Philadelphia police detective. His green eyes right now danced with teasing humor as he mentioned the man he'd once considered a rival.

"There wasn't any contest," Daisy said as she rested her head on his shoulder. "I just kept my attraction to you, both emotional and physical, under wraps, and I think you did the same with me."

"We lost time," Jonas added regretfully.

"But we have time now," she said lightly, her hand on his chest where she could feel the beat of his heart. Valentine's Day was next week, and she was looking forward to it this year in a way she hadn't for years.

Jonas leaned down and kissed her, the kind of kiss that spoke of dreams together.

After they'd pulled apart again and were staring into the fire, Daisy said, "I hope everything goes smoothly for Mom and Dad's dinner at The Farm Barn. Lydia was helpful this morning." She told Jonas about Lydia's idea for the invitation for her parents.

"That's a great idea. Your mom and dad will have time to prepare themselves and to look forward to it. Anticipation is part of the fun."

Thinking about her meeting at the venue this morning, she wondered again about Leah and Lydia's relationship.

"What's troubling you?" Jonas asked, brushing her hair away from her face.

He could read her so well. Sometimes he could read her so completely that his ability was uncanny. "After Leah visited Lydia this morning, Lydia seemed distracted. They didn't exactly argue, but something was upsetting both of them."

"At Woods I hear a different type of gossip than you hear at the tea garden."

Jonas's furniture store, Woods, attracted tourists as well as local folks. Everything in it was handcrafted. Some pieces Jonas made himself, and others were fashioned by local craftsmen in the area and sold on consignment.

"What sort of gossip have you heard?" Daisy asked.

"It's rumored that Leah and Titus Yoder are having hard times. There's a lot of talk about crops and cattle when men gather in my store. Titus's crop did poorly last year, and the price of beef has fallen."

"I suppose Leah and Lydia might have been talking about that. Lydia certainly can't buy enough produce and eggs to help make the Yoder farm profitable. If the Yoders' farm goes under, what will they do? Move home with their parents, either Leah's or Titus's? Maybe they could start over. They're still young enough for that."

"Starting over is never easy," Jonas pointed out.

Daisy understood Jonas's comment came from experience.

"When I first arrived in Willow Creek, I leased the space for my shop," Jonas explained. "I didn't know if I was going to succeed or if everything in my life was going to fall apart. Going from detective to shop owner was a change of seismic proportions. Yet I knew I had to give it time to work, throwing my attention into building furniture. Reaching out for local contacts and networking allowed me to set some stress aside."

Daisy took hold of Jonas's hand and studied their entwined fingers. Her ring sparkled in the light of the side table lamp. "Lydia admired my ring today. I really do love it," she told him for about the millionth time since he'd given it to her.

"Are you ready to set a wedding date? I'd marry you tomorrow if you want to elope. But I know you'd like a wedding with family and friends all around us, and I want that, too."

She was sure of her answer now. "I'm ready to set the date. Vi and Foster will be moving out of the garage apartment soon. I'd like them to get settled and start enjoying their new surroundings. Still, I'd like to get married before Jazzi leaves in August. I want Jazzi to have time to bond with us over wedding preparations through spring. That will distract us all from her leaving for college at the end of summer."

"We can check dates with your family and see what we can come up with that suits everybody, including your sister Camellia. I know you want her there."

Although Daisy and her sister didn't always see

eye to eye, yes, she did want Cammie at her wedding to Jonas. She and Jonas didn't know what their life together would look like yet, not exactly. Yet as she gazed into his eyes, she saw the excitement that she was feeling, too. That excitement was a wonderful way to start their new lives together.

CHAPTER TWO

"How about taking a hike with me tomorrow?" Lydia asked when Daisy had taken her call on Sunday night. "The temp is supposed to be forty in the morning."

Daisy had known The Farm Barn was closed on Mondays. "What time would you like to go?" she'd asked.

"How about seven a.m.? Neil said he'd make Frannie breakfast when she gets up and then take her to preschool."

"I'll call one of my servers and see if they want extra hours tomorrow morning. I'll text you if it's okay."

"Sounds good," Lydia had agreed with a lilt in her voice.

Daisy knew Lydia hiked more than she did. The Farm Barn's property covered about three acres, including trails through groves of white pines, a rolling landscape that led into woods heavy with maple and oak trees that backed up to the property. Seven a.m. was usually the time Lydia went out for a hike, no matter what the weather. Daisy preferred not having her toes, fingers, and nose turn numb, but Lydia didn't seem to mind.

On Monday morning, Daisy met Lydia in the parking lot at The Farm Barn. When she'd texted Lydia that the time would be fine, Lydia had said to bring Felix, and he could have a run while they walked.

Felix scrambled down from the back seat of the Journey that Daisy had bought last fall when her PT Cruiser had been in an accident. She liked this vehicle with its digitally updated features compared to the PT Cruiser she'd driven before. Felix jumped out when she opened the passenger side door, circled the vehicle, and then waited for a command from her.

Lydia waved from the back door of The Farm Barn.

Daisy had dressed for the cold this morning with a three-quarter-length yellow down jacket and cranberry scarf tied around her neck with fringes that brushed the jacket's hem. She'd even added a hat under her hood. Lydia was dressed similarly. Her jacket was red and shorter, and her hat with a red pom-pom on top matched it. She looked like a cardinal against the green of the pines behind her.

Lydia raised a hand to beckon to her.

Felix looked up at Daisy, his big brown eyes asking if he should go to Lydia.

Daisy nodded, and he ran to her friend to say hello. After greetings, Lydia looked contemplative as they started off. Noticing the blue circles under her friend's eyes belying the cheerfulness of her red outfit, Daisy wondered if something had kept her awake last night.

"Did you have any trouble getting a server for this morning?" Lydia asked.

"No, I didn't. Tamlyn wanted extra hours. She's always willing to work more. Before she came to the tea garden, she was a round-the-clock house-keeper, pretty much on call whenever she wasn't working explicit hours."

"So I imagine working at the tea garden is a re-lief for her. I know it's hard to get good servers. I have trouble keeping them. They move on to something else where they think they can make a better income or grow with the establishment."

Daisy's breath puffed in front of her as she hiked, keeping pace with Lydia. "There's not much room for growth at the tea garden. I had one server leave to go to nursing school. My full-time kitchen girl Friday is taking online classes now. She might leave eventually, and she'll be hard to replace. And then there's Foster. When he graduates this spring, I'm not sure what he'll do. He'll be hard to re-place, too. My servers have to have a rapport with the public and be able to converse with almost any-body. Some of my customers become quite chatty, and they feel they know everybody at the tea gar-den. That means they intend to find out all about my employees' personal business."

"Our customers pretty much just want to con-centrate on the food, and whoever joins them for dinner."

Felix jauntily trotted alongside Daisy, snuffling as he went. Every once in a while, he'd dart to a nearby cedar or maple. Most of the time, though, he stayed beside Daisy.

Lydia pumped her arms as she walked. "Did Jonas spend a lot of time training Felix? He's so good with you, and he takes commands so easily."

"No, Jonas didn't have to train him. His previous owner's son had done that for her."

"You said she's in an assisted-living facility now?"

"Yes, at Whispering Willows. We take Felix to visit her every once in a while. He still misses her, though I think he's happy with us. After our hike, I'll drop him at the store with Jonas before I head to the tea garden. He has company all the time there."

The ground was hard. As they usually did when they hiked, Lydia led Daisy and Felix to a gravel road. It was narrow enough for one vehicle but perfect for them to hike. Now and then their boots dipped into potholes or they scrambled over rocks that had washed onto the rustic road. At some points, the grasses were high on either side and the path was almost hidden. Daisy knew it wound into the woods behind the property where they were headed.

As the sun shone down on them, the scent of pines to their right grew stronger. Bare branches waved in the breeze. Cold nipped Daisy's nose, and she tucked her chin into the circle of her scarf.

They had grown silent for a few yards when Daisy asked Lydia, "What do you think about when you hike?"

"I try to leave all my thoughts behind at The Farm Barn," Lydia answered with a chuckle.

"But you don't," Daisy guessed.

After a sideways glance, Lydia responded, "I know you said when you bike instead of hike, you can let all your thoughts kind of blow away from your head. But when I hike, it's like they come into vital focus. I don't solve any problems, but sometimes I can see what I should do next. Hiking can be a form of meditation for me. Do you know what I mean?"

"I do, especially when you do it alone."

Lydia glanced at Felix. "Sometimes I wish I had a dog to accompany me. You know, somebody silent who just wants to be with me? If I want to talk, they would listen. If I want to run, they would run beside me."

"You want a partner."

"You make it sound like a marriage," Lydia said, amusement in her voice.

"I guess any good relationship has that commitment, and some mind-reading tendencies. Sometimes I can't believe how well Jonas knows me."

"That's good, right?" Lydia asked.

"I suppose it is," Daisy said with a smile. "And it's not as if I want to hide my thoughts from him. But sometimes I do like them to be private."

They trudged up a hill, and they were both breathing harder. Lydia shook her finger at Daisy. "Privacy is hard to come by in a marriage. Now that Jonas is living with you, isn't your relationship different?"

"It is . . . with deeper intimacy and more bonds. Even between Jonas and Jazzi, I can tell a difference. They're like father and daughter now. It's nice to see." As a widow, Daisy had empathized with both of her daughters as they'd missed their dad. Although Jazzi had been adopted, she'd been close to him, too.

"Neil is so good with Frannie. That's why—" Lydia abruptly stopped. "Never mind," she said. "I'm not used to someone listening so well. I might spill all my secrets."

Daisy wanted to ask—*What secrets are those?* But she didn't. She could, however, listen to whatever Lydia wanted to tell her. "Leah seemed upset when we met with you. Is everything okay?"

"You have a sister," Lydia pointed out. "So I imagine you know how it is."

"Yes, I know we can be at odds. I imagine your situation is more complicated."

"Leah and I were so close when we were children, as close as twins could be. We both rebelled at times against what our parents wanted, or against what our parents thought we should do. Leah was always more passive about that. I think she felt the same things as I did, but she never vocalized them. She followed restrictions and orders much better than I could. During our *rumspringa*, things really changed between us. She didn't explore much. We started having different friends. She didn't want to have English friends. I did. That's what *rumspringa* is about, to find out what's in the world. She didn't want to find out what was in the world. She just wanted her world to be what she wanted it to be, which was Amish, but with some modifications. I wanted to break out of all the rules, though not in a bad way like with alcohol and drugs. Some kids we knew did that during *rumspringa*. But I met Neil."

Daisy understood the importance of that meeting before Lydia continued with, "Everything changed for me after that. Neil was my focus. I woke up each day wanting to see him. I didn't care about going to a singing and having some Amish boy ask me to go home with him afterwards in his buggy. I wanted Neil to take me to the ice cream drive-in in his car. I wanted to walk into a restaurant with him and be proud he was by my side. We went to baseball games, and he took me to meet his parents. I couldn't take him to meet mine. They would have locked me in my room and thrown away the key."

Daisy knew some Amish parents were stricter than others. "Are you close to Neil's parents?"

"We lost them both about five or six years ago. Neil was really broken up about it. They'd been good to us, and I wish they'd been alive to see Frannie born. But that's life. I'm just grateful that Leah wants to be close to Frannie. I think Frannie looks at Leah as a second mom, and that's good. I still crave that family connection, even though my parents rejected me and everything about my life. Leah is completely happy in her life, except she wants kids. She has no desire to live beyond restrictions."

"And you?"

"I left my faith for love and a desire to live without rules. But I soon learned everyone's life has rules and restrictions."

As Lydia went silent, Daisy wondered if her friend had regrets.

* * *

Daisy welcomed Jazzi's boyfriend Mark to the house whenever he felt like dropping in . . . or whenever the two of them wanted to spend time there together. Mark had proven to Daisy that he was responsible and an all-around good kid after an incident last fall. Tonight the fire was licking at the logs that Mark had laid in the fireplace while they all sipped hot chocolate with marshmallows in the living room area. Felix trotted from Jazzi and Mark to Jonas and Daisy, not sure where he wanted to settle. Daisy had given him his own treats in the kitchen.

Jazzi patted the floor next to her, where she sat on the rug. Felix seemed to think about his loyalties for a minute, and then he went over to her and settled between her and Mark.

Mark took a swallow of his hot cocoa and focused on Daisy. "I've accepted the offer from the University of Delaware."

Daisy asked, "Electrical engineering?"

"It's a combined major—electrical engineering and robotics. The program is five years and includes a master's. The financial package the university offered was a good one."

Jonas sat forward and set his hot chocolate on the coffee table coaster. "Do you feel good about your decision?"

"I do," Mark answered with a nod. "My parents have been saving for years to send me to college, and I'm really grateful that they did. I hope to keep my loans to a minimum. I have to do well so I don't let them down."

Jazzi stroked Felix's silky fur. "Mark's known since he was kid he wanted to work in robotics."

"When I was ten, my parents gave me a kit for Christmas. I still have that thing in my room, and it beeps every once in a while."

They all laughed.

"Do you have any idea where you want this career to go?" Jonas asked.

"I've always wanted to work for NASA," Mark said with a shrug. "But I know it's early days and college could lead me in a couple of different directions."

Their conversation after that led *them* in all directions, including Mark's and Jazzi's plans for dinner out the next day—Valentine's Day. She and Jonas would be having dinner at a favorite restaurant in York.

Daisy brought in chocolate whoopie pies with peanut butter filling, and they snacked and talked more. Planning graduation was going to be exciting. Daisy told herself she'd be prepared because, after all, she'd been through graduation once before with Vi. But she wasn't prepared. Where had all the years gone?

After Mark left, Jazzi plopped in the armchair across from the sofa. Pepper jumped up onto her lap as if to say it was her turn now. Jazzi stroked the cat under the chin, looking thoughtful as Pepper purred.

"What are you thinking about?" Daisy asked, her shoulder solidly against Jonas's, feeling as if she needed his support to get through this next life change. He'd been there through several already— Jazzi searching for her birth mother as well as Vi getting pregnant, married, and giving birth to Sammy. They'd navigated around all of those, and they would navigate this.

"I'm still not sure what to do about college." Jazzi pushed her straight, long hair over her shoulder, as if brushing her hair back would help her go forward.

"Do you have a front runner?" Jonas asked.

"I could go to the University of Delaware for social work, but I'm not sure I should."

Daisy had been proud that Jazzi had been accepted there, as well as at other colleges.

"Tell me what you're thinking about," Daisy invited.

Jazzi stroked her hand from Pepper's head all the way to her tail. The cat's purr increased in volume. She turned on her side on Jazzi's lap.

"I like Mark a lot." Jazzi's eyes were glistening with her emotions as she tried to put all of her thoughts into words. "But we have to keep our minds on our studies."

"You're afraid you won't do that if you're with him?" Jonas took a sip of his chocolate, tipped his mug, and finished it.

Daisy considered his nonchalance. He was trying to make Jazzi feel comfortable, and he usually could.

Jazzi's voice caught a little as she said, "If we go to separate colleges, we could grow apart. I'm not sure absence does make the heart grow fonder."

"Think about what you would do if Mark wasn't in the picture," Jonas advised her. "What would your choice be?"

"I like the Shippensburg campus. I like the conversations I had with the students there and the profs. But I can't make a decision until I'm sure."

"You have a deadline," Daisy warned her.

"I know I do. I'm hoping I'll go to sleep one night and wake up the next morning positively sure about my future."

The comment was off-handed and was meant to be a joke. Daisy said in the same vein, "So you want me to buy a crystal ball at Pirated Treasures."

"One that works," Jazzi jibed.

More seriously now, Daisy asked, "Have you talked this over with Portia? You might want to consider her input, too."

Jazzi's birth mother, Portia Smith Harding, had become important in her life. "I know I might, and I will the next time we talk. We're going to Skype tomorrow night after her kids are in bed."

Pepper raised herself to her paws and then jumped off Jazzi's lap, as if she knew the conversation was over.

Jazzi said, "I'm going to go up to bed. Maybe in the morning all will be clear." She studied her mom for a moment. "I suspect when I talk to Portia, she's going to tell me all the same things you're telling me. This will be a whole lot easier if you hadn't taught me I should make my own decisions. You could just point me in the direction you want me to go."

"Not my style," Daisy said lightly.

Jazzi kissed her on the cheek, nodded to Jonas, and went up to bed with Pepper trailing after. Not to be left behind, Marjoram jumped down from the back of the sofa where she'd been napping and followed them.

After Jazzi had gone up the stairs, Jonas put his arm around Daisy's shoulders. "I admire the way you've accepted Portia into Jazzi's life. I know it hasn't been easy."

"For fifteen years, Jazzi was all mine. She and Ryan had a good relationship, but I think I was always more protective of her because she was adopted."

"And she was younger than Vi," Jonas interjected.

"That's true, I suppose. I never wanted her to feel as if she were different from Vi as far as the way I felt about both of them. After Ryan died, Vi poured her grief into her school work, into sports activities, and into action. Jazzi, on the other hand, kept it inside. It finally came out as the decision for her to find her birth mother. I had to support her or there would have been a wedge between us. Watching her grow closer to Portia has been a happy experience as well as a bittersweet one. But a child can never have too many people in their corner, and now she has us both."

Daisy laid her head on Jonas's shoulder, glad that he was in Jazzi's corner, too.

Daisy was still thinking about last night and her Valentine's Day evening with Jonas. They'd gone out for dinner, then spent the rest of the evening alone at Jonas's townhouse. Soon he'd have to put it up for sale. But last night, he'd given her a bouquet of roses and made the most of their alone time there.

Tonight as she, Jonas, Iris, and Jazzi went in the back door of Daisy's childhood home, Daisy hoped her mom and dad would enjoy their surprise.

Her childhood home brought back a mixed bag of memories. She'd always felt closer to her dad than her mom except for the past year or so. She was glad things had changed.

One pastime she and her mom had always had similar ideas about was growing flowers in the yard. When spring and summer arrived, they'd planted perennials together, as well as seeds for zinnias and marigolds. In February, the yard's barren winter landscape was brown with not much green except for the evergreens. Come spring, crocuses would pop up, then daffodils and tulips and hyacinths. After all, her parents did own a nursery.

Daisy's mom and dad came to greet them. After hugs all around in the kitchen, Sean showed them into the dining area with its rectangular maple table, and motioned to them all to sit. "Your mom made a chocolate cream pie and already brewed tea."

Daisy knew there was no point telling her mom she shouldn't have gone to all the trouble. Her mom showed love with food, just as her aunt did. They had learned that from *their* mom.

Jonas rubbed his hands together. "I'm always ready for chocolate and tea."

"Mom doesn't make chocolate pie very much," Jazzi admitted.

Rose fluttered around, setting out dessert dishes, placing a knife on the table with the pie. "I had the pie crust in the freezer from when I made them last time, and the chocolate pudding and whipped cream are easy. I was a little worried when you all said you wanted to gather tonight, so I thought a sweet and tea would help."

Jonas and her father waited until all the women were seated before they took their seats. Sean agreed with his wife. "I suppose you have an announcement of some kind to make. Jazzi, have you chosen a college?"

"Still thinking on it," she said with a frown. She'd tied her hair in a low ponytail tonight. With a touch of makeup, mascara, and lipstick along with a crewneck, pale-blue sweater and dress jeans, Jazzi looked ready for college.

"If not college, then what?" Sean asked, dishing out the pie.

Daisy took a flat box from her purse wrapped in shiny blue paper with a silver ribbon. She handed it to her mother. "This is for you and Dad for your anniversary. Vi and Foster wished they could be here tonight, but Foster had class, and Vi said Sammy has a cold. But they want you to know it's from them, too."

Sean and Rose exchanged looks. Sean joked, "A present instead of a problem. That looks good to me."

Everyone laughed.

"You open it," he said to his wife.

Rose looked a bit flummoxed as she removed the silver ribbon and then tore off the paper. After she lifted the lid from the white box, she looked puzzled. "It's a menu for The Farm Barn."

"It is," Daisy said. "We're having an anniversary dinner for you there on Sunday. All of your family and a few friends are invited. We're hoping you enjoy the whole night as your anniversary present. Check out the menu."

"All our favorites!" Rose said happily. "From chicken pot pie to ham and fried chicken. The side dishes are our favorites, too—cornbread muffins, banana bread, potatoes au gratin, and string beans with ham. This menu looks delicious."

"Eating is my favorite pastime," Sean said. "We'll have a whole evening to do it the way it looks."

"Ned Pachenko is going to play oldies on his guitar," Daisy added. "You can give me a list of your favorite songs. I thought it would be a nice touch after we eat. The music was Jazzi's idea."

Rose got up and came around to hug her granddaughter and then Daisy and then Iris. With Jonas, she just put her hand on his shoulder. "This is an absolutely wonderful present."

"And one of the best parts of it," Daisy said, "is that Camellia will be here. She promised me she'll drive down and stay overnight."

"Oh, that's wonderful," Rose said, putting her hands together and pressing them to her lips. She was wearing her favorite bright pink lipstick, and her cheeks were rosy. She looked downright ecstatic.

Rose resumed her seat beside her husband, took his hand, and squeezed it. "We have wonderful children and grandchildren, don't we?"

He nodded. "We do. I guess we did something right."

Rose gave Daisy a look that said she was remembering some of their sadder times. But Daisy smiled and said, "You did do something right, and even your grandchildren are building their future. Jazzi will soon make a decision about college, and Vi and Foster are going to be moving out of the garage apartment in a week or so."

"I know you'll miss them," Sean said. "What will you do with the apartment?"

"I'll leave it empty for now."

"I'm sure the good Lord will have a plan for it," Iris said. "He'll show it to you in good time."

"You sound like Rachel," Daisy teased. "She essentially told me the same thing." Rachel Fisher, a childhood friend of Daisy's who owned Quilts and Notions, not far from Daisy's Tea Garden, was Amish and always had wholesome wisdom for her. Iris did, too.

Jonas addressed Sean. "Foster had me take a look at a used car a friend of his was selling. It belonged to his parents. Foster got a good deal and will be able to move some things from the apartment in that instead of trying to pull a wagon with his motor scooter."

They all laughed at that picture.

"A horse and wagon would be better than his scooter," Sean agreed. "I hear snow's predicted for this week. I'm glad he finally found a car they could afford. We're looking forward to visiting them when they get settled in at their new place." Her dad glanced at Daisy. "You'll have to tell us what they need so we can get it for them as a housewarming gift."

After she swallowed a mouthful of chocolate pie, Jazzi informed them, "They need a new microwave. The second-hand one they were using sparked."

"A microwave it is," Sean said. "I'll deliver it to

the apartment so they can use it now." He glanced at Daisy. "Is that okay? I know you and Foster's dad want them to build their own future and find their own financial footing."

"I don't think a microwave will spoil them too much," Daisy agreed with a smile. "Thank you, Dad." He lifted his hand as if to say, *It's really nothing*, and then he cut another slice of pie.

CHAPTER THREE

Daisy was helping Tamlyn Pittenger ready the spillover tearoom for Thursday's afternoon tea service. As she was setting teacups and saucers at each place setting, Tamlyn was making sure the napkins were placed just so with the silverware. A few customers were enjoying late morning and lunchtime snacks in the main tearoom where Foster and Iris were catering to their needs.

Tamlyn tapped Daisy on the shoulder. She was Daisy's youngest server . . . in her early twenties. At the tea garden, she wore her long brown hair in a knot on the back of her head. She had full cheeks, wide lips, and her bangs almost touched her brows.

Tamlyn said, "Foster's motioning to you."

Daisy glanced over her shoulder and, indeed, did see Foster beckoning to her from the other room. There was some urgency on his expression and in his wave.

Tamlyn assured Daisy, "I can handle this. Go ahead and see what he wants."

As soon as Daisy crossed to the doorway be-

tween the rooms, Foster motioned to Neil Aldenkamp, who stood at the sales counter. "Mr. Aldenkamp needs to talk to you. I think it's important."

Foster often looked wind-tossed with his russet
brown hair askew. In addition, his rimless glasses
had a tendency to drop down his nose. But his
smile was always engaging. He had a kind heart
and a sturdy sense of responsibility. Daisy had witnessed it with his caring for Vi and Sammy, and
she loved him like a son. "Any idea what it's
about?"

"I asked, but he wouldn't say," Foster explained.

"I'll take care of it. I think the tearoom is ready
for afternoon service, but if Tamlyn needs anything, can you help her?"

"Sure, I can."

Daisy approached Neil with a smile, hoping this
was a friendly visit. He was a handsome man, somewhat rugged in appearance with a square jaw,
broad shoulders, and a stocky frame. She guessed
he was about five-ten, but with his flannel shirt,
jeans, and work boots, he seemed to look taller in
the confines of the tearoom. He gave her a smile
that didn't quite work. In fact, it looked a little nervous.

"Can we talk somewhere private?" he asked.

Flummoxed for a moment, Daisy answered, "Sure.
Let's go into my office. Is everything all right with
Lydia?"

"Lydia's fine. This is related to business."

As Daisy led him past the kitchen doorway and
into her office with its Plexiglas window, she closed
the door. She hoped this had nothing to do with
any difficulty with her parents' anniversary dinner.
On the other hand, that seemed to be the most

likely reason he was here. She gestured him to the ladder-back chair and took a seat behind her desk. If this was business, then she needed to address it as such.

"I hope there isn't a problem with my parents' dinner."

"Not with the dinner per se," Neil acknowledged, adjusting the large square black watch on his arm as if he needed something to do. "I need to give you something, and I hope it doesn't cancel our contract for the dinner." He pulled a folded envelope from his jeans pocket. He opened it full length and straightened the wrinkle.

Daisy could see it was a business-sized envelope. There wasn't any writing on the outside.

With a frown, Neil reached across her desk and laid it on the blotter. Looking embarrassed now, with his cheeks a little ruddy, he explained, "That's a revised bill for your parents' anniversary dinner. It will be higher than expected. We're having distributor issues with our chicken line and with our fruit. As I think you know, we buy free-range and organic. We're having a problem with our suppliers, so the bill will be higher than expected. If you want to cancel the dinner, I understand."

Daisy couldn't cancel the dinner with it only a few days away! Her parents would be disappointed, and it was a matter of pride with her that she could do this for her parents. All the arrangements were made. Camellia had made plans to visit. Canceling was out of the question.

Neil said again, "I'm sorry, Daisy, but this can't be helped."

Daisy knew in any business, especially the restaurant business, problems could arise at the drop of a hat. She tried to always have a backup plan, but maybe the Aldenkamps didn't do that . . . or maybe their business couldn't afford to do that. When you dealt with a supplier and a distributor you appreciated, it was hard to make a switch.

She heard the clank of cookie sheets from the kitchen. The digital frame on her desk that flashed photos of her family and their pets completed a round of photos. Her gaze met Neil's. He was watching her expectantly.

The white business-sized envelope was sealed. Using the letter opener on her desk that was decorated with a teacup on the hilt, she inserted the pointed end into the fold and sliced along the seam. Afterward, she slid the folded sheet of computer paper from inside the envelope. As she straightened it, she heard Neil shift, and his wood chair creaked.

Thought of afternoon tea service vanished as she quickly scanned the numbers. She was surprised and a little shocked, but she had to quickly assess the situation and make a decision. She could cover the added expense if for some reason Iris and Camellia didn't want to go in on this with her. The charge was going to be a third more than expected.

Looking Neil in the eyes, she kept her voice even. "I want to go ahead with the dinner. It would be a disappointment for everyone."

Immediately, Neil stood to leave, obviously not wanting to continue the conversation and Daisy's feelings about it. Daisy was silent, because she really couldn't think of anything else to say.

At the door, Neil stopped to face her. "I want to assure you that Lydia had nothing to do with this.

It's no one's fault really, and if it is, The Farm Barn is absorbing some of the expense. I know your parents' anniversary dinner will be the quality you expect. I promise you that."

After a last long look of assurance, he left Daisy's office.

As soon as Neil was gone, Daisy went into the kitchen. Tessa looked at her with questions in her eyes. "You don't look happy. What happened? That was Neil Aldenkamp, wasn't it?"

"Yes, it was, and he had some news for me. Or rather I guess you could say it was a request for more payment than I was going to give him."

Tessa stopped scooping chocolate chips into the mixer bowl. "Explain."

So Daisy did.

Eva had overheard, and she looked somber. "You had a contract, didn't you?"

"Yes, we did," Daisy assured her. "But now the contract changed. I agreed to it. What else could I do three days before the dinner?"

"You can give him a bad review online," Tessa said with a frown.

"Tessa, you know I wouldn't do that. But I am concerned. Maybe this is just a supplier-distributor issue. But it still worries me."

Tessa gave a stir to the chocolate chips that were in the bowl with the dough. "I think it's odd. Are you going to call Lydia about it? Maybe she would do something."

"No, I'm not going to do that. At the dinner, I'll find out if she knows about it. But I'm not going to step between a husband and wife. This is what happens when you mix business with friendship. It's not always a compatible combination."

* * *

Daisy was excited as she and Jonas approached The Farm Barn with her parents on Sunday evening. The big red barn loomed in front of them with its door trimmed in white. The windows looked inviting, too, with the same white trim. Jonas opened the door for all of them, and Daisy let her parents step inside first.

Guests at two long tables shouted, "Happy Anniversary." Everyone her parents loved and admired most were seated around the tables, from Rachel and Levi—Rachel's parents had helped the Gallaghers start their business by planting trees on their property until they grew old enough to sell— to Vi, Foster, Sammy, Jazzi, Foster's dad Gavin, and his children Emily and Ben. Tessa and Trevor, a local journalist she was dating, sat next to a few of the Gallaghers' friends. Bouquets of roses had been positioned in vases at intervals on both tables.

Although the inside walls of the barn were rustic, the high beams sturdy and long, the decorations tonight were frilly with tulle mixed with gingham and big black and rose-colored bows. The luxury vinyl floor with its wood-tone colors was a backdrop to it all.

Lydia came to greet them, wearing a high-necked blue-and-white-checked dress with long sleeves. To Daisy, she looked a bit nervous as she welcomed them and showed Rose and Sean to their seats of honor. Her brown eyes went to Daisy often, as if checking with her to see if everything met her approval. So far, the atmosphere did.

Did Lydia know that Neil had come to her office with the revised bill?

Camellia had been waiting for her parents and gave them both a hug. Camellia was always perfectly and stylishly dressed. She'd cared about her appearance since before she was ten. Daisy had been more of a tomboy, brushing her hair aside, and as a teenager not giving a whit if she wore makeup. Tonight Camellia looked like a model in sleek black slacks and a pale gray silk blouse. Her brunette bob reached her shoulders now. Her lipstick, a shade darker than her mother's, filled out her pretty bow mouth. Her mascara was lush, and her eyeliner said she'd spent time on it.

Daisy mentally judged her own appearance. She'd worn camel wood slacks with a camel and black tunic top. The bell sleeves, camel and trimmed in black like the edge of her sweater, added a little flair. Jonas had gifted her with black onyx dangly earrings last Christmas. To show them off, she'd braided the sides of her hair and attached the braids in the back with a gold clip. She'd pass inspection, even by Camellia's standards.

Daisy's parents decided to stand and go from guest to guest, saying hello before the first course was served. Daisy soaked in the enjoyment on her mom and dad's faces as they spoke with their guests, exchanged anecdotes, and caught up with people they hadn't seen for a while.

Jonas slid his fingers between Daisy's on her lap. "They're enjoying themselves already. Even Camellia looks happy for a change."

Camellia was speaking with Vi and Foster, and her mood seemed lighter than it had been in a long time. Was that because she was going to take the RV trip she had planned?

Jonas looked particularly handsome tonight, Daisy thought. He was wearing a blue striped oxford shirt, open collared, under a navy sweater-type bomber jacket. She thought the blue suede collar trim looked particularly sexy, but then she always thought Jonas looked sexy. His spicy after-shave reminded her of the bottle now sitting on the vanity in the bathroom. She had worried whether her bedroom and bath were big enough for the two of them. She'd worried that everything was too confined for Jonas. But it wasn't. They were both enjoying the intimacy it created. He'd assured her often that her house was just right for them. Yet she also knew he wanted to add the money he'd make from the sale of his townhouse into some kind of investment for her property. They were considering it.

Her mind flooded with pictures of their evenings and nights together . . . with how she couldn't wait to marry him. Her engagement ring caught the rays from the overhead lights, and it sparkled with possibilities.

Suddenly she heard raised voices near the kitchen. Turning to look that way, she saw Neil and Lydia having an argument. It was definitely an argument, because Neil's face was flushed, his stance defensive. Lydia's hands were moving as if she were trying to explain something to him but wasn't making headway.

All at once, Neil turned on his heel and stomped into the kitchen. Lydia put her hand to her forehead, leaned against the wall for support, and then stood upright again and squared her shoulders. She swiveled her head toward Daisy and then looked away.

"I wonder what *that* was about," Daisy said to Jonas.

"Maybe Neil just told her about the extra expenses he charged you."

Daisy's thoughts about Lydia lingered for a few moments as Gavin approached her and Jonas.

He grinned at them and asked, "Are you ready for Vi and Foster's move?"

She focused on the in-law who had become a friend. "You know I'm not," she admitted with a smile. "Are the arrangements made for helping to move them?" Foster and Gavin were supervising that.

"I think so. We have a couple of trucks. It's not like they have that much, mostly toys for Sammy. The new place will be great for them. You know it will."

"I know," she admitted. "I just want to stay close to them, and I'm afraid the distance is going to make it more difficult. They're a busy couple."

"Everyone's busy," Gavin decided. "But I'm glad you took time out to do this tonight. It looks as if your parents are enjoying it."

"How's the construction on the homeless shelter going?" Jonas asked. "I haven't driven by there lately."

"I think we're on schedule. The funds are holding out. I tried to get the best deals I could on everything from lumber to drywall. We're hoping the snow the experts are predicting this week doesn't amount to much. The town council is talking about installing parking meters in the private parking lots and the public ones for extra funds. I don't know how that's going to go over," Gavin said.

"Somehow we'll pull together," Daisy assured him. "That's what Willow Creek does."

Gavin motioned toward the kitchen and the servers who were starting to distribute platters of food. "I think it's time to take our seats. Everything smells wonderful, doesn't it?"

"Especially the fried chicken," Jonas said, rubbing his hands together.

"That's one thing I don't make often," Daisy confessed.

"Just as well," Jonas said with a laugh. "I'd have to use heavier weights and do extra stomach crunches."

"Where do you have your weights?" Gavin asked.

"In the rear of the garage," Jonas answered, as if he didn't mind that.

"But . . ." Daisy drawled, holding up one finger. "We're discussing moving one of those huge sheds into the backyard for a workshop and weight room."

"Rather than an addition on the house?" Gavin asked.

"Possibly," Jonas said.

Gavin thought about the idea for a few beats. "Either would work. Are you thinking about a little barn out back?"

Jonas bumped Daisy's shoulder with his. "That's what Daisy suggested. I don't want it to look like a sore thumb. I want it to look like it fits in."

Now the servers were adding dishes of vegetables to the platters of meat and pot pie. Daisy knew they had to take their seats.

Gavin split off from them and went to sit with his kids.

The food *was* delicious. Jonas, as well as Daisy's dad, enjoyed their fair share of the fried chicken. The younger folk ate with gusto, too. Even Camellia, who always said that she was on a low-carb diet, gave into childhood cravings tonight. *This is what an anniversary gathering should feel like,* Daisy thought to herself. She couldn't help but consider her and Jonas being married for twenty-five years, thirty years, forty years. What would they be like together? What would their family be like?

But it was more important just to enjoy the present every single day, as precious as it was.

Dessert was just as delicious as the rest of the meal. The apple strudel dough was flaky and fell apart from simply looking at it. The apple filling was cinnamony with just a touch of nutmeg. The kitchen had prepared a blueberry and whipped-cream trifle with large pieces of angel food cake folded in. The fry pies, a specialty of The Farm Barn, contained fillings with blueberries, apples, and cherries.

After dessert was served, the servers came around with more coffee or tea for anyone who wanted it. Lydia approached Daisy with her coffeepot and stopped by her shoulder. She bent to Daisy's ear. "Would you like to go for a hike with me tomorrow morning? I really need to talk to someone, and I think you could help me gain perspective."

"Sure," Daisy answered. "What time would you like to go?"

"How about seven a.m. unless we're iced over or snowed in. I checked the extended forecast, and it might snow later in the day."

"Seven a.m. is fine. I'll wear wool socks and long underwear," Daisy joked.

Lydia gave her a weak smile. "I'm looking forward to the hike."

As Lydia moved away, Daisy wondered what else they would be discussing besides the weather.

Daisy drove to The Farm Barn in the morning with Felix in the back seat. She spoke to him on the way. "It's cold out there, boy. I even brought my earmuffs today. I don't have fur like you do."

He gave a little woof, as if he understood perfectly what she'd said.

"I'll warn you, Lydia will probably want to talk more than hike. You'll just have to nose around us, okay?"

Felix obviously understood inflections, like her voice going up at the end of the sentence and the question. He woofed again, and she had to smile.

Felix had seemed a little perplexed this morning. He was going with Daisy rather than with Jonas to work. He'd wanted to jump into Jonas's SUV, but Jonas had pointed to Daisy's Journey, a car-like crossover. Jonas had said to him, "I'm taking Jazzi to school, and you're going with Daisy on a hike."

Felix knew the word *hike*. She could swear the dog had almost grinned at her. His tongue had lolled out of one side of his mouth, and his feathery tail had swished back and forth and back and forth in a speedy rhythm. So here they were.

Breakfast with Jonas and Jazzi had held her up a bit. When she pulled into the parking lot at The Farm Barn around 7:10, she saw that there were no cars around other than Lydia's. This was the restaurant's day off for everybody but Neil and

Lydia. Daisy knew on Mondays Lydia spent most of her time planning menus for the week and scheduling servers. From what Daisy surmised, Neil oversaw any financial dealings.

As Daisy parked and switched off the ignition, she remembered again the altercation between Lydia and Neil last evening. Maybe it was nothing serious. Maybe she'd find out this morning exactly what had caused it.

As Daisy exited her vehicle, she took a bolstering breath of the cold air and felt the burn in her lungs. When she'd left home, the temperature had been about thirty-five. The weather could be as changeable as the clouds in the sky these days. After Felix jumped to the ground from her vehicle, she glanced up at the sky that was heavy with hulking gray clouds that portended snow. She could feel the dampness in the air and shivered. Was that shiver simply from the weather?

She told herself she was being silly. She was alone in a parking lot at a restaurant that was empty. The thing was—Lydia should have heard her drive up. Often she met Daisy outside. There was no sign of her friend.

After another look at the sky, Daisy wondered if they'd finish their hike before snow fell. Felix liked to catch snowflakes on his tongue and romp in the snow, so that would be no problem for him. Daisy's boots were practical enough, her coat warm enough, and her gloves thick enough. She was ready for this hike.

At first, she went to the rear door of The Farm Barn. Since she was a little bit late, Lydia could be waiting inside. The front door was kept locked when the restaurant was closed. She found the back door unlocked when she tried the knob. She said to Felix, "Stay." He sat.

Inside the kitchen, she saw that it was empty, as was the dining room area. No one was bustling about now. Neil probably had taken Frannie out to Leah's place or was still at home with her, giving her breakfast. Lydia had often told Daisy she let Neil and Frannie have breakfast time because the little girl loved when her dad made her pancakes with smiley faces out of chocolate chips.

After a last look around, Daisy left the kitchen. Outside, she said to Felix, "Maybe Lydia is waiting for us on the trail. Come on."

After walking toward the grove of pines, Daisy called Lydia's name. After a minute or so, she called again louder. "Lydia."

There still wasn't an answer.

A chill ran up Daisy's neck. Felix was looking up at her as if he were waiting for instructions.

"I'm glad you're with me. Let's head out." A few snowflakes began drifting through the air. Felix lifted his nose and sniffed, then bounded off.

"Felix," Daisy called after him. He *never* did this. He usually waited for her or Jonas and followed commands. He never ran off.

Today was obviously different.

She called for him again, but he was on a mission. Daisy didn't like that idea at all. Hopefully he'd spotted a rabbit or a squirrel. Hopefully he'd spotted—

Felix had stopped about twenty yards ahead of Daisy. She saw something on the single-vehicle fire road. The splash of color was red. Felix whined, hunkered down, his paws stretched out in front of him. He barked several times before Daisy reached him.

When she did, she gasped and fell to her knees. Lydia was sprawled there, blood around her head . . . on her face. Her red pom-pom hat lay on the stones a few feet away.

Felix kept barking.

Daisy tried to keep from screaming. She felt for a pulse on her friend's neck. There was none. She leaned her face down close to Lydia's lips and nose. There was no breath of air.

Panic in her chest, her fingers trembling, she took out her phone and called 9-1-1. Then she called Jonas. She said, "Lydia Aldenkamp is dead, and I need you here."

CHAPTER FOUR

Shivers skipped up and down Daisy's spine . . . over her arms and legs. Or maybe she was just shaking all over. Red, white, and blue police strobe lights seemed to be lighting up the clouds.

A swirling fog of thoughts and feelings surrounded Daisy as she sat in the back seat of Jonas's SUV. She pulled the corners of a blanket tighter around her. Without conscious thought, she recognized the fact that Felix sat beside her, leaning into her. Staring at the black leather seat in front of her, she felt incapable of putting two sentences together. Heat flowed from the dashboard vents, but the passenger back door was open, and a cold wind swirled inside the vehicle.

Was that why she was shivering?

Police officers passed by the open door. Another siren sliced through the morning air. It *was* still morning, wasn't it?

She heard Jonas shout to someone.

Deep voices approached the SUV. Jonas was saying, "She's so pale. I want her to go to the hospital."

The word *hospital* caused a different type of alarm to go off in Daisy's mind. She reached out of the blanket and wrapped her arm around Felix's neck, as if the dog could anchor her. She rubbed her cheek against his head, and that action seemed to ground her.

She turned to Jonas and the EMT and called, "No hospital."

"Daisy—" Jonas began as he slid onto the seat beside her.

She shook her head and held her hand out to him. "I'm not going to tell you I'm fine, but I don't need to go to the hospital."

Suddenly, Zeke Willet, a detective with the Willow Creek police department, appeared at the open door with a thermos. He unscrewed the top, poured coffee into it, and handed it to her. "Drink this, then we'll see how fine you are."

Her hand was still shaking, and she was afraid she'd spill the coffee. Jonas steadied her hand as she brought it to her lips. The liquid was hot and black. It smelled strong. As she swallowed it, then took another sip, the brew seemed to help her shivering.

She looked up at Zeke, registering the worry on his face. She wasn't the one he should be worried about.

Without a word, he stood there at the door, watching her drink. She finished one cup, and he poured more in. The EMT had moved away, but she had the feeling he hadn't gone far.

After her second cup of coffee, she said firmly to Zeke, "Tell me what happened to Lydia."

Zeke leaned into the car with his navy down jacket seeming to fill up the doorway. "I have to get your statement before I can tell you anything."

"Take my statement now," she advised him. "I might forget something."

"You might remember even more if you're feeling better," he countered. "Drink more coffee and sit with Jonas and Felix for a while. I'll be back."

"Can you hold the cup now?" Jonas asked her, his jaw tense, his mouth tight, his eyes brimming with worry.

"I'm okay," she said.

With a shake of his head, as if her words frustrated him, Jonas pulled shut the SUV door. Felix hunkered down on the floor between them. After Daisy finished another cup of coffee, Jonas wrapped his arm around her as best he could, kissed her cheek, and leaned his head against hers. "I'm so sorry this happened to you, Daisy."

She felt tears come to her eyes, and she knew she couldn't let them fall now. If she did, she'd be even more of a mess than she was. She had to give Zeke a coherent picture of what had happened and what she'd found.

She didn't really know how long she sat there with Jonas and Felix. She really didn't. But Zeke did come back. He and Jonas changed places. This time, Jonas stood outside Zeke's open door, but he made sure he had Daisy in his sights. She gave him the most positive expression she could muster. Even with the cold air streaming inside, she wasn't shivering any more. The coffee had done its job.

"Are you ready, Daisy?" Zeke asked.

She was sure she was ready to get this over with. She gave him a short nod.

"I need you to tell me why you came to the property, and exactly what happened." Zeke's notebook and pen were at the ready.

Pulling in a breath, telling herself just to relate the facts, she began without hesitating. "Lydia usually went for a hike every morning."

If Zeke had questions about that, he kept them to himself. His expression said she should continue.

"Lydia claimed the hike helped invigorate her for her workday. We were supposed to hike this morning. She usually meets me in the parking lot at The Farm Barn. I was about ten minutes late today, and she wasn't there waiting. The back door was unlocked, so I went inside first and called, but nobody was around. I thought I'd look around outside with Felix in case Lydia had started up the trail. He likes Lydia, and I knew he'd find her easily. I called for a while out back, but . . ."

As a vision of Lydia's crumpled body played in Daisy's mind, her throat almost closed. She coughed then went on. "Felix and I headed for the trail we usually took with Lydia."

Zeke interrupted her. "Are you sure you didn't see anyone else around? You didn't *hear* anyone or anything else?"

"I definitely didn't *see* anyone else. As far as hearing someone, it's pretty silent out here. I think I would have heard a noise. There are branches cracking in the woods a lot, so I don't know if I would have registered anything unusual about that."

Taking time to scribble something in the small

notebook, Zeke gave her a few moments. Then he prompted, "So you headed for the trail, which is really a fire road through the back of the property."

Daisy nodded again. "There are other trails. But we usually walk up the fire road until we decide if we want to go that way or through the woods. Felix usually stays by my side, but today he clambered off as if chasing something." Her voice grew low, and her words slowed as she remembered. "He wasn't chasing anything. He'd found something. He'd found Lydia. Oh, my God, Zeke. Her crumpled body . . . the odd angle of her leg . . . the blood on her face . . . What *happened* to her?"

"The forensic team is all over the scene. As you know, the trail is just a fire and work road that leads to the rear of the property," he reminded her.

"Could a delivery truck have hit Lydia?" she asked, her mind hooking onto one of the only possibilities.

Zeke gave her a sympathetic look. "Lydia was wearing a bright red jacket and beanie. She would have stuck out easily in the winter landscape. Anyone would have noticed her."

Picturing Lydia in her winter gear, Daisy realized that. "Certainly there should be some evidence of what happened. Are there tracks? What do they show?"

"That's what forensics has to determine," Zeke said solemnly.

"It's not like this is a main highway, and there would have been a hit-and-run," she murmured.

With a grunt, Zeke finally looked up. "The circumstances are suspicious, and we're going to investigate. You need to go home and try to forget what you saw."

Daisy knew that would be impossible.

Once Daisy and Jonas were at home, he insisted she take a hot shower. More than once, she told him she was fine, and he didn't have to worry. He obviously didn't believe her. Still, he didn't argue with her . . . he simply took care of her. After she'd stepped out of the shower, dried off, and wrapped herself in a towel, Jonas was ready with one of his long flannel shirts. As she dropped the towel, he buttoned the shirt for her.

He said, "Let me dry your hair."

She was about to protest when she saw his face. He looked beyond worried, and she knew that he wished she'd gone to the hospital. But shock or no shock, she *was* better now.

Instead of arguing with him, she listened to his concern. He went on to say, "I'll dry your hair, and then I'll light a fire in the fireplace and make hot chocolate. You'll get warmed up that way. I know how cold you are on the inside, Daisy. It isn't only about being cold physically. In my line of work, I saw dead bodies. I know what it does to a person. In this case, it's worse for you, because you and Lydia were friends."

She knew he was thinking about his partner, who'd been killed in the line of duty the same time he'd been shot in his shoulder. He did know how she felt. He and his partner had been involved. He'd loved her . . . and watched her die.

Felix came into the bedroom then and seemed to study both of them.

Believing the pooch, as well as the cats, was always part of the conversation, Daisy said to Felix, "We have to run that noisy device, and then we'll come out to the living room with you and Jazzi."

The golden retriever glanced at Jonas as if checking out if he agreed or not. At Jonas's nod, Felix trotted down the hall, away from the bedroom.

"Sometimes I think he's a mind reader," Jonas said.

Daisy gave him a smile. They both needed it.

Marjoram and Pepper became Daisy's companions on the sofa. Marjoram sat in the bread-loaf position on the back of the couch, on the afghan that Daisy's mom had given her. Pepper settled onto her legs longwise, as if to secure her on the sofa. By the side of the sofa, Felix looked up at her.

"You're all in cahoots to keep me here, aren't you?" she teased.

As if in agreement, Marjoram yawned, Pepper kneaded Daisy's legs, and Felix just gave a huff and laid his head on the sofa edge.

Jonas leaned down and gave her a kiss on the forehead. "They know their jobs."

Daisy added, "And they do them so well."

Jazzi called from the kitchen, "I'll make the hot chocolate while Jonas lights the fire, unless you want tea."

"Hot chocolate with marshmallows, whipped cream, and a peppermint stick, if there are any in the cupboard."

"The works," Jazzi agreed, "for all of us."

"You have to go to class," Daisy said, suddenly realizing Jonas must have gotten hold of Jazzi before she'd left for school to tell her what happened. Daisy must have still been fuzzy not to think about that until now.

Jazzi called into her mom, "Study hall this morning. But I want to stay with you today."

Jonas pulled the armchair across the wood floor, closer to the sofa. "Zeke is going to question you again. You know that, don't you?"

"Of course, I know that. Do you think he'll wait and do it before I sign the final statement?"

"Yes. I have a feeling he's going to want to interview other people before he comes back to you."

"Nothing I can tell him will give him a hint about who did it."

"You can't be sure of that, Daisy. You know that."

She did know that. The littlest thing could tell a story. She'd seen other murder victims. One woman had been wearing an amethyst pin. That pin had been a clue to the motive for murder.

The doorbell rang, and Daisy jumped. Her startle reflex was on high gear.

Jazzi called in from the kitchen, "Vi texted me. It's Vi, Foster, and Sammy. Is that okay?"

"That's fine. It will be great to see Sammy."

A minute later, Vi, Foster, and the baby blew in in a flurry. Sammy clambered to be let down right away. Vi helped the wiggling toddler shed his coat, then studied her mom.

Daisy said, "He can crawl better than we can walk."

Sammy practically zoomed over to Daisy. As soon as he saw the coffee table, he managed to get his little hands on the top of it to pull himself up to a standing position. Then he walked around it to Daisy at the sofa. He climbed over Felix, and Felix didn't seem to mind.

Vi picked up Pepper and held her while Jonas settled Sammy on Daisy's lap. The toddler gave her a big hug and patted her cheek. He studied her face while she looked into his. He was so angelically cute.

"Take off your coats," Daisy said to Vi and Foster. "Enjoy the fire. Maybe I can put together a quick brunch."

Vi said, "Mom, you're not doing anything."

Jonas agreed, "I'm sure that Foster and I can make a wonderful brunch. You always have a loaded refrigerator."

"And I should trust you to do that in my kitchen?" Daisy asked with a sigh.

Foster nodded. "You know I can supervise. I can serve anything as good as we have at the tea garden."

Vi joked, "He thinks he can use all the skills that he's learned from Iris and Tessa and you. He should use them more at home."

Foster shook his finger at his wife. "You know we're both busy. Sometimes it's just easier to order a pizza."

Once Foster crossed to the kitchen, Vi approached her mom. She scolded in a low voice, "You have to stop doing this."

Daisy counted to five. "What? Going on a hike with a friend?" Sammy was still on her lap, but she didn't want to get excited, not for the wrong reasons.

Jonas said calmly, "I'm sure Vi and Foster were worried about you."

"I'm sorry, Mom," Vi said. "But I do worry. Why does this happen to you?"

"I truly don't know," Daisy answered. "Rachel thinks it has something to do with me caring about people, at least that's what she thinks about solving the murders. I admit in the past, I put myself in danger, but this situation is entirely different."

Vi said, "Maybe the way it happened was different, but now that it happened, what are you going to do? If you get involved, it won't be any different than any other time."

Get involved. Daisy wasn't even sure what that meant right now. Although she'd protested that she was fine, Jonas had been right. She *was* shaken up. She didn't know if this upset was going to leave in a day or a week or a month . . . maybe not ever.

Jazzi had insisted on staying home from school, and Daisy hadn't protested. Vi, Foster, and Sammy had just left after enjoying brunch when Daisy received a text from Tessa. **Can we come over? Few customers at the tea garden. Trevor told me what happened. He has info.**

Daisy showed Jonas the message and didn't hesitate to text back. **Yes. Come.**

Jonas gave her an odd look. "Are you sure?"

"I want to know what happened. We know Zeke isn't going to tell me much, if anything at all. Trevor might have found out something we need to know."

Jonas's eyebrows shot up. "Need to know?"

"You know what I mean," Daisy insisted, ducking her head and clasping her hands in her lap.

Jonas sat on the edge of the sofa beside her hip. "If you want to get involved, that's your choice. But

just remember what the consequences are. And if
you want to get involved, you know I'll be by your
side. That's how we roll."

Daisy took his hand, squeezed it, and brought
his fingers to her lips.

Tessa and Trevor must have been close by, because it wasn't five minutes later when the doorbell rang. Jonas let them in and told Daisy to stay
put. She listened. She was still feeling the aftereffects of everything that had happened—her
mind spinning, her body not sure it was entirely
out of shock.

Tessa and Trevor were dating. Daisy was surprised it had lasted as long as it had. But they
seemed happy together, even though there was no
serious commitment. Jonas took their coats, and
Daisy could see there was snow on their shoulders.

"How fast is it coming down?" she asked.

Trevor knocked snowflakes from his brown hair
as he ran his fingers through it. "Not fast. Not
really laying."

"Tea all around?" Jonas asked. "We could put
a spot of Wild Turkey in it. I know Daisy could
use it."

"That's fine with us," Tessa acknowledged. "Don't
put any in mine, though. I'm the driver. My all-
wheel drive vehicle does a better job than Trevor's
sedan."

Jazzi came down the stairs with the two cats and
saw everyone gathered in the living room. After
she greeted Tessa and Trevor, she said, "Tea for
me, too."

This time Tessa was the one who said, "I don't
know if this discussion is for your delicate ears."

"If it's something Mom can hear, I can hear it,

too. She was really upset. I'm more stable than she is right now."

"Jazzi . . ." Daisy warned.

"You know I'll hear what you're going to tell her anyway. I'm going off to college next year. Imagine all that I'm going to see and hear there. Besides, I want to know what happened to Lydia, too. She was a nice woman."

"Tea for all," Daisy said, proclaiming it so.

Jazzi said, "I'll help Jonas. The cats want treats, and I'll get a biscuit out for Felix, too."

Fifteen minutes later, they were all gathered around the sofa, even the pets. Felix stayed by Daisy's side, even when Jazzi presented him with his treat. Pepper had hopped onto the coffee table, while Marjoram sat on the back of the sofa. It was as if they were all waiting to hear whatever Trevor had to say.

The reporter took a few sips of the spiked tea as if he needed to brace himself and started with a simple statement. "A vehicle stopped about fifty yards from the accident site." He continued with, "And it revved up and raced to the spot where Lydia was probably standing."

Daisy's hands went to her face again, and she imagined the sight of Lydia's body . . . broken, bleeding, and dead. She'd said she was ready for this. She had said she wanted to know. But did she?

Jonas had settled on the floor next to Felix, right by Daisy's side. His hand snuck under the afghan and took hold of Daisy's. She squeezed his fingers tightly. He gazed up at her, and she gave a nod that this was okay. She did need to know.

Trevor went on, "Swerve tracks show where the

vehicle turned and raced back the way it had come. It couldn't have been an accident. It was more likely a premeditated homicide."

He took a few more gulps of the tea this time and leaned forward, his focus on Daisy. "You're fortunate you weren't with Lydia when it happened."

If she had been with Lydia, her life could have ended, too. That thought sobered her . . . enough that even two cups of tea with Wild Turkey wouldn't brace her to remember what had happened today. Who would want to do this to Lydia? And why?

Although Daisy went to work at the tea garden the following day, her thoughts skittered around everything that Trevor had told her, as well as what she'd seen and heard. As soon as she walked in the back door, she could feel the difference in the air, a tension not usually evident at the tea garden. As she went to her office, stowed her purse, and donned her apron, she wasn't sure what she was going to say to her staff.

At first, she said nothing, and they all went on with their day, doing what they did in the morning—Tessa making scones, Iris making chocolate-chip cookies, and Eva readying the teapots along with cups and saucers and serving plates. When Foster arrived, he gave Daisy a studying look but didn't say anything about what had happened. Tamlyn kept her distance. Even Cora Sue—who usually bubbled with the latest news, asked how everyone was, and bopped around the place with concern for every event—said nothing to Daisy.

Iris hugged Daisy several times but didn't comment. Daisy had spoken at length last evening to her mother and Iris.

Daisy knew if her staff was tiptoeing around *her*, they would also be tiptoeing around her customers. The gossip was bound to come flooding into the tea garden, and she wanted to talk with them about how to deal with it.

She hadn't opened the tea garden for service yet. Before she turned the CLOSED sign over to OPEN, she clapped her hands for everyone's attention. They all gathered around her.

She said, "Let's sit and have a chat."

There were exchanged looks, and even Tessa seemed worried. Daisy stayed standing. She had to direct this conversation, even though everyone could say what they thought about it.

"I'm certain you all heard about the accident with Lydia Aldenkamp."

They all nodded but didn't comment.

"I'm not sure what you've heard, but here are the facts. Lydia and I were supposed to go on a hike yesterday morning. I took Felix along as I usually do. She wasn't in the parking lot waiting for me. When I checked inside, no one was there. Felix and I started on the trail, thinking maybe she had already gone ahead."

"It's good you had Felix along," Foster murmured.

Daisy nodded in agreement. "He usually stays by my side, but he ran off ahead of me. Not far up the fire road, he found Lydia. Someone had mowed her down with their vehicle."

A gasp escaped Cora Sue, and Tamlyn's mouth rounded in an O. Even Eva looked shell-shocked.

Daisy concluded with, "The police are investigating."

"Do they have any idea who did it?" Cora Sue asked. "Was it a hit-and-run?"

"Nothing's for sure right now," Daisy answered, though privately she had already deduced that someone had done this to Lydia on purpose.

"How awful," Tamlyn said.

Eva looked stricken. "She has a little girl, doesn't she?"

"Yes, she does. I haven't been in touch with her husband yet. I will be soon, but I'm sure he has to come to terms with what happened, too. Anyway, the reason I brought all this up is because our customers are going to be gossiping. I'd advise you to listen to them, but keep your opinions to yourselves. Don't initiate talk about it. If you do hear anything that you think is important, let me know. I'm still shell-shocked myself. What I saw was horrible. But I'm going to put my heart and soul into working today and trying to move those pictures out of my mind. Please don't feel you have to be careful what you say around me. We're going to serve our customers as we always do and have a good day."

Cora Sue jumped up first, came over to Daisy, and gave her a hug.

Daisy's eyes misted over. In turn, each of the people she worked with hugged her. She had a good staff.

After everyone had scattered again, Iris remained, her hand on Daisy's shoulder. She kept her voice low when she asked, "Are you going to help with the investigation?"

Daisy stuffed her hands into her apron pockets. "I could have been with Lydia yesterday when it happened. I could have been hurt, too. I'm considering what I should do."

"Be careful," Iris advised her, and then gave her another hug.

CHAPTER FIVE

When Zeke showed up at the tea garden later that day, Daisy wasn't surprised. He looked rumpled, as if he hadn't slept all night. That wasn't a surprise, either. He'd be working day and night until the Willow Creek P.D. solved this crime.

Zeke was a good-looking guy with a lot of high emotional walls similar to the ones Jonas had used to protect himself. Zeke's hair looked as if he'd run his hand through it about a hundred times so far today. It was short but long enough to stick up. In jeans, he was wearing a navy wool sports jacket with a blue turtleneck underneath. Maybe he supposed that gave him a more casual air when he interviewed suspects. She imagined he'd be interviewing a lot of people today, and she was just one of them.

She asked him, "How about tea and a blond brownie?"

He frowned. "I'm not here for a social visit."

"Don't I know it," she said.

His look was determined but studying as he finally relented. "All right, feed me. That's what you like to do."

She almost smiled in spite of the seriousness of this interview. "Go to my office and I'll be right in. We're serving Earl Grey this month, unless you'd like something else."

"Whatever you give me is fine. I haven't eaten since . . . I don't remember when."

"You know the way," she said, motioning to her office.

A few minutes later, she carried a tray inside and set it on her desk.

Sitting on the chair on the other side of the desk, he scowled. "That doesn't look like tea and a blondie."

"I just added a dish of cabbage apple salad. You need more than sweets and tea to keep you going. You can still ask questions while you chew. I won't mind."

She and Zeke had always had a rather blunt relationship. They told each other the truth. Through that honesty, they'd become friends.

Zeke stared down at the salad, which also included walnuts and dried cranberries, and picked up the fork. "All right, I'll eat. But while I do, I want you to tell me everything that happened all over again. You'll have to come in to sign your statement."

"I'll stop over later." She knew telling the facts over and over again was part of the investigation. The detectives were always looking for something that someone had left out and any inconsistencies. They searched for details and leads.

While Zeke ate, she went over what she'd told him as best as she could remember it. She didn't

like remembering it, but she had come to terms
with the fact that she was the one who had found
Lydia. It was possible her memories could help
solve the murder.

After she finished recounting what had happened, she added, "Trevor told me what he found
out. The vehicle was intent on running her down.
Is that correct?"

"Daisy—" Zeke warned.

"Zeke," she sing-songed back, "don't you think I
have a right to know?"

Zeke looked at her askance. "All right. I'll tell
you one thing. We're investigating it as if it was a
homicide."

Finished with his salad, Zeke now took a couple
swallows of tea. He didn't start on the blondie
right away. Rather, he said to Daisy, "I'm looking
into Lydia's background. Tell me what you know
about her."

After Daisy thought about it, she realized she
didn't know much. She knew what Lydia had told
her . . . the basics. But not really the ins and outs
of Lydia's life. Still, anything could help Zeke, so
she began with, "Lydia was a good mom and loving
with her child."

"That was her reputation, or you saw it firsthand?" he shot back.

"Firsthand," Daisy answered resolutely. "We just
started getting to know each other in the fall, after
I planned Jonas's birthday party at The Farm
Barn. We connected, and that's why we went hiking together. She loved dogs, too, though she didn't
have one. I think Felix could tell, and that's why he
enjoyed romping with her."

"She was fit?" Zeke asked.

"Yes. Because of the hiking, I suppose. She told me she had to stay fit to take care of her daughter and work long hours at The Farm Barn. She was the kitchen manager, so she was at the facility for everything. She made the schedules for the servers, planned what they were serving, and oversaw the kitchen."

"What did her husband do?" Zeke asked, finally taking a bite of the blondie.

"I got the impression that he dealt with the suppliers and the distributors." She quickly told Zeke about the increased cost when she'd had the anniversary dinner at The Farm Barn for her parents.

Zeke looked as if he was interested in that, but he didn't delve into it further. Rather, he asked, "What about Lydia's background?"

"You mean before The Farm Barn?"

"If you know anything."

"I know she was born Amish. She has a twin sister, Leah. Leah embraced her faith, but Lydia didn't. During Lydia's *rumspringa*, she fell in love with Neil and left her Amish community to marry him. In love, she only cared about a life with him. That's what she told me. Even though she hadn't committed to her faith yet and wasn't officially shunned for leaving, her parents shunned her. Still, from what I understand, she and Leah stayed close."

"Is Leah New Order Amish?"

"Yes, she is. She's part of the same district as my friend Rachel."

After Zeke finished his snack and took a few more swallows of tea, he wiped his fingers on the napkin that Daisy had provided. He leaned forward now from the opposite side of her desk and placed his hand on the wooden surface. Daisy could see the concern in his eyes and the worry around his lips. He usually wore a poker face, but with her, he sometimes showed what he was feeling.

"I know you're involved in this, Daisy, but I don't want you to be. You found your friend and now you think you have to figure out what happened to her."

"I haven't made any decision about that yet," she said truthfully.

"Maybe not, but you have connections all over this community—with the Amish, with everyone who comes into your tea garden, and with your family. Your parents even hear gossip at their nursery."

She tilted her head, studying him. "So what are you saying?"

"I'm saying you're a smart woman with great deductive reasoning skills. I don't want you involved in this investigation, and I'm sure Jonas doesn't want you involved, either. He goes along with whatever you do because he supports you. After all, love creates a bond that's somewhat like a chain."

"Not in a bad way," she protested.

"In your case, that's probably true. But I'm asking you, if you hear anything important, come tell me about it, or tell Rappaport. Don't *act* on it."

"I don't want to waste your time if I hear something and I don't know if it's true or not. Sometimes I have to follow up."

He sighed and leaned back in the wood chair. It creaked. "That's exactly what I'm talking about. Don't be concerned about getting to the bottom of something. Text me if you want. Email me. I don't care. If it's not something I want to follow up on, I won't. This was traumatic for you, Daisy. Don't deny the PTSD. You've dealt with it before. I know it's not exactly the same thing. The way you found Lydia . . ." He trailed off and shook his head. "That's not a sight you're going to forget any time soon. Believe me, I know. Confide in Jonas and let him help you. But as far as I'm concerned, I want you to serve tea and scones and spend time running around the yard with Felix."

Silent for a moment, she leaned back in her chair, then gave him a weak smile. "You're a good guy. Do you know that, Zeke?"

"Sometimes I wonder," he admitted, rubbing his jaw. "I know I haven't been so good in the past. I'm hoping I've learned from my mistakes. I want *you* to learn . . . not from your mistakes but from your experience. Got it?"

"I got it," she said with a nod, knowing he wanted what was best for her. He really was a good friend.

The following morning, Daisy drove to Neil Aldenkamp's house instead of the tea garden. His ranch-style home, in a pleasant area of Willow Creek, was small. Lydia had told Daisy it had two bedrooms. Daisy had never been here before. She and Lydia had always connected at The Farm Barn or at the tea garden.

As she parked in the short driveway, she considered the fact that paying condolences was just something neighbors did in Willow Creek. She had prepared a chicken and rice casserole as well as a blueberry coffee cake for Neil and Frannie and settled both in a wicker basket. As she removed it from the car and shut the driver's door, Neil appeared on the other side of the storm door. He must have heard her drive up.

Neil was dressed casually in a flannel shirt and jeans and held Frannie in his arms. Even though the little girl had her arms wrapped around his neck, he managed to open the door for Daisy. She carried the basket inside. She couldn't help but see the weariness on his brow, the sadness in his eyes, the tight hold he had on his daughter, as if she were his lifeline. She didn't know if he'd want her to stay.

"I'm so, so sorry, Neil. I don't know what to say."

"Can you have a cup of coffee with me?" he asked. "I really need to talk to someone."

"Sure, I can stay."

He jiggled Frannie until she took her arms from around his neck and simply held onto his shoulder. "You remember Daisy, don't you?"

Frannie had big brown eyes and rambling brown curls that danced across her forehead and along her cheeks. She nodded and tilted her head against her dad's chest. "Daisee," she said softly.

Daisy smiled at the child. "I brought along blueberry coffee cake." She checked with Neil, and he nodded. "Do you think you'd like a little piece?"

Frannie bobbed her head up and down and stuck her thumb into her mouth.

"I'll settle her with the coffee cake and a glass of milk. And then maybe we can talk," he decided.

The living room to the right of the foyer was decorated with comfortable furniture, including a gray-plaid sectional sofa. The kitchen was directly in front of them. It was almost a galley-style kitchen. Off to the left was probably the route to the two bedrooms and bathrooms.

Neil set his daughter on the floor, then took the basket from Daisy and carried it into the kitchen. Frannie had jumped up and run ahead of him. "Settle yourself in the living room," he suggested to Daisy. "Frannie has her own table and chair, and she can sit there for her snack. Do you want a piece of coffee cake with your coffee?" he asked.

"No, thank you. The cake is for you."

In the living room, Daisy took off her jacket and laid it next to her on the sofa. Frannie was already sitting at her little table. He arranged her snack there along with a puzzle that might have been her favorite, Daisy guessed.

Once Neil had brought Daisy a mug of coffee and settled in the armchair across from her with his, she asked, "How's Frannie doing?"

"She doesn't understand why her mommy isn't here. I don't know how to explain it to her. Leah was here and took her into the bedroom to play when the police arrived the first time to question me."

Daisy held the mug of coffee in her hands, letting it warm her palms. The scent of the brew wafted up to her nose. Neil had added cream at her direction, and she wished she could enjoy it as she would any cup of coffee. But these circumstances made that difficult.

"The first time?" she repeated.

Anger or maybe frustration darkened Neil's cheeks. "Oh, yes. After they delivered the bad news and questioned me, they came back again Monday night. Fortunately, Frannie was in bed that time.

Yesterday they had me down at the station. I know I'm a suspect, and I don't know what to do about it."

"The husband is always the first person they look at in a case like this."

"Like on TV?" he asked sarcastically.

"Unfortunately, that part of the investigation *is* like TV. How long did they grill you down at the station?"

"For three hours! They videotaped it, of course, and they voice-recorded the questioning they did here."

"The detectives will be checking every little detail," Daisy told him. She wanted to ask him if he'd been honest with the police, if he'd told Zeke and Morris Rappaport the truth, but she couldn't quite bring herself to do that. This man was obviously suffering. She could tell it in the set of his shoulders, the slackness of his jaw, the way he wound his hands together and dropped them between his knees.

She glanced over at Frannie, who was maneuvering a fork the way a three-year-old did, stabbing a bite of coffee cake and letting the crumbs fall off as she tried to poke it into her mouth. Neil needed to be straight with the police for Frannie's sake. If they found anything that tied him to Lydia's murder, they'd arrest him. However, Daisy could see that he was already scared, and she didn't want to make that worse. They sat in silence for a few moments as they both took swallows of their coffee.

Neil seemed to need the brew to brace him for what he wanted to say. He started with, "I need your help, Daisy. I was going to call you later today."

"Help with Frannie?"

He sat forward. "No. Leah has that covered. I know you've solved murders before. Lydia told me all about it. I'm the detective's number one suspect, but I had nothing to do with what happened to Lydia. Maybe you can discover who wanted to hurt her. I need your help, Daisy, I really do."

Neil's gaze pleaded with her.

What could she say to him? "Neil, you should know better than anyone who might have wanted to hurt Lydia. Can you think of anyone?"

He looked away and didn't meet her gaze. "No, I don't know anyone who would have wanted to hurt her like that."

Like that. Just what did that phrase mean?

Jonas made supper for them that night—sliced potatoes mixed with sauerkraut and crushed pineapple topped by pork chops. While the casserole baked in the oven, he worked on top of the stove making the homemade version of stew for Felix. Beside him, Jazzi stirred sweet-and-sour carrots. Jonas had directed Daisy to sit at the island and do nothing.

She felt odd watching him cook.

Jazzi put Daisy's thoughts into words and addressed Jonas. "You never told us you took cooking classes," she teased.

Jonas grinned at her. "I didn't, but I know how to read cookbooks. I even found one that was titled *Cooking for Dummies.*"

"You didn't," Jazzi protested.

He laughed. "Not exactly, but I did find cookbooks in the library with easy recipes for the single man."

"Did you cook when you were a detective?" Daisy asked, sipping a cup of Earl Grey tea and watching Jonas's broad back and strong arms as he stirred Felix's stew in the Dutch oven. Sometimes it seemed as if she'd known Jonas all her life. However, there were other times when she realized she still didn't know every detail about him.

His gaze met hers, and there was a knowing in his eyes that made her realize he'd guessed again what she was thinking. "As a patrol officer, a canine handler, and then a detective, I was on the fast-food track to being unhealthy."

"Too many donuts?" Jazzi joked.

"Whatever I could grab on the run. If I did cook at my apartment, it was a fried egg, or a Pop-Tart from the toaster. I didn't gain weight because it seemed like I was constantly moving. But I was burning empty calories."

"Somehow you changed all that," Daisy noted, setting down her Royal Doulton teacup into its saucer. The pattern was called Jasmine, and it was one of her favorites.

"When I moved to Willow Creek, everything in my life changed," Jonas explained. "I was familiar with Willow Creek before I moved here. I'd had a case that took me to Lancaster to investigate. After that, I often drove up here for stress relief. Sometimes just seeing a horse and buggy on the road convinced me to slow down and appreciate life more. I wandered in and out of furniture shops in this whole area. I chose Willow Creek because of . . . the willows . . . and the creek, the Amish communities, the peacefulness I felt when I'd drive through here. As I was nearing the end of my time in physical therapy after the shooting in Philadelphia, I knew I had to change my whole lifestyle, not just my profession."

Jonas and his partner Brenda had been shot at by a suspect in a murder case they were investigating. Brenda, who had also been Jonas's lover, had died. Jonas had just learned she was carrying his baby, or so he thought, and he'd been devastated. It wasn't until after he'd moved to Willow Creek that he'd learned there had been a possibility that Zeke had been the father. They'd been friends on the force, enemies for a while, but fate had brought them together again when Jonas saved Zeke's life during a murder investigation in Willow Creek.

Jonas had spoken to Daisy at length about Brenda and everything that had happened as their friendship had grown . . . as their love had taken root. Now he could speak of some of it to Jazzi, too. She knew his story and respected everything he'd gone through.

"So in addition to taking up woodworking again, you learned to cook," Jazzi deduced.

"I did. Cooking made my townhouse smell good. With Woods, my hours are much different than I'd ever experienced as a police officer or as a detective. So I had long evenings with nothing to do. I cooked, I read, and I worked out. When I couldn't sleep, I didn't let my mind go crazy. I'd drive to my workshop at the back of the store and work on something. It was good therapy, but I didn't make woodworking an obsession like police work had been."

Jazzi gave the carrots one last stir and poured them into a bowl on the counter. "I'm surprised you didn't start trimming bonsai trees."

Jonas shook his head. "I'm glad you don't filter everything before you talk."

"Oh, I filter it," Jazzi said. "But I don't have to do that with you, and it's nice."

After Jonas switched off the burner under Felix's food, he removed their casserole from the oven.

Daisy attempted to keep her thoughts in the present. Jonas had built a fire, and they decided to bring their food to the table near it to make it a special occasion. Daisy intended to have lots of special occasions before Jazzi went off to college. Several times, however, she had to consciously direct her attention back to the food, back to the conversation, and back to the present. She couldn't forget the sad look in Neil's eyes or the way Frannie had sat at her table, innocent of the way her mother had died. She couldn't forget Zeke questioning her again about exactly what she had seen.

She'd brought apple muffins home from the tea garden for dessert. Jazzi brewed more Earl Grey tea, and they all had a cup with their dessert as Felix enjoyed his dinner with gusto. The foods Jonas made him agreed with him and satisfied him in a way canned dog food alone couldn't.

After dinner, Jonas took care of the fire, and as usual, Pepper and Marjoram followed Jazzi up to her room. In relative silence, Daisy and Jonas readied themselves for bed. Daisy could feel Jonas's gaze on her often. He climbed into bed first and sat against the headboard.

After she climbed in, he asked her, "Do you want to talk?"

She shook her head.

He didn't try to convince her otherwise. Instead, he opened his arms to her.

She went to him, seeking another type of intimacy that could say so much more than words.

Hours later, in the throes of slumber, Daisy found herself walking. She passed a field with flowers on one side—zinnias, petunias, and marigolds—all colors of the rainbow. On the other side of her, trees rose up to intertwine in a canopy. She should have stepped into the flowers. She should have stopped in the midst of them and invited Jonas to join her. But she didn't. She wandered into the dark tangled mess of tree branches, wild grass, brush, and laurel. Vines hung around her arms. Tendrils caught her at the waist and dragged through her loose blond hair. She swiveled, trying to break loose. She couldn't. The vines tightened and tangled her more. She called out as they wrapped around her, suffocating her . . . stealing her breath . . .

Jonas called her name.

The vines tightened around her chest until her eyes popped open. When they did, Jonas's hand was on her shoulder, his palm on her cheek. "You were having a nightmare, Daisy. You're safe now. I'm here."

She felt the sweat on her brow, the lump in her throat, the strain in every muscle of her body. It had been a dream. Simply a bad dream.

She inhaled a deep breath, gazed into Jonas's eyes, and knew exactly what the dream meant. "I can't let this go," she said in a whisper. "I'll never be able to relax or feel safe until I find answers. Lydia was my friend, and I could have been killed with her. It's not okay. Frannie needs answers about what happened to her mother, too. I have to do it, Jonas."

He slid his hand from her cheek and gathered her close. "Whatever you need to do, Daisy, I'm here. I'll help you any way I can."

Daisy closed her eyes and leaned against him, knowing a new day was coming . . . also knowing she was going to face it head on.

CHAPTER SIX

The next morning, after making sure Daisy hadn't had aftereffects from her nightmare, Jonas left to work in his workshop before he opened Woods. Wanting just to feel *normal*—whatever that was—Daisy asked Jazzi, "How about pancakes this morning? You have time before classes."

"What about you? Are you going into work?"

"I called in, and I'm covered for this morning."

Jazzi gave her mother a curious glance. "Pancakes sound good. Gram's recipe?"

Daisy's mom's homemade pancakes were the best. "Yes, her recipe." Daisy reached to a top knotty pine cupboard and plucked out a jar of pure maple syrup one of her customers had given her after a vacation to Vermont.

After Jazzi pulled an electric griddle from under a bottom cabinet, she set it on the island.

Daisy pulled the flour canister closer. Soon, with Jazzi's help, they'd mixed up the batter, and Daisy ladled pancakes onto the griddle.

Jazzi took a seat at the island. "I always want to turn them before I should."

Daisy studied the pancakes that were cooking. "You have to wait until the bubbles pop up all over."

"But then they get too dark," Jazzi protested.

Daisy laughed. "Just peek under the edge and see if they're ready." She did exactly that, and the one she examined was golden brown. Sliding the spatula underneath it, she flipped it. Soon she'd flipped all six of them, while Jazzi pulled down plates.

"What kind of tea should I brew?" her daughter asked.

The kettle was already on the stove, with steam beginning to issue from the spout. Shortly it would be whistling. "How about the apple spice? That will be good on a cold morning."

It wasn't long before they were seated at the island, enjoying their pancakes.

"Mom," Jazzi began, but then stopped, as if she were hesitating about what she should say.

Daisy knew her daughter. This morning, Jazzi was dressed in a color-blocked royal blue and white tunic. She wore it over a white turtleneck and jeans. Her long black hair flowed around her shoulders, glistening in the kitchen light. But her brows were raised a bit, and her shoulders tense, even as she used her fork to cut off part of the stack of her pancakes.

"What's on your mind?" Daisy asked, sure there was something.

"Are you okay?" her younger daughter asked her.

Daisy laid down her fork and studied Jazzi. "I'm okay. Why?"

"I heard Jonas in the kitchen in the middle of the night. That's unusual. When I started down the steps, I saw he was making tea, so I went back up. He had two mugs on a tray."

"I had a bad dream, and I couldn't get back to sleep. That's all."

"Mom, that's *something*, not *nothing*. I can only imagine what you dreamed."

"Don't." The word came out more vehemently than Daisy had intended it to.

Jazzi quickly continued. "I know you want to protect me from everything, but you can't. You can't protect yourself, either. Some things just get into your psyche, and you can't shut them out. I don't only mean bad stuff. When I got the idea that I wanted to search for my birth mother, I couldn't stop thinking about it. It bothered me day and night. It was always there until I did something about it."

"I'm glad you did something about it. You needed to find Portia. That was important to you."

"Don't change the subject, Mom."

Daisy laid down her fork. "What *is* the subject, Jazzi? Let's get to the bottom of what you want to ask me."

Dipping a forkful of pancakes into syrup, she hesitated before bringing it to her mouth. "It's not that I want to ask you anything. I want to tell you something."

"I'm listening."

"These murder investigations have affected you."

To do something with her hands, Daisy cut off a piece of pancake and poked it into her mouth. She really wasn't hungry anymore. "I tried not to let the investigations affect you," Daisy said.

"I know that. And for the most part, they haven't. I mean, I enjoy researching with you now and then. That part of it is sort of fun. It's like a puzzle. When you find the smallest clue, it can change everything. And I know you want to help people."

"But . . ." Daisy drawled.

"You need to help yourself."

"By stopping?"

Jazzi finally ate the bite of pancake and shook her head. "I've never been the one to say that, and neither is Jonas. We know you care, and that's why you get involved. But because of these investigations, you've had panic attacks and even claustrophobia."

Jazzi wasn't wrong about that. Daisy had handled both. At least she'd thought she had. "Then what are you suggesting?"

"Remember when I got drunk, and you knew it wasn't about the drinking, but it was about what was underneath? I was confused about Portia."

"I remember." Daisy recalled that night all too well.

"You found me a counselor, a really good one. At least, I think she's good. She helped me. And you told me if I ever need to see Tara Morelli again, I can call her."

"You're suggesting I see her."

"Yes, for self-care. You've talked to me and Vi about that a lot. You're planning a wedding. I'm going to college, and Vi is moving out. That's an awful lot to deal with, don't you think?"

Daisy almost smiled. "At the time, I thought dealing with Vi's pregnancy was a lot, but I got through it."

"You did, but you want to do more than get

through this, don't you? You want to enjoy the wedding plans. You want to be excited for me going to college. You want Vi and Foster to be happy, right?"

"All of the above," Daisy agreed.

"Then why don't you call Tara, talk to her about what happened, and put it all in perspective."

"Oh, it's as easy as all that," Daisy said facetiously.

"It can be easier than it is now," Jazzi advised her.

Jazzi never ceased to amaze Daisy. She was wise beyond her years sometimes. Just maybe she had a point.

Her conversation with Jazzi ringing in her thoughts, Daisy decided to visit her friend Rachel before going to the tea garden. The interior of Quilts and Notions always made Daisy smile, no matter what her errand. It was so bright with multicolored quilts hanging from racks. Place mats and potholders, all handcrafted, fanned out on shelves. The area with bolts of cloth, threads, and buttons fascinated Daisy. She wasn't a seamstress herself but was amazed at the creations some of her friends and fellow Willow Creek residents made. A revolving corner rack held books on subjects from quilts to the history of Lancaster County.

Rachel stood at the counter, studying her computer. She was New Order Amish, and could use electronics for business. Her district was more lenient than some, her bishop understanding of how the Amish world had to connect sometimes with the English world.

Hearing Daisy's footsteps, she looked up. "*Wilkom,* Daisy."

Hoping she could have a few minutes of conversation with Rachel, Daisy unzipped her fleece coat.

Rachel's sudden turn toward Daisy made the strings on her *kapp* float forward. "How are you, *mijn vriend?*"

"I'm . . ." Daisy began.

"Do not say you are fine," Rachel warned her. "I know what happened. Gossip is all over town."

"It was an awful experience," Daisy conceded.

Rachel muttered, *"Es waarken maulvoll gat."*

As Daisy and Rachel played on Rachel's family farm while Daisy's parents consulted with the Eshes about starting trees there for their nursery, Daisy had picked up much Pennsylvania Dutch. She knew Rachel's comment meant there was nothing good about it.

"There *was* nothing good about it," Daisy agreed.

"Knowing you, you want to help the police again, ain't so? Do you think that's wise?"

"Wise or not, I feel I could have been in danger with Lydia. That scares me, but it also makes me angry."

"You are slow to anger," Rachel said.

"Usually, but this—" She stopped, her throat tightening. "I visited Neil, Lydia's husband, to give him my condolences. That little girl is so sweet. She didn't deserve this to happen to her. On top of that, Neil feels he's a suspect. The husband always is."

"He does not have an alibi?"

"Not much of one. He said something about driving to Columbia to look into other distributors and producers for The Farm Barn."

"Someone should know whether he met with them, yes?"

"He said no one was at the establishment."

"No alibi," Rachel agreed.

Daisy related to Rachel what had happened when she and Iris had met with Lydia; the fact that Leah had come in, and they'd both seemed stressed over something. "I know you don't like to gossip, but I need some background. What do you know about Leah and Titus Yoder?"

"Business is slow today," Rachel said, looking around the shop and outside the door. "Do you want to sit a spell and have a cup of tea? It seems silly asking *you* that."

"I'm always ready for a cup of tea. For some reason, sipping a cup of tea with somebody helps me absorb information better."

"Take off your jacket. We can sit in the quilting corner."

Rachel had arranged three ladder-back chairs in a back corner of the shop. Sometimes women brought in quilt tops they were finishing and asked for advice. Rachel was also part of a quilting circle that met once a week. They usually got together at each other's homes, but one night a month, they came into the shop.

At Quilts and Notions, Rachel used an electric teapot to boil water for cups of tea. She also used teabags that Daisy had supplied.

"Earl Grey with vanilla?" she asked Daisy.

"That's perfect," Daisy said, shrugging out of her jacket and hanging it over the back of one of the chairs.

Rachel unfolded a wood tea table and set it up between two chairs. On it, she set two fluted mugs with a hummingbird pattern. The water was finished heating in a matter of minutes. She plopped the teabags into the mugs, then poured the water over them.

"Honey?" she asked Daisy, pointing to the little earthenware jar on the sideboard.

"You know how I like my tea," she teased.

"I should after all these years."

Soon they were sitting across from each other, Rachel in her ankle-length royal blue cape dress with a black apron, and Daisy in her pale gray slacks and violet puff-sleeved sweater. Daisy stirred honey into her tea while Rachel squeezed a slice of lemon into hers. Daisy knew Rachel was probably considering what she wanted to say. She didn't talk about other people lightly.

Rachel began with, "If you ask anyone in our district about Leah and Titus, they would say they stick to themselves. I mean, all Amish are private in a sense, but Leah and Titus, they don't have much to do with anyone but their parents, and in Leah's case, her sister Lydia."

"Why do you think that is?" Daisy asked. "They're New Order Amish. I consider that to mean they're a little more in the world than Old Order Amish. Am I wrong about that?"

"Our district's ordnung is interpreted by our bishop a little more leniently than others. But Leah and Titus, maybe because of the strictness of their parents, adhere more to the old ways. And then there is still embarrassment about Lydia leaving her faith. You know Lydia's parents shunned her when she left."

"I do."

Rachel picked up her mug and stared into the

tea, took a tentative sip, and then gazed at Daisy. "Leah didn't have a *rumspringa*. She had no desire to stray from her roots. I think Leah and Lydia's parents saw their twins, who looked so much alike, and thought they should be the same. They didn't take into account their different personalities."

Sipping her tea, Daisy considered that.

Rachel went on, "My Sarah and Hannah are alike in many ways, but different in just as many. Like Vi and Jazzi, ain't so?"

"Like me and Camellia," Daisy added.

Rachel gave her a huge smile.

Remembering history that Lydia had confided in her, Daisy said, "Both women seemed to have had trouble conceiving children. Lydia told me she had two miscarriages before she had Frannie."

Rachel fingered the handle of her mug. "I don't know if Leah had miscarriages, but I do know she desperately wants to be a mother. All she's ever wanted was to be a wife and mother and have a large brood of *kinner*. I've been told she and Lydia were inseparable as children. Although they were fraternal twins, they seemed to have that twin bond. I can't imagine what Lydia's leaving did to Leah."

Daisy considered that. "She left for a man and true love."

"Maybe so," Rachel said with a nod. She hesitated and then admitted, "I think Leah and Titus married more for convenience."

"Not love?" Daisy asked, hurting for the twins.

"There seems to be love now, but that's not the way it started. Both sets of parents considered Leah and Titus a good match."

"So it was an arranged marriage?"

"Ah, hard to say. Leah could have said no. But as
I said, all she wanted was to marry and have children. Titus was considered a good catch. He had a
large working farm, horses, some cattle, and the
means to build them a good life. They both had
the same upbringing and values. They both
wanted the same future. Isn't that what marriage is
all about?"

"But there has to be love and passion, too."

As if she were hesitating to say what she was
thinking, Rachel took a few slow sips of tea. Finally, she gave a little shrug. "That's more of an
Englischer's way of thinking. If a marriage is built
on a solid foundation, love and more can follow.
Believe it or not, my parents and Levi's parents
thought we were a good match. My parents advised me to accept his invitation for a buggy ride
after a singing."

"Did you *want* to accept?"

"At first, no. I thought Levi was a little too
stodgy for me."

Daisy had to laugh. Levi could be quiet. But
when she'd seen him care for and play with his
children, then he was anything but stodgy. "But
you came to think differently of him, right?"

"I did. And yes, the love you speak of sparked
quickly. But it was by no means love at first sight.
We grew on each other as we grew in love. By the
time we married, we couldn't imagine life without
the other." Her gaze dipped to Daisy's ring. "That's
how you and Jonas feel, true?"

"Yes, it is. I wouldn't think of marrying without
that feeling. I was so young and impulsive with
Ryan, and that was right for me at the time. But
Jonas and I have been slower to sort our lives and

see how they fit together. We've always had that spark," she teased mischievously, knowing Rachel would never talk about the passion. It just wasn't her way.

The bell over Rachel's shop door dinged, and Daisy knew their conversation was over. She finished her tea and set down her mug.

As Rachel rose from her chair to see to her customer, she said, "I'm going to visit Leah tomorrow to express my condolences. Would you like to ride along?"

"I definitely would," Daisy answered. Maybe she could discover a clue as to who wanted to hurt Leah's twin sister.

Friday morning streamed with sun and a cold breeze as Rachel's son Luke hitched up the family buggy. Daisy had encouraged her friend to take the courting buggy—a two-seat open buggy—but Rachel had just smiled. "No, we'll use the other one," she'd said. "That way, you'll be warmer."

Rachel's family buggy was called a cabin buggy and sported a gray fiberglass top. The windows could be opened. Daisy and Rachel had them closed now to be as warm as they could be. In addition, Daisy covered her lap with a wool blanket. Battery-powered turn signal lights helped keep Rachel safe on the road, and the orange triangle at the rear of the buggy indicated that it was a slow-moving vehicle.

Inside the buggy, Daisy watched the scenery slip by, surprised how much she enjoyed traveling this way. As children, she and Rachel had ridden in buggies, wagons, and courting buggies. She'd even driven them. Last fall, she'd driven one for Rachel when her friend had experienced an unexpected injury.

A sheen of frost lay over the fields as they traveled back roads to the Yoders' farm and didn't encounter any traffic. Horses dotted the landscape behind wood fences. Later in spring and summer, they'd encounter vehicles used for tilling, hauling, and working the fields, some drawn with mules. But now all was quiet.

They clopped past a farm where goats cavorted in a pen. The wash line from barn to house had already been hung with the family's clothes. It was a common sight around Lancaster County.

They also drove by a phone shanty or two. Amish neighbors often shared a phone encased in a four-sided wooden structure with no windows. Answering machines took messages, and families checked the shanty at the end of each day. Like Rachel, some of the Amish farms had phones in their barns for necessities.

When they reached the Yoder farm, a red pickup truck was coming out of the lane. Daisy recognized the driver. It was Neil Aldenkamp.

Rachel saw him too and commented, "He probably just dropped off Frannie. I imagine he has a lot of arrangements to make."

"Lydia managed The Farm Barn," Daisy said. "She knew their operation inside and out. I suppose Neil's going to have to do that now. The truth is," Daisy said, "I don't know if Neil realizes the expertise he needs to run The Farm Barn. I could be wrong about that. I hope his servers and staff can help him."

"Do you think it will stay open?" Rachel asked.

"No clue," Daisy said. After all, wasn't this visit about picking up a few clues?

Rachel shot her a sideways glance and turned into the lane that led to the farm. It looked to Daisy as if some of the fencing needed repair. As Rachel's horse—this one was named Brownie—clomped up the lane, the buggy wheels threw a few stones.

Daisy took in the property with interest. The house itself was two stories and set between tall blue spruce. A wide porch crossed the front of the house.

"Did Titus and Leah build this?"

"Oh, no. It belonged to a relative of Titus who had passed on. Titus managed to buy the property for an honest sum before he and Leah were married."

The house was essentially a box shape, the roof slightly pitched. Smoke puffed out from a chimney.

After Rachel parked the buggy, Daisy attached Brownie to a hitching post. Rachel pulled a carton from the floor of the back seat while Daisy carried a basket. She'd brought corn chowder and corn cake. She knew Rachel's box contained a casserole and a batch of oatmeal cookies wrapped in foil. Together they climbed the gray-painted wooden steps to the porch. The railing surrounding the porch looked as if winter had taken its toll on it, because paint was chipping off here and there.

Daisy rapped on the wooden screen door, since Rachel's arms were full. The man who came to the door looked serious and questioning until his eyes fell on Rachel.

"*Guder mariye*," he said to Rachel.

"*Guder mariye* to you too, Titus. This is *mijn vriend* Daisy Swanson. We came to pay our condolences. Daisy was a friend of Lydia's."

Titus stepped back and motioned them inside. He said to Rachel, "I can carry that for you," and took the box from her arms.

Titus wore the traditional Amish dress for the area—black pants with suspenders and a dark blue long-sleeved shirt. His beard, signifying he was married, had at least a decade's worth of growth. His brown hair was cut in a bowl cut, and his eyes were blue and probing.

The living room was sparse with a sofa, armchair, and an oak rocker. Daisy spotted a tall canvas container, almost like a laundry basket with rope handles that lay on its side. Wood toys—from blocks to a truck—tumbled out. The clean planked white oak floors led into the kitchen, where Daisy could hear a child's laughter. A black wood stove on a brick hearth in the dining area sent warmth throughout the first floor.

Leah looked up from where she was sitting beside Frannie as the child colored on a large piece of paper.

"*Guden mariye,*" she said in what seemed like an automatic greeting. A small smile drifted to her lips, and she noted the box that Titus set on the table.

Daisy brought her basket over to join it. "We're so sorry about Lydia."

Leah nodded, looked down, and placed her hand on Frannie's curls. "*Danke,*" she said, again almost automatically.

Titus took his black felt hat from a peg on the

wall. His black three-quarter length coat followed. "I'll let you to your visit. I'll be in the barn." He nodded to Daisy and Rachel and left the house.

Leah glanced at him, and then the closed door. "He's grieving, too," Leah said to Rachel. "He and Lydia didn't often see eye to eye, but he loved her because she was my *schwester*."

Daisy knew that word very well. It meant sister.

"We don't want to intrude," Rachel said to her. "But we wanted to show you that we care."

Daisy pointed to her basket. "Corn chowder and corn cake."

Rachel added, "Beef and noodle casserole and cookies. I thought Frannie would enjoy."

Frannie glanced up at Leah. "Cookies?"

Leah gave her niece a genuine smile. "Would you like a cookie and milk? You didn't eat much breakfast."

"I wanna cookie," Frannie said.

"They're oatmeal-raisin," Rachel said. "So they're not altogether bad for her."

Frannie watched Leah with interest as she unwrapped the cookie pouch and took a cookie from it. After she quickly grabbed a plate from a cupboard, she set the cookie on it. Lifting the soup from Daisy's basket, she stowed it in the refrigerator and removed the bottle of milk. She poured the milk into a cup and settled Frannie at the table with her snack.

Leah gave Frannie a hug before she came to stand with Rachel and Daisy. There were tears in her eyes. "I'm not sure what to say to her."

Rachel put her hand on Leah's arm. "Love her the best you know how. She'll feel that. Tell her the truth when you must."

"That her mother isn't coming back?" Leah asked, almost looking horrified.

Daisy interjected, "It's kinder in the long run if she knows the truth. Even when my girls were older, it was better that they knew their father was dying of cancer, so they could say their good-byes."

"You're a widow?" Leah asked.

"I am."

Leah glanced at Frannie again. "Lydia and I were so different, not in looks, but in nature. Still, when we were children, we were inseparable. We raided the cookie jar together at night, we stayed awake much past when we were supposed to, we snuck out to the barn to play with the baby lambs. Then . . . Lydia met Neil, and everything changed. But we could still read each other's thoughts, at least often. Sometimes life just got in the way of us being twins."

"I saw Neil recently," Daisy said. "He's worried that the police will think he hurt Lydia."

Leah was nodding. "He told me that. I can't believe they would."

"He asked me to help him if I could."

Leah fingered a string on her *kapp* as she studied Daisy. "Lydia told me about you. She said you work with the police."

"Not exactly *with* them, but sometimes at the tea garden I find out information that can help them."

"We stay away from the police whenever we can."

The Amish wanted to stay off the grid. They wanted nothing to do with the government, and the police were under that category.

"I know you do, but I'd like to ask you a question if you don't mind."

After a brief hesitation, Leah agreed. "Go ahead."

Daisy kept her voice low. "Do you know anyone who would want to hurt your sister?"

CHAPTER SEVEN

Later that day at the tea garden, Daisy was serving soup and corn cake to a couple at a table in the main tearoom as she remembered Leah's answer to her question. She'd looked Daisy straight in the eye and said, "Everybody loved Lydia. She could talk to anyone . . . feel comfortable anywhere. I can't imagine anyone trying to hurt her."

Well, someone *had*. Would Zeke Willet talk to her about any other suspects they had other than Neil? She doubted it.

Daisy had just set the bowls of soup on the table for the couple when she felt a tap on her shoulder.

Daisy studied Cora Sue's serious expression. Her bottle red hair, high on her head in a topknot, didn't bob as it sometimes did. She was usually bubbly, but right now she looked as serious as a cup of black tea.

"Do you need help?" Daisy asked. Maybe they'd gotten a call for more tables or reservations for the afternoon tea.

"Not exactly." Cora Sue nodded over her shoulder to a table by the window. "Martha said she'd like to speak with you if you have time."

Martha Hahn was a regular at Daisy's Tea Garden. She usually came in in the late afternoon for a snack before heading home. She told Daisy it gave her a little quiet time before her kids returned from school and she cooked supper for the family. Martha was the one who had recommended The Farm Barn to Daisy last fall for Jonas's birthday celebration.

Cora Sue said, "I can take over this table if you want to talk with her. We're ready for all our guests coming for tea service."

At a glance into the spillover tearoom, Daisy could see Cora Sue was right. Three tables of four each were set for a full afternoon tea service. "All right, I'll see what she wants. I won't be too long." Daisy moved toward the corner table.

Martha might have an old-fashioned name, but she was by no means old-fashioned. She wore her hair in a stylish short bob. Her sandy-blond bangs fell down to her brows. She was dressed in a zebra-print short coat over winter white leggings.

When Daisy reached her table, Martha asked, "Do you have a few minutes?"

"Customers will come in to be seated for afternoon tea soon, but I have time until then." She took the seat across from Martha. "How can I help you?"

"I wanted to talk to you about Lydia." Martha usually wore stylish makeup, but even with cheek blush, she looked pale.

"You were friends long before I knew her," Daisy said. "I'm sorry for your loss."

Pushing her empty cup of tea away from her,

Martha sank against her chair back. "And I'm sorry for yours. I know you hiked with her, and you'd become friends."

"Yes, we had. We became close after Jonas's birthday party last fall. I was so glad you recommended The Farm Barn."

"I knew it was perfect for what you wanted."

"It was perfect for my parents' anniversary dinner, too. Lydia seemed a little discombobulated that night, but everything went off well. The food was delicious, and the service was good."

Martha picked up on what Daisy had said. "Do you know why she wasn't herself?"

"No, I don't. Now I wish I did."

"Her death wasn't an accident, was it?" Martha asked.

"Have you heard something?" Daisy asked, not wanting to give away anything the police intended to keep quiet.

"I heard that someone ran her down . . . *on purpose*," Martha answered, her face a combination of grief and anger.

Daisy stayed silent.

"I know you help the police sometimes."

"I think they'd rather I wouldn't," Daisy responded honestly.

"But this time you will, won't you? Because Lydia was your friend."

Remembering her visit to Leah, Daisy admitted honestly, "I don't know what I can do."

Martha stared down at her plate dotted with crumbs from a cinnamon scone. "I have something to ask you."

"Go ahead," Daisy prompted.

Raising her head, Martha asked, "Did Lydia tell you about her marriage?"

Unsure what Martha was getting at, Daisy answered, "Lydia explained to me that she left her faith for Neil, and they married young. I'm not sure she knew what she was getting into, with both marriage and the English world at the same time. She'd been protected all of her life."

"I'm not speaking of the past," Martha insisted. "At least not the faraway past. There were problems in Lydia's marriage."

"What kind of problems?" Daisy thought about finances that could come between a married couple. Then she remembered her bill from The Farm Barn. "Is The Farm Barn in financial trouble?"

"I wouldn't know about that. But I *do* know Neil had an affair."

That evening, Daisy had many thoughts on her mind when she and Jonas cuddled up on the sofa. A fire licked at a few logs as they listened to music. It was a habit they'd developed that she especially liked, because the time helped them both unwind and connect. After a while, with the acoustic guitar playing lightly in the background, she fiddled with a button on Jonas's flannel shirt and said, "One of my customers today told me something I didn't really want to know."

"What was it?" Jonas asked, stroking her hair.

"She said that Neil had an affair."

Jonas was quiet for a few moments. "It won't take long for Zeke or Morris to find that out.

Affairs are never as hidden as people want them to be."

"You didn't know about Zeke and Brenda," she reminded him. Since his best friend and his lover had betrayed him, Daisy knew the subject could still be painful.

She felt Jonas tense for a few moments, but then he relaxed again. "No, I didn't. I suppose that was because I trusted them both. Zeke was a good friend. I never expected him and Brenda to have an affair."

"The way Zeke tells it, it was only one time."

"One time is still an affair."

Daisy knew betrayal was betrayal, no matter how many times it happened.

Zeke and Jonas had gotten over the betrayal and formed a friendship once again, though Daisy didn't know if Jonas would have ever recovered from what had happened if Brenda had lived.

Thinking about Lydia and Neil's marriage, she sighed. "I suppose I thought since Lydia and Neil fell in love when they were young, and she gave up everything to be with him, that their marriage would have been a good one. But I guess you never know what the inside of a marriage looks like, do you?"

"No," Jonas said.

She looked up at him and asked, "What do you think makes a man look outside of a marriage?"

Jonas's frown was wry. "Other than the obvious reasons?"

"And what are the obvious reasons?" Daisy asked. "The way a woman flirts . . . the way she relates to a man?"

"Possibly. But it's also the thrill of a new relationship. Sex. Something novel. Beyond that, I think there's a need to feel good around someone, to feel like you're admired, and feel like you're understood. Things happen in a marriage, I suppose, and people grow apart. When that happens, it leaves the door open."

"I suppose that's true for a woman, too," Daisy said. "But Lydia had her daughter to think about. And like I said, she'd given up everything for Neil, especially her family. Does a man think about his children—their feelings . . . their future—like a woman does?"

Jonas took her hand and rubbed his thumb over her fingers. "I don't know about other men, Daisy. I only know about me. When I make a vow, I intend to keep it. If problems arise, we'll work them out together. Isn't that what we've done up until now?"

With hope in her heart for their future, she realized that was exactly what they had done.

She had something else she needed to talk to him about. "I made a decision."

"About?" he asked.

"I'm going to make an appointment with Tara Morelli. I think it will help me to talk with her, especially since I'm going to be involved in this investigation."

On Sunday afternoon, Jonas and Daisy walked into the social center at the fire hall, ready for a meeting. A committee was planning the groundbreaking ceremony for Willow Creek's homeless shelter. The chamber of commerce was involved and had come up with a sign for the shelter to be presented at the groundbreaking. It was revealed today on a tripod at the front of the room.

Once they were all seated on folding chairs in the large room, Betty Furhman, the president of the chamber this year as well as the owner of Wisps and Wicks—a candle shop downtown—stood in front of all of them with a wide smile. After welcoming remarks, she said, "I'm so pleased the homeless shelter is coming into fruition. I want to thank Jonas Groft for the beautiful background wood detail of the sign, and Nan Conroy for her graphic talent in painting on the letters for our New Beginnings shelter."

Daisy squeezed Jonas's elbow. "It's really beautiful."

Jonas had created the long, elegant shape of the wood with curvy corners that gave it a bit of pizzazz. Nan, a Willow Creek crafter in many areas that Daisy was quite familiar with, had painted the lettering and the flourish. After she'd finished, Jonas had completed the project by adding a coat of finish that would withstand weather. When the building was completed, it would proudly be displayed above the front door.

Betty motioned toward the sign, and most people in the room clapped. Afterward, the business meeting proceeded.

Chamber business today revolved around a date for the groundbreaking ceremony, as well as festivities. Although the town had had a social in the fall that Daisy had catered, this would be an official ceremony. The mayor would cut a ribbon and speak about the unifying qualities of the shelter. Gavin Cranshaw, the contractor on the job, would explain the construction process.

Sitting a table away, Gavin smiled when he caught Daisy's eye. Because Gavin was Foster's dad, she and Gavin had certainly had their ups and downs as the young couple married and became parents. They'd even been involved in the catching of a murderer together. Good friends now, Daisy considered Gavin an integral part of her family.

Jonas murmured to Daisy, "I know Gavin will give an honest presentation of what's involved in the construction. Do you think Willow Creek residents can take that?"

"I do. I also know Gavin will try to stay on budget. His projects usually come in maybe only five percent over. He tries to factor in the price increases of lumber and other materials."

"That's the way of construction," Jonas said. "And we'll have to remember that if we do put an addition on the house."

They listened as Betty also brought up the subject of the coming spring and what flowers the town would hang on the lampposts. The town council was involved in that project, but the chamber members had a say. After all, they ran the businesses, hoping that prettying up the town would bring in more customers.

After Betty ended the meeting, everyone rose from their seats. Some left, and others chatted with each other. Gavin came over to join Jonas and Daisy. After greetings, he asked, "Are Foster and Vi packed up yet?"

"They're trying," Daisy said. "But I think a lot of the moving is going to be last minute, shoving baby things into the car and just carrying them in without boxes."

Gavin laughed. "When you have kids, things are a little disorganized sometimes."

Gavin had three children—Foster, Ben, and Emily. After his wife had died, he'd done a good job of raising them on his own.

Nan Conroy suddenly appeared by Daisy's side and tapped her shoulder. "Can I speak to you for a few minutes in private?"

"Sure," Daisy said, excusing herself from the men.

Around fifty years old, Nan had dark brown hair that dropped to her shoulders. She often wore a headband or used a banana clip, arranging it on top of her head. Her nose was a bit large for her face, but her royal-blue eyeglass frames took attention from that. She often lifted them to see better to read or do her work. She was curvy but wore loose dresses that often floated mid-calf. Tonight she was wearing an A-line cranberry long-sleeved dress that stopped just below her knees. Her short black boots were practical for the winter weather.

One of Nan's specialties was making clothespin dolls to sell online and at flea markets. Daisy had contacted her to make them for her planned Alice in Wonderland Tea the first weekend in April. Each of her child guests would receive one.

Nan was carrying a tote bag that she'd probably designed. It was a heavy cotton fabric patterned with every sort of kitchen utensil. Orange, green, and yellow made it quite eye-catching.

Leading Daisy to one of the tables, Nan set her tote bag atop it. She pulled out three clothespin dolls. The first was an Alice in Wonderland replica with blond hair, a blue bow, a blue dress, and a white apron.

"That's adorable," Daisy said admiringly. "I love it!"

Nan grinned. She pulled out a second one. This one was fashioned sideways, like a cat with a huge grin—the Cheshire Cat. The stiff brown and black fabric had been glued on to represent its fur.

"That one is cute, too," Daisy said.

The third clothespin doll she pulled from her bag was representative of the White Rabbit.

"You've outdone yourself. I love them all."

"And you think thirty-five of them will be plenty?" Nan asked.

"I'd rather have extra in case I need them. When my servers see these, they might each want one, too. Can you make ten extra?"

"Sure, I can. I'm starting a big push for the flea markets this spring. I worked all winter to make enough, but I never know." She began inserting the clothespin dolls back into her bag. While she did, she gave a sideways glance to Daisy. "I wanted to talk to you about something else, too." She checked around them to see if anybody was listening.

"What?" Daisy asked with curiosity.

"Lydia Aldenkamp and I often did brainstorming sessions about decorations for The Farm Barn. She'd been planning a new look for summer—lots of flowers, fabrics, and eyelet instead of burlap. I was going to help her with the accessories."

Daisy had almost forgotten about Lydia's murder in the busyness and chatter of the chamber of commerce meeting. Now, however, it all came rushing back. "I still can't believe she's gone," Daisy murmured.

Nan searched Daisy's face. "I heard *you* were the one who found her."

"I'd like to keep that quiet. I don't want to answer a lot of questions about what I saw."

"I can only imagine," Nan said. "But people will talk, and there was a lot of activity there that day after you found her. Patrol officers have families, and they often know things that ordinary folk don't. The chatter spreads."

Daisy knew that was certainly true. A new patrol officer had once caused an information leak that had brought an altercation to the tea garden. It had embarrassed her.

Waving her hand as if to brush all that away, Nan went on. "I brought this up because I wondered about something. Did you know that Lydia had had pranks played on her over the past month?"

"I didn't know that. What type of pranks?"

"She found nails under her tires. One time after she was in town, someone had slashed one of her tires. Another time when she was parked at The Farm Barn, someone keyed her vehicle."

Daisy's mind spun. Why would anybody do that to Lydia? "Did she have suspicions about who was doing it?"

"If she did, she wouldn't say. Do you think this is something I should tell the police about?"

"It wouldn't hurt," Daisy replied, thinking that the damage could have been more than pranks. Had there been other problems that Nan didn't know about? Had Neil known about this? "The police are probably going to want to question anyone who had been around Lydia when those things happened to her. Yes, I'd definitely tell them."

"I'll call in the morning. Will you be attending Lydia's funeral on Tuesday?"

"Yes, I will. I feel so bad for her twin and her husband."

"Leah has Frannie to comfort her if Neil keeps giving her Frannie's care."

"I don't see why he wouldn't," Daisy said.

"He'll be a widower. He might close The Farm Barn. Who knows what he'll do next."

Daisy supposed all of that was true. She was reminded how she'd changed her life after her husband had died.

Jonas came over to Daisy's side and wrapped his arm around her waist. "Hi, Nan," he said. "I think they liked our sign."

"I'm grateful they did," she said. "We both worked hard on it." She picked up her tote bag and said to Daisy, "I'll let you know when I finish the dolls."

"The dolls for your tea?" Jonas asked with a smile.

"Yes, and I'm looking forward to it already," Daisy admitted. Kids, dolls, and Alice in Wonderland. What could be more uplifting?

Daisy leaned against her fiancé, knowing he understood her more than anyone else in her world. She was so grateful for that.

As Daisy sat in Tara Morelli's office on Monday afternoon, she wondered again what she was doing there. The therapist's office was located in the downtown area of Willow Creek, two streets behind the tea garden. An old craftsman-style home, it had been refurbished. From the sign outside, Daisy knew that an acupuncturist and a reflexologist also practiced in the building.

Tara's office was located down the hall from the front foyer. Stairs accessing the second floor led to other offices. Jazzi had told Daisy all about the office, since she'd once been a client of Tara's. But now Daisy assessed the area herself. After Tara had closed the door and welcomed Daisy inside, Daisy had glimpsed a bathroom connected to the office. She'd also noted a litter box inside. She'd been trying to distract herself from why she was here. It was easy to do that in the pleasant room.

Floor to ceiling built-ins climbed up one wall. A desk space was at the center with a rolling high-back ergonomic chair. The bookshelves were painted a very light gray. If Daisy really wanted to distract herself, she could try to read the titles on all the volumes on the shelves, as well as scan the knick-knacks and photos there. The area rug over the wood floor was rectangular in shades of light coral and gray. The same tones of gray were present in the subtly patterned wallpaper around the rest of the room. A love seat in coral and off-white sat against one wall. Right now Lancelot, a large yellow tabby with big golden eyes, lounged on it. He focused on Daisy every so often.

Daisy sat across the room in an off-white fabric armchair that faced another just like it. A round, dark coral ottoman sat between the chairs. A table against the wall next to her chair held a charcoal-and-white-patterned light and a box of tissues.

Tara, who sat across from her, held a legal pad on her lap. Tara Morelli might have been in her late forties. It was difficult to tell. Her highlighted hair waved around her face, and her bangs flowed to the side. Her nose was slim and long, and her mouth was wide. When she smiled, her green eyes lit with pleasure, and a dimple appeared at the corner of her mouth. She was wearing khaki slacks with an off-white blouse and short jeans jacket.

Suddenly Lancelot stood, arched his back, blinked at Daisy, and jumped to the floor with a plop. He headed straight for her and jumped up onto her lap. She accepted him easily, letting him settle on her raspberry-colored slacks, not minding the idea of pet hair on them one bit. She let him smell her hand, and he brushed his face against it.

"Are you comfortable with him there?" Tara asked.

"I am. I told you when we spoke on the phone that I love cats. Jazzi talked about Lancelot often from her sessions."

"He must have thought you looked nervous," Tara said conversationally. "Are you?"

Of course, Tara was aware of Lancelot's vibes as well as Daisy's. "I don't know if nervous is the right word. I'm not afraid of you or Lancelot or the session. I feel comfortable here. The room reminds me a little of the tea garden. It's trying to promote peace and calm."

Tara nodded. "That's exactly what I try to promote. However, sometimes we have to wade through rapids to get to the peace."

"I suppose that's what I'm afraid of, if I'm afraid of anything."

Tara paused, then noted perceptively, "In my experience, someone who's fearful doesn't help the police solve murder investigation cases."

"The cases just happen." Daisy knew she probably sounded defensive.

Tara didn't judge. She merely waited.

Daisy finally gave in to breaking the silence. "I think that's what I'm here to talk about. My relationships with my daughters, Jazzi and Vi, are stable. My mother and I are getting along better than we ever have. I consider my family to be loving, and my friends to be supportive."

She considered her life and her plans to marry. "I suppose Jazzi has told you all about Jonas?"

"She has, but your counseling sessions are confidential. I would never tell Jazzi something you said. I would never tell you something that Jazzi said, unless both of you were here together and I had your permission."

Daisy nodded, knowing that was true. She and Tara had spoken about the confidentiality agreement before Jazzi's sessions had started.

"Jonas has formed a good relationship with Jazzi, and he and I . . . well, sometimes I have to pinch myself. I can't believe I found him."

"Or he found you," Tara said with a smile. "How does Jonas feel about your involvement in murder cases?"

"Since he's a former detective, he's often helpful. I think he'd like me to not get involved simply because he's protective. But it's not as if I go looking for something to solve. And now, he said he'd help me in any way he can."

"Now?" Tara asked.

Daisy stroked her hand down Lancelot's ginger back. The fur on his back was darker than the lighter golden fur on his sides. His face actually had white cheeks. Right now, she needed him on her lap more than she could say.

When he looked up at Daisy as if to give her encouragement, she told Tara, "I think I need to talk about finding Lydia's body . . . about feeling as if I might have been in danger that day. Lydia's husband asked me to help him. Lydia was my friend. I'm worried about her little girl."

Tara had made a few notes and now looked thoughtful. "Tell me what you expect from our sessions."

In the dead of night, Daisy had considered exactly that. "I want to figure out why I'm drawn into murder cases and dangerous situations. I have to find out why confronting a murderer doesn't always make my knees shake. I have to find out why solving the case is sometimes more important than my own safety."

Tara's gaze lifted to Daisy's. "Okay, let's get started."

CHAPTER EIGHT

Daisy and Jonas drove to the Fountain of Life Cemetery on Tuesday morning. It sat atop a rolling hill surrounded by pines and sycamores. Jonas had driven his vehicle, and Daisy sat beside him with her hands folded in her lap.

"What are you thinking about?" Jonas asked, obviously noticing how quiet she'd been.

"I'm thinking about cemeteries and the place they've had in my life."

Driving up the hill, he hesitated before asking, "Do you think about Ryan when you visit a cemetery?"

"I do," she admitted softly. "But I think about Jazzi, too." She felt the need to explain. "During Ryan's funeral, rain fell. Afterward, Jazzi saw a rainbow. Since then, she's looked for rainbows, considering them a sign that her dad is watching over her. We look for signs, don't we?"

Without a moment's hesitation, Jonas reached over and squeezed her hand. "We still want to be connected to our loved ones. The signs give us hope."

"Butterflies as well as rainbows," Daisy said. "My mom always claimed that whenever she saw a butterfly, that was her mom looking over her. Butterflies and rainbows. I suppose they help on a day like this."

Jonas didn't comment again but drove along a narrow lane laid with gravel. It led to a cemetery plot where a green canopy had been raised. They'd passed security at the entrance to the cemetery, and Daisy supposed they had been hired to prevent reporters from bothering mourners. She'd been fortunate that her name hadn't been connected to Lydia's murder, at least in the broader public. There had been a circus of reporters around the tea garden after the first murder she'd become involved in. That had been scary. Jonas had helped shield her from the worst of it. That's when she'd first noticed his protective streak. He knew she liked to take care of herself, and he respected her ability to do so. But his warrior side emerged when she was threatened.

When Jonas parked behind a line of cars, Daisy recognized Detective Rappaport's nondescript black sedan. Jonas did, too. He commented to Daisy, "You'd think Morris would have that dent fixed so nobody could recognize his car." The detective and a fence post had connected on an icy road in January.

"That would take time to do. And he doesn't like to use his truck for police work. He'd have to be without the car for a few days," Daisy noted. "Why do you think he's here for the funeral?"

"Probably to watch Lydia's husband."

Although Daisy wished Neil was in the clear, she knew the husband was always the prime subject in cases like this. Especially since Neil didn't have an alibi.

Twenty minutes later, Daisy stood with Jonas to the back of the rows of chairs lined up before the casket, bracing in her winter dress coat against the breeze. Leah and her husband were in the front row, sitting beside Neil. Leah looked meek and small in her black wool cape and black bonnet, as if she were trying to disappear. She almost looked as if she felt she shouldn't be there. Her husband Titus was stoic in his long black overcoat and black felt hat. From what Daisy could see, the twins' parents hadn't attended, and Daisy thought that was sad.

She leaned toward Jonas. "It's such a shame Lydia's parents aren't here."

He frowned when he murmured, "Lydia's parents shunned her, and that's true even of her funeral."

"How can parents *be* like that?" she protested.

"They're Amish, Daisy. You know that sometimes their rules are more important than family . . . more important than any bonds they have."

Jonas did understand, and she did, too. But it was just hard to take in. "I wonder where Frannie is."

"Probably with one of Neil and Lydia's friends. I wouldn't bring a child her age to a funeral, either."

As a biting wind whipped through the tent, Daisy stood closer to Jonas, her body against his. Her purple wool dress coat protected her somewhat, but she was still chilled inside. Not only from the cold.

Reverend Kemp, the minister from Daisy's church, had known Lydia and Neil. From his comments about Lydia, Daisy expected they had been regular attendants at the services. He spoke of Lydia's kindnesses to others, her love for her daughter, the works she had performed at the church. He read from the first letter to the Corinthians, chapter thirteen. *Though I speak with the tongues of men and of angels, but have not love, I'm only a resounding gong, a clanging cymbal resounding in the wind.*

He ended with, *And now abide, faith, hope, and love; these three. But the greatest of these is love.*

Daisy had tears in her eyes when he finished. She saw that Leah was openly crying. Titus handed his wife a white handkerchief.

Everyone stood in place after the minister had finished. Neil must have kept two roses by his side, because now he gave one to Leah. Together they went to the casket and placed them on top. They stood there a few moments, each engulfed in grief. Leah turned away first and returned to her husband's side. Neil stared at the casket, as if he still couldn't believe Lydia was gone. A few minutes later, he went back to his chair, looking like a broken man.

Jonas leaned into Daisy's shoulder. "Are you going to speak with Detective Rappaport?"

After the chamber of commerce meeting, Daisy had revealed to Jonas what Nan had told her. "I suppose I should. He's behind the canopy near the pines."

This plot was at the edge of the cemetery, and

Daisy knew Detective Rappaport didn't want his presence to be overly obvious. As she turned to find him, she realized there were quite a few people gathered behind her. Lydia had made many friends at The Farm Barn. She noticed one young woman particularly overcome with grief. She was petite. Her curly blond hair was disheveled, and she had dark circles under her eyes. Daisy had seen her serving at the restaurant. She recalled her name was April.

As Daisy threaded her way through the funeral-goers to reach Detective Rappaport, someone tapped her on the back of the shoulder. She turned and saw Martha Hahn. "Hi, Martha."

Martha was shaking her head. "It's a sad day today."

"It is," Daisy agreed, motioning to the rows of people who had gathered for the funeral. "Lydia made lots of friends."

"Yes, she did," Martha said.

April was standing a few feet away, and Daisy nodded to her. "Some of Lydia's servers are here."

Martha seemed to notice April's tearstained cheeks. "Lydia and April Jennings were particularly close. April lost her parents in an accident when she was twenty. Now she's twenty-two and on her own. She's one of those people who Lydia took her under her wing. April even stayed overnight at Lydia's now and then, probably because she was missing her parents and felt lonely. Lydia considered her servers as family. Because her parents particularly ignored her, I think she believed she had to take care of others. She didn't want anyone to feel as abandoned as she had."

Martha waved to someone at the edge of the

crowd. "That's my ride. I'll see you soon at the tea garden."

After Martha walked away, Daisy continued on to the edge of the cemetery, where Detective Rappaport was standing. She said to him in greeting, "You're more noticeable back here than you would be if you were in the crowd."

"Maybe I want to be noticed," he responded succinctly.

"Who are you keeping your eye on?"

He didn't deny that he was. His gaze was obviously targeting Neil and Leah, who were standing together near the casket.

Her voice low, Daisy said, "I know Neil doesn't have a decent alibi. Does Leah?"

Detective Rappaport's gaze focused on Daisy now. "I know you and Lydia were friends. *You* probably know more than I do."

Always taciturn, the detective was adept at modifying the conversation. "You didn't answer my question," Daisy said.

"I usually don't," he replied with a shrug.

"Aren't we beyond all that, Detective?"

After a sigh, he finally answered, "Leah doesn't have one, either. Doing chores on her farm where nobody saw her doesn't count."

"And did Neil explain his whereabouts?"

Rappaport leaned against the trunk of the bare-branched maple tree. "He dropped his child off at preschool, but after that, he took a drive. That doesn't count as an alibi."

"Do you know where Frannie is today?" Daisy was often surprised at the facts Detective Rappaport could find out that nobody else knew.

"She's with her preschool teacher. That woman

is an important part of the network. She's organized and time-oriented, so I can believe the time
she told me when Neil dropped off his daughter
the day of the murder."

Knowing the detective's interrogation skills from
personal experience, Daisy imagined he'd grilled
the preschool teacher thoroughly. Morris scanned
the crowd, and his attention settled on Neil once
more. "He acts like a grieving husband, doesn't he?"

"Acts?" Daisy asked, catching the implication.

Again, Morris shrugged. "Anyone can be a good
actor with a little practice."

To Daisy, Neil's grief seemed genuine, but she
didn't say so to Rappaport. He'd think what he was
going to think.

"Did Nan Conroy call your office?" she asked,
feeling obligated to tell Morris what she knew.

"I think she called Zeke's number, but I don't
think he's had time to talk to her yet. Why?"

"She told me that in the past month, Lydia had
had pranks played on her. Someone put nails
under her tires . . . actually slit one of her tires.
Someone also keyed her car."

Morris swung his full attention to Daisy. "And
you think this could have something to do with
her murder?"

"It could if someone was angry enough with her
to do it. Maybe that anger got out of hand."

"Maybe," Rappaport agreed. "But vandalism
doesn't always lead to murder. I don't have to tell
you what I'm thinking, do I?"

"No. I'm a mind reader," she said with a sigh.
"You're not going to tell me to stay out of the investigation, but you're going to hope that I will."

"You *are* a mind reader. That doesn't bode well for Jonas."

She couldn't tell if the detective was serious or not. Then one side of his lips suddenly twitched up. He was holding back a smile. Once in a while, he *did* have a sense of humor.

After Daisy finished with Detective Rappaport, a few more of the customers of the tea garden stopped to talk with her. That was true of other chamber of commerce members, too, business owners who were sad about The Farm Barn and wondered if it was going to close. Daisy didn't have any answers.

When Daisy glanced at Detective Rappaport, he'd moved away from the trees and into the group. He was standing in the row behind Leah and her husband, and Daisy didn't recognize the man he was talking to. A patrol officer in civilian dress also came to watch the gathering? Maybe *she* was the one getting paranoid now. Would the department do that?

They would do anything to solve the murder. She knew that. She was about to approach Jonas to see if he wanted to leave when Neil Aldenkamp appeared beside her. She believed she could see evidence of tears on his face.

He wiped away wetness below his eyes. "Thank you for coming. I know you care. Some of these people are just curious, and that's why they came. I saw you talking with Detective Rappaport. Is he ready to arrest me?"

She felt sorry for Neil. How could she believe he

had anything to do with his wife's death? "Neil, I wouldn't know that. Really, I wouldn't. The police are very close-mouthed about these investigations. They only tell me what they think I already know. My coming here today had nothing to do with the investigation. I wanted to support you and Leah. Is Frannie okay?"

"She's missing her mom." He looked away as he seemed to choke up. "Her preschool teacher is watching her today. Megan was a friend of Lydia's. She babysits for us when Leah can't."

Daisy waited, because she suspected Neil had something else on his mind. She didn't know why she thought that, but she didn't believe he would have started a conversation today of all days if he didn't. She imagined he'd want to pick up Frannie, go home, and lick his wounds. Still, she could be reading him all wrong.

"I have a favor to ask you," he said.

"What is it? If I can help, I will."

"I'm in a real pinch. A friend of mine has a wedding reception planned at The Farm Barn. I have no one to manage the event. Lydia did all of that. She probably did things I can't even think of."

"Can't one of your servers step up?" Daisy asked, suspecting where this conversation was going.

"Our servers are just that, servers. April's the only one who's shown any initiative to speak of. But she and Lydia were close, and April is having her own breakdown right now."

"How would you like me to help?"

"I'd like you to manage the wedding reception."

"I've never done anything like that," she told him honestly.

"Yes, you have," he protested. "You manage the

tea garden every day, and I heard you planned your daughter's reception. I know your aunt is your partner and you have a kitchen manager. Nevertheless, you are the main force at Daisy's Tea Garden. I've heard about your special tea events that are very much like receptions. The last one, the Storybook Tea, was all over the news. So don't tell me you can't handle a reception."

"Neil, I don't know . . ."

As her voice trailed off, he jumped right in again. "Lydia has a flash drive with the names of the people she contacts for each of the particular services. So all you'd have to do is contact them. She uses a baker in Lancaster for the wedding cakes. She uses a supplier in York for the linens and silverware and glassware for anything special. Our chef would be able to tell you what he needs and where he gets it. The menu for the reception is already planned."

"It sounds to me as if the event is already on a roll. Why me?"

"Because you have class, and you can intuit what people want. I know nothing about decorating The Farm Barn for a wedding reception. I'm sure you might have ideas for that."

This time of year, dried lavender and tulle would work, depending on what the bride's preferred décor was.

"The couple wants to go ahead with the reception. Please consider managing it for me . . . for Lydia."

Daisy understood that he knew that last supplication would touch her. It had. She would have done anything for Lydia . . . and now, for her daughter. Keeping The Farm Barn on its feet would be the best thing to do for Frannie.

"I have an event coming up at the tea garden in a month, an Alice in Wonderland Tea. I have to put all my creative energy into that. I don't want to short-change anybody."

"How about if we start with a date," Neil said. "It's March eleventh."

"That's less than two weeks away."

"Can you fit it into your schedule?"

"Let me talk to Jonas and my staff. I want to make sure I have the time to give to you for planning before then."

"Will you give me your answer soon?"

"I'll give you my answer by Friday."

"That's fair."

Jonas strode over to Daisy then and wrapped his arm around her. "Are you cold? Are you ready to go?"

She nodded. "Neil and I were just finished. Neil, take care of yourself and Frannie. I'll give you a call by Friday."

"Thank you, Daisy."

He didn't have anything to thank her for . . . yet.

To Daisy's surprise, a tourist bus had parked in the public parking lot on Friday around lunchtime, and visitors had poured into Daisy's Tea Garden. She didn't have time to think about Lydia's murder or Neil's request as she served tea, salads, and baked goods.

Cora Sue sidled up to her around two. "Things have slowed down," she said. "Why don't you take your break? We've all had ours at one point or another."

Daisy looked around the tea garden. Remaining customers were finishing their orders. Everyone had been served efficiently, and activity had wound down.

"I grabbed a couple of cucumber sandwiches earlier, but I could use fresh air. Maybe I'll take a walk down to Woods. I'll be back in half an hour."

Cora Sue nodded and gave Daisy a knowing smile. "Tell Jonas I said *hi*."

Daisy smiled back. "I will."

Like many other store owners in town, Jonas had decorated his front window with the coming of spring in mind. He'd placed two porch rockers there, one in white and one in natural wood. Their caned seats were part of their beauty. Anyone could imagine them on a front porch or in a living room. Beside them, he'd placed a side table that had one leaf dropped and one leaf open. On it he'd set a pink-and-yellow-flowered tea service that Daisy had lent him. A highboy sat to the side of the rockers with a stuffed cat in gardening duds on top of it. The other shelves held miniatures from tiny flowerpots to bunny rabbits to tiny gardening implements. Underneath it all, he'd positioned a scalloped oval jute rug. It was reminiscent of one that might be placed on the front porch. The tableau would have drawn her inside, even if she hadn't wanted to see Jonas.

There were several customers in Jonas's store. She found him almost immediately at the back counter with the cash register. He was filling out a sales slip for a man standing there. His manager, Tony Fitz, seemed to be explaining the styles of chairs that sat in cubicles against one wall. Jonas would customize any finish, from the robin-egg blue to the walnut to the white.

Daisy waved at Jonas and motioned that she'd look around until he was finished. There was always something beautiful to see, from the granite-topped islands to the hope chests to a mirrored dresser. Two Mennonite women standing in front of that dresser were engrossed in conversation. Daisy could tell that they were Mennonite from the *kapp*s on their hair and the pattern of their dresses—one was green-flowered and the other had a pretty blue design. They were holding jackets over their arms, so Daisy considered them serious customers who wanted to look around for a while.

She herself had her eye on a writer's desk for her living room. She could use that, not only for her laptop, but to work on her recipes, which she usually wrote longhand. The front of the desk came down with two supports that slipped out of either side. That formed the surface of the desk. When it wasn't in use, it could be closed, hiding a shelf and cubbyholes where she could keep her notes. It seemed like a good idea.

Since it was sitting next to the dresser, she approached it with a smile. The grained walnut finish was exactly the kind she liked. She ran her hand over the glossy top of it.

She was ready to open the front by a little turnkey handle when she heard one of the women tell the other, "I heard Leah was a sight at the funeral. She couldn't stop crying. She's had so much tragedy. Having a stillborn baby could ruin a woman."

Daisy knew Leah and Titus sold produce at a stand on their farm. The community heard things when they milled about it.

"It was a terrible experience," the other woman agreed. "And she hasn't been able to conceive since. Now her sister is gone. One loss always compounds another, and the way her parents treated Lydia . . . that was a sadness all of its own."

Daisy hated to eavesdrop. She really did. But learning more about Leah might tell her more about what could have happened to her sister.

Daisy opened the front of the little desk quietly, not wanting to disturb the two women or interrupt their conversation. It was better if they didn't notice her.

"Lydia told me all Leah ever wanted was a husband and lots of babies. No wonder she loves Frannie as she does. But there is heartache coming her way."

Daisy went still and listened intently.

"Did you see how rundown the farm is looking?" the woman in the blue dress asked.

"Life is tough everywhere, but Titus Yoder is not the type to ask for help. All he'd have to do is approach a neighbor or two. His fences would be repaired in no time. He'd have help with the fields, too."

The woman in green began to move away, and her friend followed.

Daisy stayed put, thinking about everything they'd said. She was running her fingers over the inside of the small secretary when someone beside her asked, "Interested? If your fingerprints are on it, you have to buy it."

Daisy knew that voice. Trevor Lundquist was standing over her, looking down at her with a grin.

"Are you Jonas's new salesperson?" she teased.

"I'd be good at it, don't you think?"

"I think you might chase his customers away. I am looking at this to buy, though. It really would be perfect in my living room."

Trevor leaned close and whispered in her ear, "I bet if you tell Jonas that, he'd make you one, and you wouldn't have to buy it."

She laughed. "You're probably right. On the other hand, I'm helping his store and the community if I buy it."

"Other than the desk, I wanted to talk to you about something," Trevor said seriously. "Cora Sue told me you were here when I stopped at the tea garden."

"What's on your mind?"

"I'm working on next week's blog. My subject's going to be Amish versus English roots in this area."

"Because of what happened to Lydia?"

"The fact that she and Leah are twins sparked the idea. But I was wondering . . ." He paused, then continued, "Do you think Rachel Fisher would speak to me about it?"

After considering Trevor's inquiry, Daisy answered, "That depends on what your motives are. Rachel would be interested in those, too."

He thought about her concern. "My motives are pure, I promise. I think you've been influenced by the Amish, and other Englischers have, too. On the other hand, have the English influenced the Amish? I'm just posing the questions."

"You'll have to plead your case to Rachel yourself. I'm sure she won't be part of it if you're going to show anything Amish in a negative light."

He shrugged. "I'm hoping to make it an optimistic article based on facts, merely the facts."

Daisy knew the detectives were going to proceed with the facts for their investigation. Maybe that's what she should consider doing. She was also going to accept Neil's offer to oversee his friend's wedding reception. That occasion could reveal facts, too.

CHAPTER NINE

On Sunday evening, Daisy stood in the middle of what had been Foster, Vi, and Sammy's apartment. Now it was her apartment again, and it was empty . . . so empty. This apartment above her garage was decidedly tight on space. She supposed it had the square footage of a small cabin—one open room, except for the bedroom that had a connecting bath with a sink, commode, and walk-in shower. The living room area had once held a platform rocker that had been tucked in beside a sofa. A small table had been positioned in the kitchen area. Daisy had made and shared food there so many times. Most of the furniture had been selected from a thrift store, and Gavin had helped with that expense. Gavin had gifted Vi and Foster with a new bed as a housewarming present. The old one was still here.

What Daisy recalled most vividly was Vi giving birth to Sammy in the bedroom. Daisy had been a witness to that miracle. Jonas had been here, too, in a supportive way, trying to take care of anything that any of them needed.

Today most of the color was gone from this apartment . . . the sounds were gone from this space . . . the love was gone from this space.

Daisy was so lost in her thoughts of everything that had happened in the apartment, all the times they'd shared, that she hadn't heard Jonas come up the steps and into the living room area. When he reached her side, she brushed away a tear. Standing behind her, he wrapped his arms around her and held on tight.

"I'm sorry I'm so emotional."

"Nothing to be sorry about," he said, close to her ear. "You liked having Vi and Sammy and Foster close. You want to experience every moment of your grandchild's life that you can. You care a lot. I care, too. I've gotten used to seeing the three of them around the property, stopping in for a cup of tea when Foster needs to talk about something. Since Sammy started walking, he and Felix are so much fun to watch."

Daisy took in a deep breath and squared her shoulders. Seeming to sense her resolution, Jonas turned her around to face him. "Vi isn't moving away, just into the country. Ten minutes and you can be there. What are you afraid of?"

"I want to be close to them, but I don't want to intrude on them. I'm also afraid that at a distance, they'll be so busy they'll forget we're around."

He hugged her again. After he leaned away, he said, "I bet I can tell you what Tara would say concerning your fears about all this."

Daisy gave him a small smile. "Okay, counselor, give me your best advice."

"She would say, and I would say, that you probably need to talk to Vi and Foster about your fears. Put them out in the open and tell Vi what you need."

Daisy knew Jonas was right. Instead of thinking of herself, she had to think of Vi and Foster and Sammy. They were starting on a new, joyous part of their life.

"Let's go see their new living quarters and help them get settled," she decided.

Jonas took her hand, and they walked to the stairs together.

Ten minutes later, Jonas and Daisy drove down the lane to Glorie Beck's old house and parked in back of a pickup truck, Foster's new car, and another SUV. Daisy had met Glorie when her granddaughter Brielle had become one of Jazzi's closest friends. For eighty years, Glorie's house had been clapboard. Nola, Glorie's daughter, had wanted to make changes to the house so upkeep would be simpler, but Glorie wouldn't let her.

However, renting it out was a different story. Nola's ideas for updating had come to fruition. The white clapboard was now cream siding. The porch, with its little roof, was still gray, as were the floorboards. The window trim was also still gray but freshly painted.

Daisy said to Jonas, "I imagine Glorie didn't want the house changed too much. She wanted to still be reminded it had been her home. The renovations they made are good ones, no matter who rents the house. She updated the heating system to include air conditioning. Nola had insisted she do that if she wanted to rent it. And Brielle told me Glorie had a window installed in the large pantry off the kitchen. It's small but will be a great nursery for Sammy. I can't wait to see it."

"All of that had to cost Nola," Jonas reminded Daisy.

"I'm sure Nola received a fine settlement with her divorce," Daisy said. "From what I understand, her husband Elliott just wanted to wash his hands of all of it. He let her keep their house to sell it as she wished. That enabled her to build the one for her and Glorie and Brielle. I hope he tries to have a relationship with Brielle. She needs her father in her life."

"But he hasn't been in it much up till now," Jonas recalled.

"I know, and that's sad. Nola's trying to make up the time she lost with Brielle while she was growing up."

Ned Pachenko came out the door and jogged down the steps to meet Daisy and Jonas. In his twenties, Ned attended college with Foster and was manager of the store downtown, Guitars and Vinyl. He'd played his guitar the last two celebrations Daisy had held at the tea garden and was going to play for her Alice in Wonderland Tea, too. His blond curly hair, long in the back, brushed his sweatshirt.

"I'm just headed to the SUV for another load of boxes," Ned explained.

Jonas asked, "Do you want me to help?"

"Sure, that would be great. We have all the essentials inside, but I have a box of Sammy's toys and books from their bookshelves."

Daisy's Aunt Iris had taken over the afternoon

tea garden service so Daisy could be here. In support of the move, Daisy's mom was babysitting Sammy, so the adults could put the place in order before they brought him home.

Daisy went inside and marveled at how already the house had taken on Vi and Foster's personalities. The wood floors gleamed after being sanded and polished, and a perky gold, green, and blue rug lay under the small coffee table Vi and Foster had used at the apartment. Their sofa fit in fine, as did the platform rocker. A valance that Daisy's mom had made in a brown and tan check hung over the window above the sofa.

Daisy's gaze swerved over to Vi, who was so busy she hadn't heard Daisy come in. She was lining shelves in the white metal kitchen cabinets that had been popular long ago. They were well-maintained. There was a counter with a gray speckled Formica that had seen better days, but that didn't seem to matter. Vi had already set her mug tree on it, and the new microwave that Daisy's dad had bought the couple as a housewarming present held a prominent place. The white gas stove looked old, as did the refrigerator with its rounded top, but they worked just fine, and that's all that mattered. There was a flight of stairs that led up to a loft, and already Foster was attaching a baby gate so Sammy wouldn't try to climb those stairs.

Suddenly Daisy heard a car in the driveway. When she looked out, she saw Glorie and Brielle. Brielle was driving, and after she disembarked from the car, she came around to open the door for Glorie.

Using her cane, Glorie helped herself out of the car. Her curly light brown hair was streaked with gray and looked like a wispy cloud around her face. As usual, she was wearing jeans and an oversized T-shirt. It looked way too big. This one was orange.

Brielle reached the back door of the sedan and brought out a plastic container. She stayed beside Glorie as they came up the walk, and Daisy opened the door for them.

"I brought brownies," Brielle said. "I'm ready to help however I can. Is Jazzi coming?" she asked Daisy after giving her a hug.

"She'll be here later. She's helping at the tea garden today."

A moment later, Jonas and Ned brought in the boxes that had been in Ned's SUV. After Vi and Foster gave them all hugs, Vi waved at the little house. "What do you think?" Her expression was hopeful.

"Take me on a tour," Daisy said, just wanting a little time with Vi.

Vi waved to the loft. "That's going to be Foster's office up there where he can do his web business. It's not completely set up yet, but Ned's going to help him with the computer and printer."

"That's a good idea for Foster's workspace. I saw the baby gate," Daisy noted.

"Sammy's just going to have to get used to the idea he can't go up there, and we have to remember to attach the gate every time we go up and down. But it won't be that different from the one at the apartment." They had had a gate there, too, at the head of the stairs.

Vi showed Daisy into the bedroom. "I splurged

and bought a new bedspread at A Penny Saved," her daughter said, with a flush in her cheeks.

The new spread found at the thrift shop was a comforter with big squares of all different kinds of flowers, and a dust ruffle in a pretty mint green. The window wore matching material in the curtains.

"It's pretty," Daisy agreed. "So nice and fresh for the room. Perfect with the light oak of the bed's headboard. And I like this light salmon color you painted the walls."

"When Glorie said we could paint, we didn't want to go too wild. We kept the cream in the living room and the kitchen, but I thought this would be nice for us. Come see Sammy's little room."

The space *was* small, but it had a window and enough room for the full-size crib, a rocking chair, and a changing table. Quacking ducks danced across Sammy's yellow curtains. "I want to hang decorations in here, too," Vi said, "but I don't want to just slap something on the walls. I'd like to do a gallery of pictures in Foster's and my bedroom, too. What do you think?"

"I think both are a great idea. You're really making this your own."

"We appreciate everything you did for us, Mom. Really, we do. I don't know what we would have done after we married if we'd had to find a place of our own somewhere and pay rent. But this—" She stopped. "This really seems like ours, and I hope Glorie lets us rent it for a long time."

Daisy considered this to be as good a time as any to tell Vi how she felt. "I was glad I could do it for you, and I had the benefit of being close to you.

I'm afraid . . ." She stopped, took a breath, and continued. "I'm afraid now that you're here, we're not going to see each other as much, and we won't be as close."

"Oh, Mom, don't think like that," Vi assured her. "You are always welcome here, and we know we're always welcome at your house. We'll make sure we see you often."

Daisy didn't want to make Vi feel guilty about having a life of her own. "Look, honey. I said that because that's how I'm feeling, and I wanted you to know it. You and Foster and Sammy are going to have your own life now. I'll be around if you need me, and so will Jonas. But I also know how life speeds us on our way."

There was a twinkle in Vi's eye when she said, "Once you and Jonas are married, the two of you might not have time for us."

Daisy laughed, and then she said, "I guess we never do know what life's going to throw at us, do we? So what I'm going to promise you is simple— that I'm always here, just a text or a call or a visit away. Okay?"

Vi gave her mom a big hug. "Very okay."

Everyone in the main part of the house had taken a break to eat Brielle's brownies and to pop open cans of soda and bottles of water. Brielle had settled on the floor in the living room next to Ned, while Glorie sat in the platform rocker. Foster had brought a wooden chair in from the kitchen. On the sofa, Jonas waited for Daisy.

Glorie was saying, "I was just telling Foster if Vi needs a cup of sugar, I'm not that far away over at the house."

"I can be the runner," Brielle assured them with

a teasing look in her eyes. "I can run back and forth."

"Until you go to college, young lady," Glorie reminded her.

"Yes, Grammy. Until then."

Talk revolved around the colleges Brielle was thinking about attending, the car Foster had bought, and the songs Ned might play for the Alice in Wonderland Tea. Then the talk turned to something that was still on Daisy's mind—Lydia's murder.

Ned said to Daisy, "I imagine my store has been a lot like the tea garden with gossip about Lydia Aldenkamp."

"I try not to listen to the gossip," Daisy admitted. "But I do keep an ear out for any information about someone who might have wanted to hurt Lydia. Have you heard gossip that matters?" she asked Ned.

"My customers talk about everything while they're looking through records, including the murder. I had an old guy in last week who wanted to buy a guitar."

Brielle asked, "Old meaning forty . . . or old meaning seventy?"

Ned gave her a conciliatory smile. "Actually, I think he was in his sixties, but he told me he heard The Farm Barn has been in financial trouble for a long while . . . at least a year. I've heard that from other customers, too. The bottom line is—nobody understands it, because it always seemed to be doing so well. They had a packed parking lot for family dinners, and they've been holding a bunch of wedding receptions."

"Even so," Daisy said, "profit margins are tight

in the food industry, and help is hard to keep." She told everyone that Neil had asked her to help with his friend's reception because he was simply unfamiliar with everything Lydia had done.

"And you decided to do it?" Glorie asked her.

"I did. I'm meeting the couple tomorrow. I actually asked myself what would Lydia expect me to do, and I believe she'd want me to help Neil. So I'm doing it for her."

Daisy sat in the office at The Farm Barn on Monday afternoon, studying the couple in front of her. Neil had introduced her to his friends, reiterating to them that Daisy was more than capable of managing their reception on Saturday. Bob and Allyson Mueller had known Neil and Lydia a long while.

After Neil left to pick up Frannie at preschool, Bob smiled when he said, "Neil and I went to high school together. We had some hard times and got into a lot of mischief, too."

Bob looked like a football player who had maintained some of his boyish charm. His blond hair was thin, but he combed it to the side. The crinkles around his eyes were friendly, and so was his smile.

"I think a lot of your mischief had to do with girls," Allyson joked.

"Maybe mine," Bob said with a wink. He told Daisy, "I didn't meet Allyson until about five years ago. Neil, on the other hand, was luckier."

"Luckier?" Daisy asked, thinking it wouldn't hurt to get history on the couple. She could customize the reception that way.

Allyson cocked her head. "Bob's told me about

his adventures, but when I think of Neil and Lydia, I think of happy-ever-after and dreams coming true. It's so romantic what happened with them."

"I don't know if I've ever heard the whole story," Daisy said. "I'd be glad to hear it. I like a happily-ever-after saga."

Bob shrugged. "I think Allyson makes more of this than she needs to. But their story tugs on your heart. Neil and Lydia met during Lydia's *rumspringa*."

"It's hard for me to imagine *rumspringa* for Amish girls . . . and the boys, too. Imagine being closeted in a life like the Amish lead—no TV, no electricity, no movies or makeup or fashion—and then suddenly having the whole world open up before you," Allyson pointed out.

"Not all Amish kids experience *rumspringa*," Bob said. "Some of the youth don't really explore the outside world. They don't want to. Most return to their rules and restrictions. But Lydia was different."

Allyson wrapped her fingers around her husband's arm, as if to give him the affection that she was feeling right at that moment, and the idea that happily-ever-after could be possible for them, too.

"I didn't know Lydia as long as Bob did," Allyson said. "But I *do* know she looked at everything differently after she met Neil. She told me that she bought clothes that her sister would never think about wearing, hoping Neil would like them. She got a job waitressing in a restaurant and made friends with the other waitresses. They taught her about hairstyles and makeup, and that whole world opened up to her when she realized she was pretty and not plain. Without a *kapp* and dress like other Amish girls wore, she was an individual . . . unique . . . attractive. Her changed attitude wasn't all about Neil, but most of it was. I can understand that. When you're in love, everything looks shiny and new. You believe life is one big adventure to enjoy with that special person." She tapped Bob's arm, and he smiled lovingly at her.

Bob looked thoughtful and serious when he related, "It wasn't just the English world and Neil that changed Lydia. All of it made her look at her Amish faith differently. She wanted to see Neil more than she wanted to go along with her family's restrictions and all the rules she grew up with. She was only nineteen when he asked her to marry him. He patiently waited a year until she was sure she wanted to choose a life with him."

"He must have really loved her," Daisy said, knowing patience wasn't always easy to come by when you were in love.

"Oh, he did," Bob confirmed. "He didn't see anybody else during that time. He was totally dedicated to her and what she wanted. If she had rejected him instead of her faith, I don't know how he would have survived."

Now Daisy was completely involved in this story, and she wanted to know more. After all, maybe it would help to figure out who had wanted to hurt Lydia. "It seems they've built a good life together."

"It's taken me years to build up my computer business," Bob mused. "Solving people's problems, going to their houses, forming networks and connecting took a long time. Word of mouth was everything for my business. I watched Neil struggle. While he waited for Lydia, he was earning a college degree and working two other jobs. He was a janitor and a handyman, and finally got the idea to start a painting company that took off. Lydia continued to work as a waitress and took bookkeeping courses. She helped get Neil's business off the ground."

"What happened with his painting business?" Daisy asked.

"He sold it," Allyson said. "Afterward, they put their funds into The Farm Barn."

"And now, that is succeeding," Daisy said. "That's why you're having your reception here. It's going to be fabulous. The way Lydia would want it to be."

Allyson's eyes filled with tears. "After Lydia died, we thought about having the reception somewhere else, but Neil said he wanted to do this for us. He said you'd do an excellent job because you and Lydia thought about decorating and families and parties pretty much the same way. Is that true?"

Daisy didn't know for sure if that was true. But she did know she would do her best.

For the next hour, Daisy took notes and reviewed the menu with the couple, as well as the plans Lydia had laid out on her flash drive. As they were finishing up, Neil came in, Frannie holding his hand. When Frannie saw them, she ducked her head close to his jeans-clad leg and shyly hid her smile.

Suddenly she let go of Neil's hand and ran to Allyson, whom she apparently knew well. Allyson scooped her up in her arms and set her on her lap. "How are you today, Princess?"

Frannie grinned. "Good. Daddy's gonna take me to Auntie Leah's so he can work."

Neil grimaced. "Out of the mouths of babes. We just spent a fun time at the playground, didn't we?"

Frannie bobbed her head, as if it had been a happy time.

Allyson asked Neil, "What are you going to do with Frannie on a daily basis now?"

"Leah has helped Lydia with Frannie's care since she was born, so she'll continue to do that. Thank God," he said gratefully.

At the mention of God, Frannie looked at Allyson, her hand on Allyson's face. "Daddy says Mommy's in heaven."

Tears came to Allyson's eyes. She took hold of Frannie's hand and then kissed the little girl's cheek. "Your Daddy's right. She is there, and she's watching over you. You'll always be her little girl, and she'll always be your Mommy."

"Auntie Leah and Daddy aren't going to heaven now," Frannie said.

"Not for a very long time," Allyson told her.

The rest of the adults struggled to keep their composure, including Daisy. Whoever had taken Lydia's life had forever marred this family.

Daisy was going to do her best to make sure Neil and his little girl had some answers.

CHAPTER TEN

As Daisy drove down the lane to Rachel and Levi Fisher's house, she remembered her childhood days here. She'd played hide-and-seek in the corn stalks with Rachel and her brothers. They'd cooled off in the pond with Daisy in her shorts and tank top and Rachel in her dress. They'd had very different lifestyles, yet their friendship had been solid.

Gazing up at the roof of the house, Daisy noticed that the clothesline from the house to the barn was full of fresh laundry. Rachel's oldest brother and his wife lived and farmed on the Esh property, the farm next door. That was the farm where Daisy had learned about living in a house without electricity, taking care of the horses who pulled the buggies, and helping with chores that the family rose at sunrise to accomplish.

The door of the Fisher home led into a mud room. Daisy knocked on the door of the mud room, where coats and boots and tools were stored, hoping the Fishers had finished supper. She didn't want to intrude.

Luke, Rachel's son, opened it. Wearing a coat, he grinned and said, "Hi, Daisy."

"Are you on your way out?" Daisy asked.

"Ya, sure am. Last check of the barn for the night." He tipped his black felt hat to her as Rachel entered the mud room.

"Daisy, it's *gut* to see you. What brings you out on a cold night?"

"I'd like to talk to you for a bit. Am I interrupting anything?"

"No, Mary already went to bed. Levi is out in the barn. Sarah's over at Hannah's house."

Levi's maam Mary—his grandmother—lived with the family. Rachel and Levi's older daughter had been married last fall. She lived in a house on the property that the family had built themselves.

With a gesture of welcome, Rachel beckoned Daisy into the kitchen.

Rachel's kitchen was always filled with delicious aromas. Tonight Daisy caught a whiff of roast beef and something sweet. A gas light shone overhead.

Rachel motioned to the table. "How about a blueberry fry pie and a cup of tea? I made the fry pies last night so the men would have them when they were working outside today. Lots of repairs to do from winter." Rachel was already putting a tea kettle on the gas stove. Next she took a white teacup and saucer from a handmade hutch in the corner. "Take off your coat and sit yourself down, and we can talk."

Daisy hung her coat over one of the cane-seated chairs. Rachel studied Daisy. "*Du gucksht gut,*" she said in her upbeat way. Daisy knew the phrase meant, *You look good.*

"*Danke*," she said.

"But inside isn't so good?" Rachel asked. "Your heart is hurting?"

"My heart is hurting for Leah, Frannie, and Neil. It's tough to get over what happened. And we moved Vi and Foster."

"I heard. How did that go?"

As Rachel took the fry pies from under a cake holder and set them on the table, Daisy explained about the day and some of her feelings. "I think they'll be happy there," Daisy admitted. "They'll have more space. Much as I don't want to admit it, it's probably good that they aren't as close to us physically. I don't want them to ever feel that they don't have the freedom to live their own life."

Fondness for Daisy's family twinkled in Rachel's eyes when she said, "But they'll have Glorie to watch over them."

Daisy laughed. "I suppose so, and that makes me feel good."

As they enjoyed the fry pies and tea, Daisy told Rachel about the reception that she was going to be managing for Neil. "Once I settle into the swing of it, I think it'll be fun. It's more complicated than organizing a special tea for the tea garden, but I'm pretty sure I can handle it."

The talk after that turned to Rachel's daughter's new life as a married woman, and Luke courting someone from the family's church district.

Daisy admitted, "I stopped by to ask you a few questions about your district."

"What do you need to know?"

Daisy carefully considered the questions revolving in her mind. "What does your district feel about Leah still being involved in Lydia's life after Lydia was married? That's unusual, isn't it?"

"As you know, our bishop is a little more lenient than some. Some of the community has looked down on it, but others haven't. After all, they were twins. And Leah consulted with the bishop. The word about that traveled around quickly."

"She consulted him about staying close to Lydia?"

"Yes. She didn't want to do anything against our rules. After Lydia's baby was born, Leah asked if she could care for her. I think our bishop saw that Leah had a strong desire to mother. He hoped it would be good for the sisters as long as Lydia's lifestyle didn't influence Leah."

How to make sure of that? Daisy wondered.

Rachel must have read her mind, because she explained, "Leah had to check in with the bishop periodically. All seemed to go well."

But *had* all gone well? Daisy knew that appearances didn't always reflect the truth.

Rachel went to the counter, picked up the porcelain teapot, and poured them two more cups of tea. "Another fry pie?" she asked.

"Goodness, no," Daisy answered. "I really should get going."

However, Rachel sat in the chair again and gave Daisy a studying look. "Not before we talk about your wedding."

That suggestion surprised her. "My wedding?"

Eye to eye, Rachel asked, "When is the date?"

Daisy fidgeted with the handle of her teacup. "We haven't decided on an exact date yet, but we're thinking July."

"A hot month."

"I know, but that will give us plenty of time to plan."

"Just what are you planning?" Rachel asked, with a casual nonchalance that made Daisy smile.

"We're thinking about a small gathering."

Rachel shook her head, as if that idea didn't fit. "I can remember that barbecue at your house when the detective brought the smoker."

"Yes . . ." Daisy drawled, suspecting where this was going.

"That was not that small. You have a lot of friends who want to come, Daisy. They want to see you happy."

She sighed. "I know. We're thinking about having the ceremony and reception in our backyard. What do you think about that?"

"You have the space."

"We do. I can envision the canopies. What do you think?"

"I think it's your wedding, and you and Jonas should do what gives you pleasure."

Daisy knew her wedding would be very different from an Amish wedding. An Amish wedding occurred during the week, and the whole district was invited. Preparations took a long time for that many people. The bride wore a simple blue dress rather than an elaborate white one, and the service often lasted about three hours.

"So you have been thinking about this?" Rachel asked with her eyes twinkling.

"How could I not? I want this badly, and so does Jonas. We'd elope, but . . . I want Jazzi and Vi to be involved."

Daisy could hear the mud room door open, and someone stomped inside. After a few moments, Luke appeared in the kitchen.

"Any fry pies left?" he asked with a grin.

"About a half dozen, but you have to save some for your *dat*."

"I will." He went to the counter, washed his hands in the sink, and then lifted the covering on the cake holder, removing two fry pies.

"On a plate or napkin," Rachel advised him.

After he did that, he said, "I won't interrupt your talk."

"We were talking about weddings," Daisy said with a smile.

Luke's face grew bright red. "So my mudder told you I am courting?"

"She did, but we were talking about *my* wedding. You can relax."

He chuckled. "*Gut*, because mine is a long ways off."

"Time does fly," Rachel reminded him. "You have to make the most of it."

Time does fly, Daisy thought, her mind leaping to another subject entirely—Zeke, Detective Rappaport, and their investigation. Had the trail to solving Lydia's murder gone cold? Did they have any solid leads?

Did she want to know what those leads were?

Daisy and Tessa had decided to have a tasting night with Jonas and Trevor at Daisy's house the following evening. Jonas and Trevor took Felix for a walk while she and Tessa worked in the kitchen.

These would be some recipes to try for spring. She hoped their customers would like them. She and Tessa had both come up with a creation. The whole first floor smelled of savories and baked goods.

"Where's Jazzi tonight?" Tessa asked. She pulled smoked salmon and cream cheese cups from the oven.

"She had a meeting at school about graduation. It's going to be here before I know it . . . before *she* knows it."

The kitchen's sliding glass doors opened, and Jonas and Trevor came bounding in with Felix. "Felix says he's hungry," Trevor joked.

"I'm sure Felix would like some of what we're making," Tessa said with a wink.

"We'll wash up, and then I'll make sure Felix is served his supper," Jonas agreed. "I made him a new batch of stew last night."

"You cook for this dog?" Trevor's brows practically rose to his hairline.

"We do," Daisy said. "The food we make lasts a few days, and then we mix it with other food. We think it's healthier."

"You do know you're treating him like a child," Trevor said, suppressing a grin.

"You'd be amazed how much we do for the cats, too," Daisy joked.

They all laughed.

"The kitchen smells wonderful," Jonas said, putting his arms around Daisy and giving her a quick hug. "Can't wait to try everything."

Within the next half hour, Daisy and Tessa had set out their offerings on the island. Daisy had decided to treat this like a special occasion. They could all use a little joy right now. She'd set four

Royal Albert Enchantment salad dessert plates on the counter to use for their sampling. Each snack plate held an accompanying teacup. She'd also set out the footed soup bowl and saucer set. The bowl had two delicate handles, one on either side, and it looked something like a teacup. The dishes were rimmed with blue lace with gold highlights, a bouquet of flowers in the center. She didn't use them often, because she only had a set for four.

"You've outdone yourself tonight," Trevor said, looking over the counter. He used a ladle to spoon some of the creamy carrot soup out of the tureen. "I do think this china is too fancy for us. I don't want to break anything."

"China is to be used," Daisy said. "It's pretty to look at, but it's much more enjoyable when you eat off of it."

There were baby quiches with bacon and broccoli, tea sandwiches with turkey and pear. "Can I eat desserts in between the sandwiches and soup?" Trevor wanted to know.

"You can eat our selections any way you want to," Daisy told him.

He lifted an elderflower and almond cookie from a tiered plate along with mini rhubarb muffins. The lemon-raspberry scone was a new recipe, as well as the cherry tomatoes stuffed with ham salad. They made plenty of each, because they knew a simple tea service wasn't going to fill up these guys.

Soon they were all gathered around the dining room table that Daisy had refinished as a rehab project when she'd first moved to Willow Creek. It had been therapeutic to do. She'd laid out cloth place mats printed with daffodils.

After Trevor took a seat, he said, "I feel like I'm at a tea service."

Tessa whacked his arm. "That's exactly what you're supposed to feel like. You should come into the tea garden sometime and actually enjoy one. We're not merely about whoopie pies and chocolate-chip cookies."

"I need the sweets to keep up my strength. Journalism is a hard business."

"How's your blog doing?" Jonas asked.

Trevor had started a blog last fall, hoping to capture advertisers and make money from it. "I'm getting more interest. I'm thinking about doing podcasts along with it, but that's still in the thinking stage. I'm on Instagram and Snapchat, and the followers are mounting. You wouldn't believe the number of people interested in our corner of the world."

"I believe it when the tourist buses arrive at the tea garden," Daisy said. "Hopefully we'll have a good spring and summer."

"You're going to have a busy summer, especially if you get married," Trevor said with another wink. "Have you thought about a honeymoon?"

"We haven't set the official date yet," Jonas said.

Trevor spooned soup into his mouth. "Still, where would you two like to go, if you could choose anywhere you wanted?"

Jonas gazed at Daisy. "The beach, the mountains, the desert?"

After she thought about it, she said, "I've always wanted to see the Grand Canyon."

"That's a possibility." Jonas's smile was just for her.

They ate in silence for a few minutes, enjoying

the food and sipping tea. When their plates were almost empty, Trevor said to Daisy, "Tell me what you've learned about Lydia's murder."

Daisy looked confused for a moment. She'd been trying to forget about all of that. Yet on the other hand, she knew Trevor wanted to find answers as well as she did.

"I haven't found out anything about the murder, but I have discovered more about Leah and Lydia's relationship, and Lydia's marriage. Something there that was a surprise."

"What kind of surprise?" Trevor asked.

"Someone told me that Neil had an affair, and that the marriage was in trouble."

"Uh-oh," Trevor said. "If you heard that, the detectives probably did, too."

"Every couple has good and bad times," Jonas reminded them all. "Daisy and I have."

"Yes, but when murder is involved, everyone comes under suspicion," Daisy reminded them.

Jonas stood, went over to the counter, and brought the tiered tray of sweets back to the table. They all took another scone, tart, or cookie. They needed that kind of sustenance for this conversation.

Jonas said, "The detectives are surely doing a deep dive into the couple's backgrounds. Neil is probably their prime suspect."

Trevor finished another scone. "I spoke to Rachel about Amish values," he told Daisy. "She was quite open about it. They have so many restrictions. I can see why teenagers would leave the faith."

"Did Rachel talk about that?" Daisy asked.

"Not so much. But I drew conclusions from

what she said. On the other side of it, the Amish community is protective, tight-knit, and safe. I imagine it's hard for teenagers to leave that co-coon. It might be hard for anybody to leave that cocoon. It sounded like Lydia did and didn't look back."

"Everyone looks back," Tessa said. "You can't help but look back. I can't help but look back on what happened with Reese and me. I was a suspect in his murder. I think there are always things we think we should have done differently."

Daisy had been pulled into solving the case, be-cause Tessa had been a suspect. She'd dated an art gallery manager who had a past she hadn't known about. That was often the case when motives led to murder.

For the most part, the staff at The Farm Barn midweek was congenial and friendly, ready to help Daisy any way they could to get ready for the wed-ding reception. Daisy was spending the morning at the restaurant becoming familiar with the staff. The particulars for the event were mostly ready, but now she had to give assignments to the servers for the reception itself. She was about to do that when she went to the office to see if Neil had any other details he wanted her to take care of. He was around today, and she was glad of that in case questions popped up. But when she went to the of-fice, the tone of his voice stopped her. He was on the phone.

"There's nothing I can do about it," he was say-ing. "If the money isn't in the account, it's not in the account."

Daisy listened. If Neil wasn't part of a murder investigation, she wouldn't have eavesdropped. She could learn something important.

"I told you, I just don't have the money, and if you give my account to a bill collector, they're not going to squeeze anything out of me, either."

Had Lydia experienced the same financial problems when she was running The Farm Barn? Had she known about them? Or had Neil kept them secret?

Deciding not to interrupt him now, she returned to the kitchen. One of the servers, April Jennings, had been particularly helpful this morning. She almost knew the questions on Daisy's mind before she asked them. She also had the answers at her fingertips. But Daisy also noticed that April kept herself apart from the other servers. Was there a particular reason for that? Or was she just more introverted and didn't mingle?

Daisy remembered what Martha had told her about April staying with Lydia now and then. Possibly April was just still deeply grieving. Daisy knew that in grief, people could turn inward.

Daisy was standing at the service counter, her iPad in hand as she studied the diagram of the tables that she'd laid out before her on the desk. Jake Starsky, one of the servers who seemed to be able to get along with everyone with an ever-ready smile, approached her. He was in his twenties, and Daisy could feel the energy pulsing off him. He was handsome, and his confidence told her he could probably get a date with anybody he wanted. His dark hair was brushed up the front of his forehead and the back slicked down. The sides of his head were shaved. He was definitely young and hip. Today he was wearing an orange football jersey and jeans with holes in the knees. His muscle build told her he might work out daily.

She'd told the staff they could call her Daisy, and he did that now. "Daisy, I just wanted to give you some hints as to the serving staff."

"Hints about what?" she asked, looking up at him, peering into his face. Hopefully he'd shave off his beard stubble before serving at the reception.

"Although the servers never had particular stations, some are better at some things more than others."

"Such as?" Daisy asked.

"Jackie's the best at beverage service. She knows how to handle the glasses and the trays, and she never spills anything."

"Good to know," Daisy agreed.

"You know Nora is the sous chef, right?"

"It's in my notes," she said with a nod, wondering why Jake was trying to ingratiate himself.

"She's also good at expediting the orders."

Lydia had been so organized and detail-oriented that she had left notes about all the servers. The note beside Jake's name was "Competent." Daisy supposed Lydia's notes were essential if Neil took over a service, or if she wanted to juggle servers around in their jobs.

"I have notes on most of this, Jake. Lydia was very organized."

Flushing a bit, he agreed. "Oh, she was. She ran this place like a machine. Everyone knew their job. No one was ever out of place. I just wish . . ." He stopped, then continued, "I just wish I hadn't been on vacation when she was . . ." He hesitated, then added in a low voice, "Murdered."

Maybe he was grieving, too. "I suppose the staff is a support for each other."

"We are," he assured her.

Neil came around the corner of the office into the kitchen. Realizing that Neil and Daisy might have business to discuss, Jake said, "Just let me know if there's anything you need."

"Will do," Daisy said.

Neil's gaze followed Jake out of the kitchen. Daisy asked him, "Is Jake always that helpful?"

"What do you mean?" Neil asked.

"Oh, he wanted to give me hints on the servers and what they did best."

Neil shrugged. "Actually, Jake was away for a couple of weeks. He just returned to work after Lydia's funeral. He probably feels as if he has to catch up and step in. In lots of ways, he's a perfectionist."

Setting aside thoughts of Jake, Daisy said, "For now, everyone seems to know the drill. Lydia taught them their jobs well. Customers don't realize that servers don't simply carry dishes to tables. They have to keep track of numbers and orders and placements. Your staff seems more than competent in all of it."

"They were Lydia's staff," Neil said morosely.

"Maybe so, but they're *yours* now."

"I know I have to pull myself together, but it's hard. I try to put on a good face for Frannie, and even for Leah. But at night, I wonder how I'm going to be a single dad and run a business, too. Sometimes I don't think it's possible."

Thinking of Bob and Allyson, Daisy reminded him, "You have good friends. Leah seems ready to help you when you need it. It's all about your support group, really. Back in Willow Creek with my girls after my husband died, I wasn't sure how I was going to do it either, but my aunt and I decided to open the business, and I had my family around me. It can be done, Neil. I promise you."

He still looked skeptical. "I'd like to think that's so. If you don't need me for the next half hour, I'm going to take a walk."

"No problem. I'm going to go over table placement with the staff."

He nodded and turned to leave. When he did, April appeared. "The decorations are all in place, and everyone's ready for their assignments."

Daisy rolled up the chart and picked up her tablet. "Okay, then we're ready for final instructions for Saturday. I'm nervous about it," she said honestly, "but I hope all of you aren't."

April gave her a smile. "We've all done this before. A wedding reception should be a happy thing."

"I hope we can make it a celebration that Bob and Allyson will remember."

"Before we go out there, I'd like to talk to you for a minute."

"Sure," Daisy said, setting her tablet on the counter again. "What's the matter?"

"I really need this job, but there's lots of scuttlebutt going around about The Farm Barn closing. I want to be ready if it does," April informed her. "Do you have any openings for servers at the tea garden? I'd enjoy that."

Daisy supposed a backup plan was necessary for April to pay her rent and other expenses. She truly liked this young woman. "If you're serious about working at the tea garden, come in and fill out an application, and then we'll take it from there, depending on what happens. I don't want to steal you from Neil if he needs you."

April gave her a wide smile. "I could work both jobs."

Did April need funds that badly? Had maybe Lydia been helping her?

Just as Daisy's servers had lives and complications in them, she knew this group did, too. They'd all need jobs if The Farm Barn closed. She hoped Neil could keep the business going for all of their sakes.

CHAPTER ELEVEN

Since Daisy had returned to Willow Creek, the Rainbow Flamingo was the dress shop where she shopped for special-occasion clothes. Today, however, she wasn't here for special clothes but for something else. She had a meeting with the seamstress, who was going to sew costumes of a sort for her staff for the Alice in Wonderland Tea.

The Rainbow Flamingo was within easy walking distance from the tea garden. In the late afternoon, she and Iris headed that way to keep an appointment with the seamstress.

As they approached the shop, Iris said to Daisy, "You didn't need me to come along. You can make these decisions."

"I know, but this is a little different, and I wanted your opinion."

"It's nice for someone to want my opinion," Iris teased.

Daisy pulled open the door, and they stepped inside the shop. It wasn't a store that was stuffed to the walls. There were coordinates on racks, dresses on another. Special-occasion dresses hung on a rod near the dressing rooms.

Heidi Korn, who was now the owner of the clothes shop, came around the counter to meet them with a huge smile. Heidi often changed her hair color. They had seen it three different shades since she'd moved to Willow Creek. Now she was a platinum blonde with dark brows. She caught Daisy studying her. She joked, "Just love it?" Her hair was now chin-length and angled. "Is it true blondes have more fun? You would know, Daisy, right?"

"Heidi Korn, you get more outrageous every time I talk to you," Iris said, in a chastising voice.

Heidi laughed. "Oh, come on, Iris. You know Daisy is fun in her own way, and it's always wholesome."

In a way, Daisy admired Heidi. She studied the woman's sparkly silver manicured nails, her form-fitting cranberry-colored dress and five-inch spiked heels, jeweled around the toes. Heidi was Heidi, and she did have a good sense of taste, at least where her customers were concerned.

"Greta is waiting for you, and I can't wait to see what you think of her sketches. I know you had a long discussion with her to tell her what you wanted, and I think she's done that in the most simple way possible. Simple in a good way."

Daisy was always conscious of expenses, and even though she wanted these special touches for the Alice in Wonderland Tea, she was also very aware of the cost.

"Go on back," Heidi said, motioning behind the counter and down a hall. "Greta had some alteration requests, and she was working on those, but she's ready to help you."

Iris and Daisy walked single file down a hall past the dressing rooms. In the alteration room, there were two sewing machines, dress forms, walls studded with buttons, rickrack, and trims. Greta was sitting at an artist's table, a charcoal pencil in hand as she studied a design.

Her stool swiveled toward Daisy and she grinned. "Daisy, I have so much to show you."

Greta was a short woman, about five feet tall. She had close-cropped silver hair in a pixie cut. Daisy guessed she was in her sixties and had the wrinkles on her face to show it. Sporting no makeup, she wore slacks and a T-shirt in a grass-green shade with black and white high-top sneakers.

"Take off your jackets so we can talk about this," she invited.

Iris and Daisy hung their coats on hooks behind the door, while Greta hopped off her stool and moved vinyl chairs over near her sketching table. Daisy watched with her aunt as Greta presented a sketch to them. "You told me you want your servers to be dressed like Alice, correct?"

Daisy nodded. "Since she's the most recognizable character, I thought that would be best."

"Here you go."

Daisy studied the sketch as Greta explained, "It's basically a blue apron with a white pinafore trim."

"That's a wonderful idea," Daisy said.

Greta pointed again to the Alice sketch. "I'll be making these headbands with a bow."

"Simple and effective," Daisy agreed.

"What I thought you'd say," Greta said. "I also know you have a man server, and you have a young man who will be playing music."

"I do," Daisy confirmed.

Greta took another design from behind the first. "This is a long vest. Foster and your guitar player could wear those for the White Rabbit and the Mad Hatter."

"We'll be decorating the tea garden with everything Alice," Daisy said. "The White Rabbit and Mad Hatter will be perfect. Maybe I can convince Foster to wear bunny ears."

Iris laughed. "He'd do anything for you, and you know it."

Greta hopped off her stool again and ducked behind a dressing screen. She brought out a replica of the apron. "I made one of these as a sample. I thought you could take it along, show it to your servers, and see what they think. I can make any changes you'd like. We still have a little time."

Greta added, "I didn't make a copy of the vest since I'm waiting for the fabric." She took two smaller drawings from behind the others on her artist's table. "You can take these along and show them to Foster and Ned."

Daisy's phone buzzed, and Greta said, "Go ahead and take it. I know you business women get important phone calls."

Daisy checked the screen. "This *could* be a business call. Are you sure you don't mind?"

"Go ahead," Greta said again.

Daisy stepped into the hall, though she knew Iris and Greta could still hear. The call was from Neil.

"Hi, Neil. What's going on?"

"I just wanted to tell you that the police had me down to the station again."

"How long this time?"

"Another two hours. We didn't go over anything new. Willet wanted me to tell him about the staff."

"Personal information?"

"It seemed that way. I don't really know much. The only one I knew a little bit about was April, because she stayed overnight a few times. I think she was lonely. The detectives are digging in all the wrong places."

"Where do you think they should be digging?"

"I don't know," he confessed morosely.

"The detectives conduct their investigation in a way they believe they can collect the most pertinent information."

Neil sighed. "I guess they're doing their best. They need to focus on somebody other than me."

"Neil, have you thought really hard about this? If you can give them some sort of lead, they will follow it."

He was thoughtful and silent for a few moments. "Maybe you're right. There is something I could tell them. The chicken supplier didn't like Lydia and gave her a hard time. At least it would be *something*."

"If you think it matters, then you should say something."

"There was another reason I wanted to talk to you. Allyson and Bob are pleased with your planning for their reception. I'm glad I asked you to do this, Daisy, I really am."

"I'll do my best for you, Neil. You know that."

"I'll let you go," Neil said. "I know you have a business to run. I didn't mean to vent. I really didn't."

"How's Frannie?"

"She's best when she's with Leah. When she's with me, she just looks sad. Maybe it's the house. Maybe I should think about moving."

"Neil, if she's comfortable there, don't make a decision now. It's what she knows."

"No big decisions, right?"

"Not right away, anyway."

"I'll see you soon, Daisy."

After Neil ended the call, Daisy slipped her phone into her pocket and returned to Greta's office, where Greta and Iris were talking about Lydia Aldenkamp.

Greta was saying, "It's such an awful shame what happened to Lydia. Are you going to help find out who killed her?" she asked Daisy.

"I don't know, Greta. I don't know if I can."

"I heard the husband's pretty broken up. He stops out at the east end convenience store where my niece works. Since his wife died, he buys coffee and leaves fast."

Daisy sensed a subtext to Greta's comment. "Is that different from the way he used to stop in for coffee?"

"He used to stay and talk to everyone there for a bit. He's a friendly guy."

Neil *was* personable, that was true.

"We've had more than our share of troubles in this town," Greta said. "I know you've helped with some of them. I watch *Dateline* and those other crime shows. The police suspect the husband, and they keep their eye on him, too. I hope Neil knows that."

"I think he does. He's hoping they'll soon find other leads."

"That's a job for you, missy," Greta said. "I know you can do it."

Daisy knew she probably could do it. But did she want to?

Often South Central Pennsylvania was visited by a March snowstorm. Not simply a covering, but a real storm. That was happening tonight as Daisy checked out the window to see if Mark and Jazzi were on their way home. Not that it helped staring into the snow that was first fluttering down, and then beating down, as if it had a contest to see how much it could land in merely a few minutes. Jonas came up behind her and put his hand on her shoulder. "They'll be okay."

"I told them snow was predicted tonight. They shouldn't have gone on a date."

"They're teenagers," Jonas reminded her with a sigh, as if that covered the subject completely.

Jonas had started a low-burning fire in the fireplace. Felix napped flat out near the hearth. Marjoram and Pepper were a distance away on the deacon's bench, cuddled together as if they needed each other's company and warmth.

Suddenly Daisy leaned toward the front window, her nose almost against it. "I think I see something."

Jonas didn't comment but took her hand and pulled her over to the sofa. "If it is them, you don't want to be standing in the door all worried and anxious when they come in."

Five minutes later, Daisy was relieved when Jazzi opened the door and she and Mark burst inside. They were snow-covered from their walk from the garage to the front door. They were laughing, not at all concerned they'd been through a snowstorm. Jonas had been right. They were teenagers.

As nonchalantly as possible, Daisy encouraged, "Come on in. Take off your coats and warm up. Do you want hot chocolate?"

Mark shook his head. "I really should turn right around and go home. It's coming down pretty fast. My truck almost got stuck twice coming up the lane. There must be six inches out there."

"The radar was predicting about eight inches in a short amount of time," Jonas said.

As Jonas made that comment, the lights blinked and went out. The humming from the HVAC system and the refrigerator ceased. The house was suddenly silent, with the only noise being the popping of the flames in the fireplace.

There was a flash of light as Jonas took out his phone and checked something. "Power outages all over town." To Mark, he said, "I don't know if it's safe for you to go back out there."

Daisy instinctively reacted to keep Mark safe. "Stay overnight. We have sleeping bags. We can all keep warm by the fireplace."

Daisy couldn't see Mark well in the glow of the fireplace, but she heard the surprise in his voice when he asked, "Are you serious?"

"Sure. Why don't you give your parents a call." Who wanted their child out in this mess?

Daisy and Jonas rounded up flameless candles. Mark called his parents, and they agreed he should stay. Daisy was grateful for her gas range. At least the burners worked. As she put a pot on for milk for hot chocolate, she called Vi.

Vi sounded out of breath when she answered. "Our electricity is out, too," she said. "I'm packing things up. Nola has invited us to go over to her house for the night. They have a generator."

"Are you walking over there?"

"Foster thinks it will be an adventure. Don't worry about Sammy. We're going to bundle him up really well. We have a couple of those caps that have LED lights on the brim. Foster has a mag light, too."

Daisy wanted to protest and say it was too dangerous to walk Sammy that far in a snowstorm. Struggling with the fact that she *wanted* to give advice, she knew she'd be wise to hold her tongue. "You both have your cell phones," she said as a statement.

"We do, Mom. Please, don't worry. This will be an adventure Sammy can talk about when he's older. We'll tell him the story over and over again. It's really not that far from our house to Nola's. Brielle is coming out to meet us and help us carry things."

Vi reassured Daisy again with, "Nola already had

someone plow the road. He's going to come back again later, so we'll only be trampling through a few inches of snow. Really, Mom, we'll be fine."

They *would* be fine, Daisy told herself. Telling Vi she loved her and asking her to call once they were settled at Nola's, she ended the call.

Jonas came into the kitchen, and Daisy told him what Vi had told her.

"If the road's been plowed once already, they'll be okay."

"If Vi still lived above the garage, they all could have come over here around the fireplace with us," she said with some regret.

"I know you're still getting used to the idea of them being on their own." He wrapped his arm around her waist, and she laid her head on his shoulder.

"I am. I'm going to worry until Vi calls."

"I know you will. But in the meantime, Jazzi's here with Mark, and they're both safe."

"They are," Daisy agreed, straightening. "Let's ask them if they want whipped cream or marshmallows on their hot chocolate."

Half an hour later, Vi called that all was well, and Daisy relaxed. By the light of the fire, she, Jazzi, Mark, and Jonas played Cat-Opoly, drank hot chocolate, laughed, and talked through their game.

Afterward, Jonas went upstairs and lifted sleeping bags from the storage closet. Daisy pulled extra pillows and blankets from the linen closet. Soon they'd unrolled the sleeping bags in the living room in front of the fireplace. Felix settled between Daisy and Jonas. Daisy realized she felt contentment and peace in spite of the storm outside. She'd pushed Lydia's murder from the forefront of her mind. She realized Tara's advice to stay in the present was exactly what she was doing, and it felt good.

By early morning, plows had done their work. The electricity flashed back on. Awake earlier than Daisy, Jonas had donned snow gear to shovel and use the snowblower. Mark stayed for Daisy's baked cinnamon scones and Jazzi's scrambled eggs.

Jazzi seemed quiet at breakfast. After Mark left, Jonas went to the garage apartment to make sure the power had been restored there.

Daisy asked Jazzi, "Are you okay?"

"I'm fine," Jazzi said, taking another scone from the plate on the island.

"You're quiet."

"I'm thinking," Jazzi returned.

"Thinking about what?" Daisy knew prompting was often what a mother had to do.

"Last night felt weird with Mark here overnight," Jazzi said.

"Weird how?"

"Weird like we were closer than we usually were."

"But we were with you."

"I know. It felt odd to be lying there on the floor beside Mark."

"Are you thinking it was more intimate than usual?"

"He only held my hand a couple of times, so it wasn't that intimate," she said. "We didn't kiss in front of you."

Daisy had to smile. "No, I guess you didn't."

"Just that closeness made me aware of some things. I don't know if I'm ready for a serious relationship."

Daisy was glad she had a thoughtful daughter who knew her heart and mind. Her own heart was less anxious about Jazzi leaving and starting a life on her own. She'd miss her. Nevertheless, she was also excited to see the wonderful woman Jazzi would become.

Snow caused complications, especially for older folks. Daisy called her mom, who assured Daisy that a neighbor was going to snow-blow their walkways. However, Jonas wanted to see how the streets were faring. His four-wheel drive vehicle could maneuver those. They decided to ride over to Iris's house to see if she needed help. The snow had stopped, but the wind had picked up. The fine dusty snow was blowing everywhere and looked like a blizzard itself in some places.

On the drive, Jonas asked, "Are you considering opening the tea garden tomorrow?"

"I doubt if we'll have many customers, but you never know. When people are snowed in, they could walk to the tea garden and buy a scone and a cup of tea. It's something for them to do if they have cabin fever."

"I checked the weather report," Jonas said. "It's supposed to be forty and sunny tomorrow. Most of this is going to melt."

"I'll see what Iris thinks. We certainly don't need a full staff."

"Are you ready for the wedding reception at The Farm Barn?"

"As ready as I can be at this point. The decorations are ready to be delivered."

"And the food?" Jonas asked.

"The food suppliers are all on board, too. Neil says we're ready to go."

"Has he been easy to work with?"

"As easy as anyone running a business, I suppose. He has a lot on his plate right now, and he seems a little impatient sometimes. I certainly understand that."

"He has to pay his household bills as well as The Farm Barn bills. It's not an easy feat."

Driving down Iris's street, Daisy looked up ahead. To her surprise, a truck and a sedan were parked along the street in front of Iris's house.

Iris's bungalow had a stone finish and was about a thousand square feet of living space. This section of town was older, and mature trees grew along the street, snow lining their branches now. There were other bungalows, modest two-story homes, and some ranch-style houses. Iris's home had character. There was a single car garage on the west side. A gable with a tall Palladian window was located on the east. The oval window with stained glass decorated the entrance, along with two white pillars and a gabled overhang.

Jonas pulled up behind the other two vehicles. "That's Morris's truck," Jonas said, with a bit of amusement in his voice.

"And Marshall's sedan." Daisy recognized the college bumper sticker.

But even more surprising than the two vehicles parked at Iris's house was the sight of two men in her front yard dressed in snow gear.

"Can you tell who is who?"

Daisy almost laughed, but she knew this wasn't a laughing matter. She knew them both well. Morris was stockier with a barrel chest. Marshall was just as tall and broad-shouldered, but had a leaner form.

"I'd know that hat of Morris's with the ear protectors any day of the week," Jonas said, a smile in his voice. "He's dressed to be out there as long as he has to be."

Peering out again, Daisy said, "Marshall looks ready for the same. And how he can wear a down coat and still look stylish? That green scarf around his neck comes up to his nose."

"His watchman's cap has some swagger, too," Jonas said.

Daisy had worn her high boots, so the snow along the curb and street was no problem. Trampling to the sidewalk, she reached the point where Marshall had shoveled it. She couldn't see his face very well as it was covered by the scarf, but he lifted his hand in greeting and returned to what he was doing, his leather-gloved hands gripping the shovel.

Meeting up with Morris at the driveway, she noticed his gloves were the waterproof kind.

He yelled at her, "Who told that guy that it snowed?" He pointed to Marshall.

She laughed out loud. She just couldn't help it.

Jonas had rounded his SUV and walked up the street to the driveway, meeting Daisy at Iris's front porch.

Iris opened the door, shaking her head, her face ruddy. "What's wrong with those men? It's a competition to see who can finish first. I don't know what to do with them."

"I'm not sure there *is* anything you can do with them." Jonas's smile grew wide. "We were going to ask you if you needed help shoveling, but you certainly don't."

Iris rolled her eyes and motioned them to come inside.

Shedding their coats, Daisy and Jonas automatically slid off their boots to cross the ceramic tile in the foyer to the living room. They passed Iris's bedroom when they'd come inside. The house had an interesting layout and one that suited Daisy's aunt.

"I already have hot chocolate ready for when those dolts come inside. I usually pay our neighbor's teenager to shovel. I'm not so sure Morris and Marshall aren't too old to be shoveling snow."

"They're both trying to show you that they're fit," Jonas said.

"Fit for what is what I want to know," Iris said with more exasperation.

They sat in Iris's dining area. Iris served hot chocolate to Daisy and Jonas, along with a plate of chocolate-chip cookies. "You know what's going to happen when they come in, don't you?"

"Do you want to tell me?" Daisy asked.

"They're going to sit here and glower at each other. We won't be able to even have a decent conversation."

Daisy stirred the whipped cream that her aunt had dolloped on top of the hot chocolate. She studied her aunt. "There's only one way to end this. You're going to have to make a choice."

Flustered, Iris flopped into a chair and stared into her cocoa. "I'm not ready."

"Then there's only one other thing to do," Jonas advised her. "Pray that there's no more snow."

CHAPTER TWELVE

Business was definitely slow at the tea garden the following day. Foster had had his college classes canceled, so he had come into work with Daisy and Iris. Tessa had decided to mix cookie dough and freeze it so they'd have a supply when they needed it.

Mid-morning, Daisy received a call from Neil. He asked her if he could come to the tea garden to meet with her.

"The roads are clear," he said, "and I have something I want to discuss with you, but I'd rather do it in person."

"I'll be at The Farm Barn this afternoon for prep tomorrow . . ." Daisy began.

But Neil cut in. "I'd rather meet with you at the tea garden."

Her mind raced around all the possibilities for Neil's request. She kept busy until he arrived, one thought circling another in her mind. Was he going to cancel the reception tomorrow? Had Bob and Allyson changed their minds? Was Neil having trouble with the suppliers? Had something come up regarding Lydia's murder? So many things to think about—pieces of the puzzle that she was trying to fit together.

When Neil arrived and greeted her, she asked him, "Tea and a cheese biscuit?"

"Sure, that would be great."

It took her no time at all to set up a tea service. She served him Earl Grey tea on a Rosina vintage bone china teacup and saucer. It was a rare blue-black pattern made in England. On a cut-glass plate, she'd arranged a cheese biscuit for savory, and a coconut walnut scone for sweet. On the tray, she'd placed a honey pot and a sugar bowl.

Neil added honey to his tea and stirred. "You do make beautiful baked goods."

"Thank you. Just not wedding cakes," she joked. Bob and Allyson had chosen to order their wedding cake from a baker in Lancaster. They'd shown Daisy a picture of it, and it was gorgeous with white molded chocolate flowers and pearls.

"Bob and Allyson have specific tastes. They said you have their decorations down perfectly with tulle and lavender and rose taffeta bows on the chairs. I'm not sure Lydia could have captured the romantic spirit as well as you have."

That compliment surprised Daisy, and she almost felt as if she needed to defend her friend. "Lydia's decorations were always impeccable."

"I know they were. But most of them had Nan Conroy's ideas behind them. Lydia's mind centered on organization and efficiency. That's why she was so good at running The Farm Barn. She also knew how to delegate the right tasks to the right person. Besides Nan, April often came up with wonderful ideas to add to the equation."

"April has been a great help to me. So have the other members of the staff," Daisy acknowledged. "Jake sometimes pushes as if he wants to take over, but I don't let him do that. Did Lydia?"

After a bite of the warm cheese biscuit, Neil shook his head. "Lydia took Jake at face value. She didn't put up with any of his nonsense. But he's an enthusiastic member of the staff who is a hard worker. He's the one who moves furniture around when you need help, or can take over managing the kitchen."

"I'll remember that if I get into a bind at the reception. Is that what you want to talk about?"

Neil scanned the main room of the tea garden, and then his gaze focused on the spillover tearoom, the sales counter, the walls, and decorations. "No, I'm not here about the reception. You seem to have that well under control. Bob and Allyson are pleased by what you're doing. I'm hoping it goes off without a hitch."

"That's my hope, too." After she stirred honey into her tea that she poured into a Crownford Queen's bone china floral teacup and saucer, she took a sip and studied him. Maybe her silence would prompt him to continue. She knew the detectives often used that strategy. It worked.

Neil set his teacup on the saucer with a click. "I want to know if you'd like to buy The Farm Barn."

A small gasp escaped Daisy. She'd never expected that. "I *have* a business," she protested.

"There's no reason why you can't have two," he said with an ingratiating smile. "Women CEOs are trending."

He had to be joking, right? "Are you serious about selling?"

He looked dejected as he nodded. "I just can't run it, not now, not with Lydia gone." His face crumpled, and tears came to his eyes.

Daisy felt so sorry for him. "Neil, I understand that that's the way you feel now, but at a time like this, you shouldn't make any big decisions, especially not one this big."

Neil inhaled a long breath, then let it out. "I know that's what grief counselors advise. But on the other end, I know when a dream has ended. Running The Farm Barn isn't my passion. It was a dream that belonged to me *and* Lydia. With her gone, it's simply evaporated. Why would I want to run a business that reminds me of her every time I turn around? Why would I want to be there every day, remembering the way she flitted about the dining area, seeing her taste what the chef cooked, recalling how she could speak to all our customers with ease that made them feel at home?"

Daisy was quick to respond. "But aren't those memories precious to you? Aren't those things you want to remember?"

"Not right now, Daisy. I couldn't ask you to manage it for me when you have a business to manage of your own. But if you bought it, you could hire everybody you need to run it. You could *hire* a manager."

She had never considered running two businesses, and she wouldn't consider it now. Especially not now.

She had to ask herself some questions about Neil. Maybe The Farm Barn had been a dream of his and Lydia's, but what had happened when he'd had an affair? Had the dream shattered then, too? A marriage needed attention, and she intended to give hers as much as she could.

"I understand where you're coming from, Neil. Really, I do. When my husband died, so many of my dreams ended, too. But like you, I had two children to think of. After a while, I knew I had to change my dream, because the dream Ryan and I had had together was gone. It wasn't about business in my case. It was about family and home and where I wanted that to be. I moved back here to start over. Is that what you want to do? Start over?"

Leaning back in his chair, he sighed. "I suppose. But unlike you, I'm not about to leave here. Frannie loves Leah, and I don't want to separate them. I also have a support group for her here— her preschool teacher and Allyson. But I do need to make changes. Are you sure you won't consider buying The Farm Barn?"

Not hesitating, she answered, "I'm getting married this summer. Over the past two years, my life has been all about the tea garden and Vi and Jazzi. Vi is finding her own life, and Jazzi will be going away to college. I know what you're thinking, that that would be a perfect time to invest in something new. But I'm going to invest my time and all of my attention into my new marriage. Do you understand?"

"I understand more than you know. You're right

to put your relationship with Jonas first. I wish . . ." He shook his head. "I wish Lydia and I had carved out more time for ourselves. I wish so many things."

Just what exactly would Neil do differently? What exactly had caused his affair? Most of all, what exactly had caused Lydia's murder? Maybe this afternoon and evening, while she helped ready the restaurant for the reception tomorrow, she'd recognize clues she'd missed before.

The wedding reception on Saturday was proceeding smashingly. At least Daisy thought it was. When Allyson and Bob had walked into The Farm Barn to the cheers of all their guests, Daisy had gasped. Allyson's gown was perfection—a ball gown with a deep V-neck, long see-through illusion sleeves, and so much tulle Daisy wondered how Allyson would be able to sit in it. Seed pearls and glass beads danced across the bodice. A sparkling belt circled the bride's waist. Allyson held the train on a ring that slipped around her wrist. She looked ecstatic, and so did Bob in his tuxedo, his crisp white shirt, and black cummerbund.

In The Farm Barn's dining area, the tables had been set for around sixty guests. Space had been left open for dancing, and the DJ had apparently created a playlist of the couple's favorite songs. Besides keeping an eye on the kitchen, and the platters of fried chicken, pot pie, and pot roast being served from there, Daisy toured the dining area, checking on the services.

When Daisy stopped by Allyson and Bob's table, Allyson placed her hand on Daisy's arm. "You've done a marvelous job. It rivals Lydia's magic. I know she would be happy about all this, and happy that you were in charge."

That's what Daisy had hoped. She also hoped between setting up the room yesterday afternoon and overseeing part of the food prep, she'd hear something that would help her figure out what had gone wrong in Lydia's life. She hadn't, though. Maybe in the breakdown of the wedding reception, she'd hear gossip that could help.

Daisy had gone to the kitchen to see about the wheeling out of the wedding cake when she noticed Neil at the back door. His voice raised, he sounded angry. There was so much noise and activity in the kitchen, no one else noticed. She did.

The man at the door had russet hair, rather wild and thin, along with heavy chin stubble. He was growling at Neil, and Neil, with gritted teeth, was red-faced. They were partway inside the doorway and partway outside. The man wasn't wearing a coat, but rather a sweatshirt and jeans. She heard Lydia's name mentioned, and a cold chill ran down her back.

Just then April passed by her on the way to the kitchen. Daisy tapped her arm to stop her and whispered, "Do you know who that man is?"

"Sure do," April said with a frown. "That's Cletus Holloback, the chicken supplier."

No sooner had April told her who the man was, when Neil slammed the door on the fellow. He turned and saw Daisy and April watching him. Without a word, with a scowl on his face, he went into the reception without making a comment.

The chicken supplier. Why would Neil be having an argument with the chicken supplier? Over his prices? Neil had said the supplier didn't like Lydia. What had gone on between them?

The reception took on a life of its own as tables were cleared and the beautiful wedding cake was wheeled in. Daisy watched from a few feet away as Allyson and Bob fed each other cake with a bit of sloppiness that caused their guests to laugh. She supervised as April wheeled the cake back to the kitchen for cutting. After April cut slices, servers began carrying it, along with vanilla ice cream, to each table. The DJ began the bride and groom's playlist, and the couple danced their first dance as a married couple. The bride and groom's parents joined in, as did the other guests soon after.

The rest of the reception proceeded without a glitch. Daisy texted Jonas around seven p.m.: **I'll be home in about an hour.**

He sent back the text, **Looking forward to it,** and a smiley face.

Daisy wanted nothing more than to take a hot shower and cuddle on the sofa with him for the rest of the evening. As she made sure cleanup went as planned, she thought about her own wedding gown possibilities. She knew she didn't want a ball gown or anything too frivolous. Maybe creamy lace and sleeveless because of summer . . . possibly with a short train. She doubted she'd wear a veil, possibly flowers in her hair. She'd consult with the women in her life and see what they thought. She knew her mother would give her opinion and so would Tessa, but she might listen to Jazzi and Vi and Iris a little more. She looked forward to all of it, especially walking down the aisle toward Jonas.

Daisy was in the dining room, watching April take the bows from the chairs, when she saw Jake approach the young woman. At the kitchen doorway, Daisy couldn't hear what was said between them. Jake looked as if he were trying to convince April of something. His expression was . . . Daisy couldn't tell for sure.

She could see that April's expression seemed to be a combination of hesitant and worried. But then her eyes took on seriousness, and she told Jake something he obviously didn't want to hear. He turned away looking . . . disappointed . . . maybe a little angry. When he caught Daisy watching him, he smiled and gave a wave as if everything was just fine.

Was it just fine?

The public sale on Sunday afternoon was almost ready to start as Daisy and Jonas met Vi and Foster outside the property deep in Lancaster County. The snow had melted. With sunshine today, the temperature hovered around fifty.

Vi leaned toward Daisy and said, "I know we're just here to bid on a dining room table, but this is the kind of home I'd love to own someday."

The home had so many unique features. It was brick in a Tudor style. A pointed roof furthered that unique quality, and the arched doorway added more charm.

As they all walked inside, they saw more arched doorways, built-in bookshelves, and even a breakfast nook. Not wanting to miss the start of the sale, they went out back to the flagstone patio where the auction sale was taking place. Daisy overheard Foster saying to Jonas, "I heard the couple who lived here is moving to Southern Arizona for warmer weather. I can't imagine leaving Pennsylvania and its seasons, can you?"

Jonas ran his hand over a jelly cupboard when they stopped to talk. "I like the seasons, but I guess a couple has to do what's best for themselves as they age."

Foster said, "Vi and I want to own our own home someday. I know it's going to be a lot of years until then."

"Maybe not, if you get a good job when you graduate."

"I'm hoping I can get something without much of a commute. I don't want to be too far from Vi and Sammy."

"We've got a good network between me, Daisy, and your dad. We can put the word out what kind of job you're looking for, and maybe just the right thing will come along."

Foster looked Jonas in the eye. "You and Daisy and my dad form the foundation of our lives. We're more thankful than you could ever know."

Daisy saw the mist in Jonas's eyes and knew how much Foster's words meant to him. It meant so much to her, too.

They all registered and obtained their bidding numbers. Daisy already had her eye set on a grouping of china that would be great for the tea garden. Leaning close to Jonas, she asked, "Is anything worth your attention?"

"There's a pine bench over there. Since it seems like it's in a shabby condition, it might not go for much. I can make it into something special."

"Do you think Foster will win the table and chairs?"

"They brought Gavin's truck just in case. Foster knows how much he wants to bid, and I don't think he'll go over. Since it isn't an antique and has bumps and scratches that I told him I could easily fix, they might be in luck."

"Mom was so glad they asked her to babysit today."

"Your mom will spoil him as much as you do."

"I don't spoil him. I love him."

Jonas swung his arm around her shoulders and gave her a kiss on the cheek as the auctioneer took his stand and picked up his gavel. Once the bidding started, it proceeded at a steady pace. For the first two hours, Daisy mostly people-watched. Some came and went as objects they wanted came up for sale and then sold. There were dealers there, too, who were going to stick around for the whole auction. The house itself wasn't going to be auctioned off today. The auctioneer, Jim Thornton, was also a real estate agent who was waiting for offers to be submitted. Auctiongoers looked inside, and maybe one of them intended to buy. That was the whole point of today—make as much money for this couple as could possibly be had. It would stake them on a new life in Arizona.

Odds and ends from the shed in the back, where the pine bench had come from, went first. Jonas bid on the bench and got it for twenty dollars. He gave Daisy a smile and thumbs-up. She laughed.

"That pine bench will be a beautiful piece of furniture when you're done with it."

To her surprise, Vi bid on a set of ceramic patio pots. One was chipped, and they all needed to be painted. She won those.

Daisy asked her, "What are you going to do with them?"

"I want to set them around the front porch, sort of like you do at the Victorian. I'll paint them. Don't you think they'll be pretty?"

It was obvious that Vi wanted to make Glorie's house her own, and Daisy knew this was why they had moved. She was proud of them.

Foster said to Daisy, "I heard the table and chairs are coming up soon. They want to sell them before the lunch break."

"Jonas and I will watch and help you get them if we can."

"You know my top price," Foster said.

"I do. We won't let it go over if we can help it."

A few minutes later, however, they had to reassess. They learned the table and chairs were going to be sold separately.

"We want the table," Foster told them, and gave them the price he was willing to pay for that. "If we have to, we'll find chairs separately somewhere else."

Daisy had done that herself.

The chairs were sold first, each one by itself. This type of selling was up to the auctioneer. If he thought he could bring better prices that way, that's what he did. Finally the table came up. It was walnut with a scarred and nicked finish. One man, whom Daisy suspected was a dealer, kept bidding on it against Foster. Jonas put in a bid, too, not to hike the price but to show the man that he wasn't the only one and he couldn't take advantage of Foster since he was younger. The older fellow finally gave up, and Foster won the table right at the amount he wanted to pay.

Many people had started leaving, because a breeze had picked up. Daisy and Vi pulled on their gloves and moved around to stay warm. Foster's cheeks were ruddy with the chill, but he looked ecstatic that he'd won his prize. "Can you help me load it into the truck?" he asked Jonas.

"Sure thing. Let's go settle up." He asked Daisy, "Do you want to stay until after the lunch break? You didn't get your china."

She shrugged. "The auctioneer might sell it in lot boxes, and I don't really want to stand out here in the cold and wait. We can go." Suddenly, however, she caught Jonas's arm. "Look over there."

Leah and Titus Yoder were speaking with the auctioneer.

"I wonder what that's about," Daisy said.

"I don't think you'll want to run over there and ask them." Jonas's eyes were filled with amusement.

"No, I don't. But I do know how to find out what it's about."

Tomorrow, she was going to visit Rachel Fisher's shop.

Quilts and Notions had a steady stream of customers whether the weather was cold, hot, snowy, or rainy. Women in this area quilted, and Daisy knew Rachel's quilting circle was constantly busy.

Many of the women sold their quilts for profit. Others created them for family, neighbors in need, and charity auctions. To Daisy they were all beautiful—from the log cabin designs to wedding rings to tumbling blocks. She herself had a sunshine and shadow–patterned quilt on her bed.

There were three women choosing fabrics and threads at the quilting supply area on Monday morning. Rachel's daughter Hannah was helping them. Sarah, Rachel's other daughter, was filling the shelves with quilted potholders and place mats. There was a couple who looked like tourists examining the quilt rack, and another woman carrying a Coach purse, studying the books on the rack about Lancaster County history.

Rachel stood at the computer, checking out a woman with fabric sales. Daisy waited until the woman left.

Rachel smiled at her and said, "*Hallo.*"

"How are you?" Daisy asked.

Rachel adjusted her *kapp*. "It's been busy today."

Daisy glanced around the shop, and no one seemed to need Rachel at the moment. "We went to an auction yesterday." Daisy lowered her voice so no one would overhear her. "Leah and Titus Yoder were there."

"Bidding on auction items?" Rachel asked.

"No, I didn't see them bid on anything, but they were talking with the auctioneer. I thought that seemed a little odd unless they were going to buy and sell."

Rachel looked thoughtful. "Who was the auctioneer?"

"Jim Thornton."

Rachel let out a very low, "Ahh."

"What does that mean?" Daisy asked

As if suddenly something had made sense, Rachel gave a little nod. "I heard a rumor and didn't know if it was true. You know I don't pass anything along unless I have facts."

Daisy had to smile. "Yes, I know that, and that's why I often come to you."

Rachel gave a quick nod. "I heard that Titus is going to sell off some of their farm. Jim Thornton sells real estate, ya?"

"Yes, he does. He's selling the house where the public sale was held."

"It's possible he will be handling Titus's land if he sells," Rachel noted.

"Can the Yoders still make a living on the farm if they sell off part of their land?"

"That's the other side of the rumor I heard," Rachel conceded, her tone going even lower. "Supposedly Titus is going into business with Eli Lapp, who opened the buggy shop. Something about a partnership. It seems farming is just not enough anymore for Titus . . . for his family. I feel sorry about that, but I know it can be true. We are so fortunate. We have the farm, and we have the shop. Together we manage well. But others are not so blessed."

"Your husband knows how to handle the land. He's open to new methods," Daisy said. "I've heard Titus is somewhat stubborn about listening to others' input." Lydia had told her that.

"That happens," Rachel agreed. "The Amish try to keep the outside world out. But we have to remember we need to survive, too."

Daisy knew firsthand that Rachel and Levi guided their family the best way they knew, keeping open minds, but still being Amish . . . still relying on their faith . . . still relying on each other. Daisy hoped Titus and Leah could find that balance, too.

CHAPTER THIRTEEN

After the tea garden closed, Daisy walked down to Woods, avoiding a puddle along the way. Market Street businesses were closing for the day. Entering Woods, she was surprised to see another dog with Felix, who was resting under a table. She recognized that pup—it was Bart Cosner's basset hound, Scout. The patrol officer had adopted the dog from Four Paws Animal Shelter in the fall.

Bart was standing about a foot from a distressed, gray-painted island with a dark granite top. The veins of black and green in the granite would fit in anywhere.

No one else was in the shop, since it was almost closing time. Bart was saying to Jonas, "I like that one, too." He pointed to a natural island with a butcher-block top. He took a photo of it with his phone.

Bart's dog was low-key, and Felix seemed to suit his personality to whomever he was with. Felix got to his feet and trotted toward Daisy, the basset hound not far behind. She had two pairs of glossy eyes looking up at her. Both dogs wanted attention. With a chuckle, she stooped down and petted one with each hand. The basset hound dropped to the floor in front of her, rolling over for his tummy rub. Felix stared at him as if asking, *Really? Daisy just got here. What do you expect?*

Daisy petted the dog's belly and gave Felix some much-needed attention, too. When she was finished, both dogs lay at her feet adoringly.

"He's going to want to go home with you," Bart warned. "The kids roughhouse and play with him. They don't give him that kind of attention."

"What about you?"

"We're buds. He sits on the sofa with me and watches sports."

Jonas approached Daisy with his smile just for her.

Bart moved around the store and ran his hand over a pie safe.

"Are you redecorating?" Daisy asked Bart.

"Sort of, but not really. We're thinking about re-painting our kitchen cupboards, moving the kitchen table, and putting an island in. Nothing major."

"That's enough to disrupt your household," Jonas joked.

"It doesn't take much," Bart agreed. He texted pictures on his phone and then slipped the phone into his pocket. "I sent all the photos. She's going to have to decide what she likes. I thought this would be a start. If she doesn't like these, she can talk to Jonas about building her something else."

"My custom orders are stacking up," Jonas told Bart. "It could be a month or two."

"That's fine. We'd rather wait until warmer weather to paint anyway."

Daisy couldn't pass by the opportunity of having Bart so close and in conversation. She asked, "Are you making progress on Lydia's investigation?"

"Somehow I knew you were going to ask me that," Bart said with a grimace. "You know I can't tell you anything. Detective Rappaport would put me on desk duty."

"He's not the chief," Jonas said.

"No, but he has pull. I know better than to cross him."

"He hasn't told me anything," Daisy complained.

Bart sighed and shrugged. "It's no secret that detectives always looked to the people closest to the victim first. You can surmise what you want from that."

"Does that include family?" Jonas asked. "I can understand the detective looking at Neil, but certainly not Lydia's sister Leah."

"Lydia's family includes more than Leah," Bart said.

Did that mean Titus was under suspicion, too?

"There's nobody left but Titus," Daisy said, looking to Bart for more answers.

He wouldn't give her any answers, but he did say, "If the shoe fits."

Just what did *that* mean?

Later that evening, Daisy and Jonas sat on the sofa in front of Jonas's laptop, working on a preliminary guest list for their wedding. "I'm sorry you've never met my Philadelphia friends," Jonas said. "Many of them are still on the Philadelphia police force. It's hard to coordinate schedules."

Daisy remembered the weekend she was supposed to go to Philadelphia with Jonas for a barbecue. However, that was the weekend that Vi had told her that she was pregnant. She and her daughter and Foster had had a lot to discuss. She'd stayed home because of her daughter. Now, would she do the same?

"I know what you're thinking," Jonas said. "And don't. That weekend couldn't be helped. That was a long time ago, Daisy."

"How could you know what I was thinking?"

"I know you," he said with a wink and a look that told her he did.

"It's hard to keep the guest list pared down," she said.

"We don't have to pare it down if you don't want to."

Jonas understood the kind of wedding Daisy wanted, not a big to-do with a fancy ball gown and reception for too many people to talk to, and plans that took months to prepare for. She wanted a quiet, intimate wedding, and a reception with all their good friends.

"You already have my guest list on there," she pointed out. "It's mostly family, plus Tessa and Trevor, Cade and whoever he's dating. I added Detective Rappaport and Zeke. They're probably on your list, too," she said with a grin.

"You can claim them," Jonas teased. "I have about five good friends on the police force, and their wives or girlfriends. Plus a couple who were my neighbors."

Daisy suddenly had an idea that she thought would make their wedding even more special. "What if you invite your Philadelphia friends to Willow Creek before the wedding?"

"You mean for the bachelor night or something like that?"

"No, not that. I was thinking they could come for a weekend now, way before the wedding. They could stay in the garage apartment, since it's empty."

Jonas rubbed his jaw as he seemed to mull it over. "And they could stay in my townhouse. Maybe it's a good thing I haven't sold it yet. If we want to use Cade to sell it, we really have to do that soon. I'll give him a call this week."

"I'd like to get to know your friends, and you know that won't happen at the wedding."

"You mean because I'll have eyes only for you?"

"And I'll have eyes only for you."

Jonas wrapped his arm around her and pulled her back against the sofa. "I'll check with them and see if they can come maybe next weekend."

When she and Jonas gazed into each other's eyes, Daisy could see their future there. And when Jonas kissed her, she forgot all about the guest list.

Daisy's office at the tea garden wasn't large. When she and Iris and Tessa were sitting in it, it was cramped, but they were batting around more ideas for their Alice in Wonderland Tea.

"I read *Alice in Wonderland* again," Tessa said. "She did more than fall down the rabbit hole chasing after the White Rabbit."

"Let's start with that," Daisy decided. "Can we do an Alice in Wonderland trail into the tea garden? Is that even possible?"

"I don't know how we'll make a rabbit hole," Iris said dryly.

They all laughed.

"Do you think there's time to find a big cutout of a white rabbit for the doorway when people come in?"

Tessa, the artistic one in the group and a painter, said, "Well, of course there is. I still have my art connections. I haven't given up painting, you know, simply put it aside for a while. Trevor takes up my painting time."

Iris chuckled. "Men will do that."

"Relationships will do that," Daisy agreed. "Do you think you can get one around five feet tall?"

"Sure. I'll draw one up and see what you think. We could have a few other stations with cutouts. How about the Cheshire Cat?"

"Let's make it a dressed-up cat with a smile, not based on the Disney or Lewis Carroll book."

"Will do," Tessa said.

"How about the Queen of Hearts?" Iris suggested.

"That's a wonderful idea, and she'd round out the trail nicely." Tessa pulled some drawings from a folder she'd laid on Daisy's desk and pushed them across to Daisy.

"Take a look at these sketches I made for cookies. A pocket watch is important in *Alice in Wonderland*, and I can do a cookie shaped like one. Playing cards, too. It will take a little time, but Eva's good with a piping bag, too."

"Of course, we have to have teacup-shaped cookies," Iris said with a smile. "That tea party is essential to Alice. That's why we're having the day, right?"

Iris asked, "What kind of centerpieces do we want on the tables?"

"Didn't the flowers think Alice was a weed and chase her out?" Tessa asked.

"That's true. How about daisies?"

"It seems fitting since our facility is called Daisy's Tea Garden," Tessa said, grinning. Tessa pointed to another drawing. "How about little Alice cookies, just a blonde little girl, bow in her hair, blue dress."

"I'm getting more and more excited about this," Daisy said. "It seems to be moving my mind from the murder. That's a good thing."

"No leads from the police?" Iris asked.

"None that they're revealing," Daisy responded. She pushed her hair back from her cheek. "They're keeping all the clues bottled up, not sharing much."

"I've been thinking about the crime scene," Tessa said. "Trevor and I were discussing it. It's possible the forensic team could have found paint on Lydia's clothes or something like that. That would lead them to the vehicle."

Daisy shook her head vigorously like a child being told something she didn't want to hear. "I hate thinking about it."

Iris asked Daisy, "Did you talk to Jonas about Neil's offer to buy The Farm Barn?"

"What?" Tessa almost shouted. "You want to buy The Farm Barn?"

"No," Daisy assured her quickly. "I do *not*. That's the whole point. Yes, I told Jonas about it, but it's not in any of my plans, not now and not in the future. This is enough. I love working here with all of you. I don't want to take on something that would eat up my family time."

"That's smart," Iris said. "And you'd have to dump a ton of money into it, I would imagine."

"I don't want to do that, either. I want to put money in Sammy's college fund. Jonas and I want to possibly add on an addition. We've decided that, if anything, we'll give more time to the homeless shelter, and donations to it."

"Being a strong woman these days," Tessa began, "is all about knowing what you want, finding it, and holding onto it. You're doing that, and I admire you for it."

"Are you finding what you want with Trevor?" Daisy asked.

Tessa blushed. "Uh-oh, I should have known I shouldn't bring up personal stuff."

"You didn't answer the question," Iris teased.

"I like Trevor. I might even say I love him, sort of. I just don't know if I want to spend the rest of my life with him." Tessa turned her gaze on Iris. "And you?"

Iris waved her hand at Tessa as if to wipe her words away. "I'm waiting for a sign."

Daisy laughed. "Morris and Marshall could have a long wait."

They were all smiling when Tamlyn knocked hesitantly on the door. "Do you have a minute?"

"Sure, I do," Daisy said. "What can I help you with?"

"The tearoom's all cleaned up and ready for tomorrow. But there's something I wanted to talk to you about, something that seems odd."

Daisy's mind seemed to go in a hundred different directions at once, but she decided to wait to see what Tamlyn had to say.

"You know that Varages, France yellow with red flowers teapot set?"

Daisy studied Tamlyn. The server knew almost every teacup, saucer, and pot in the cupboard. She was careful how she served them and whom she served them to. She had special ones for guests she thought would appreciate and be careful with their teacups and saucers. Daisy didn't mind as long as everyone was satisfied.

Since the teacup and saucer Tamyln was describing usually stood out, Daisy knew exactly which one she was talking about. "Sure, I know which set you mean. I found it at Otis's Pirated Treasures. It was a good find. Has something happened to it?"

"I don't know," Tamlyn said, her finger to her chin. "A teacup is missing."

"Missing?" the three women asked at once.

"Yes. Yesterday we had two buses come in. Foster asked if he could use the set, and I told him to go ahead."

"Maybe Foster will remember something about what happened to it," Iris said.

"Maybe. Like I said, we were busy. The last time I saw it, the cups and saucers were sitting on a service table to bring to the kitchen."

"I can't imagine our customers would steal our teacups," Daisy said, almost with amusement.

"I wouldn't think so either," Tamlyn agreed. "But you never know. Crazy things happen, and people sometimes are crazy."

Daisy didn't know about crazy, but she did know about odd, and sometimes even sinister. Still, she didn't imagine how a missing teacup could cause any trouble.

*   *   *

That evening, Daisy sat in her living room, the fire blazing, Jonas nearby in the kitchen, and Jazzi upstairs. She was video-chatting with her sister. She could see palm trees swaying against a blue sky as Cammie sat under an awning attached to her RV. Cammie was all sunshine and smiles, bobbed dark hair swaying in the wind. She held up her laptop for Daisy to see the landscape and the size of her RV. "Don't you wish you were here on a beach in Florida instead of in Pennsylvania with your cold weather and snow?"

Cammie could usually push her buttons, but tonight, Daisy was happy with the people she loved, and her sister wasn't going to get under her skin. "I had enough Florida weather when I lived there all those years. You're taking advantage of the best time of the year there. I hope you're having fun."

Cammie's gaze moved from the laptop as she seemed to check her surroundings. "I'm having some fun. The beach is nice. I remember how much Mom and Dad missed you when you lived down here." Again, that little nudge at Daisy's long fuse.

"When I lived in Florida, my love for Ryan and finding my own life was more important than anything else. But now I'm glad I've come home. Mom and Dad miss *you* . . . you know . . . with you in New York. Have you ever thought of returning to Pennsylvania? Can you see yourself living here again?"

Cammie brushed her bangs aside and sighed. After a long hesitation, she responded, "I'm on this RV trip because I'm getting restless in New

York. I thought if I took a drive around the country and time off, maybe I'd decide what I really want to do."

It was rare for Cammie to be that honest with Daisy, and Daisy appreciated the sharing. "Are you trying to decide what state you want to settle in?" Daisy asked, a teasing note in her voice.

"I don't know about the state. I'm deciding if I want to stay in public relations for the rest of my life. I think maybe I need to branch out, or just focus in deeper on something. Do you know what I mean?"

When Daisy had lived in Florida, she'd been a nutritional counselor. She'd advised people with diabetes, people who wanted to lose weight, and ran some hospital programs, too. She had liked what she was doing. Had it been a passion? Possibly. She wasn't sure about that. Then Ryan had been diagnosed with cancer, and her life had changed forever. Running the tea garden with her aunt had become a vocation in so many ways. She liked being with people. She liked listening to them. She liked buying teas and mixing flavors. She loved baking. She could create recipes that Tessa and Iris would taste-test. This was as fulfilling as her nutritional work had been.

For Cammie to find that too, she had to make some decisions. "Are you tired of working with people?"

"Isn't *that* a good question? I must be, or I wouldn't be here alone. I haven't gone nightclubbing, or to the bars, or anything like that. I'm just enjoying the sand and the sun and hearing my own thoughts for a change. Maybe I'm growing up," she joked.

"Would you be comfortable developing ad campaigns from your apartment and sending them out into the universe?"

"You mean, e-mailing contacts, finding accounts, dealing with clients remotely?"

"Something like that."

"I don't know, Daisy. I think I might leave it all behind."

"And do what?"

"Maybe own my own vineyard and spend time with the grapes instead of with people."

Daisy had to laugh, and Cammie laughed with her.

After that, they talked about Jazzi and colleges, about Vi and Foster and Sammy, about their parents. They ended on a high note with Cammie saying she'd keep in touch.

After Daisy closed her laptop, Jonas came into the living room with a cup of tea for her and for himself. "How did that go?"

"I think it went well." She knew Jonas had wanted to give her some privacy with Cammie. "Our conversation made me realize how different Cammie and I are, even though we're sisters."

"She's wilder and you're a homebody?" Jonas teased.

"In some ways. I think Cammie would like to be a homebody if she could meet somebody she really loved. That hasn't happened. I think if we lived near each other, things would be smoother between us. Oh, I'm sure we'd clash. That's the way Cammie and I are. But now with my relationship with Mom healing, I think we could all get along better."

"Is that your Pollyanna attitude again?" Jonas asked with a grin.

"I suppose so. But I do think it's true. I think Cammie and I would find how much we're the same rather than look at how much we're different." She paused, then went on, "Considering sisters and how they're alike and different, I can't help thinking about Lydia and Leah. They were twins, but yet they were so different. In other ways, though, I'm sure they were the same. After all, they grew up in the same family with the same values, and I think Lydia still shared them. She just didn't want to do it as an Amish woman. I know Morris and Zeke are looking at every member of Lydia's family, but I can't believe Leah would want to hurt her sister. I just can't."

"I know you can't. But if you can't think about her sister that way, what about Leah's husband Titus? He's pretty sober and close-mouthed, so different from Lydia and the life she led. Neil is completely of the world, even if Lydia kept her Amish roots in a sense. Do you think Titus and Neil got along? Maybe there could have been friction there that started something else."

Jonas had his detective hat on, and she could see him consolidating theories. She did that now and then, but with this case, maybe she was just too close to it.

"I'm still surprised the Yoders are selling off part of their farm. If it's true they are," she said.

"Daisy, you know how hard it is to make a living farming. Levi and Rachel have told you that a lot."

"I know."

"And you're thinking about how to find out the truth about what's happening?"

"I haven't spoken to Cade for a while, and I was thinking we should renew our friendship. Maybe he could share some information about the Yoders."

"Not if they're his clients."

"No, maybe not if they're his clients. But maybe, since he's in the real estate business, he would have heard something about the transaction."

Jonas picked up his teacup and clinked it against Daisy's as she held hers up, too. "Go to it, Daisy Swanson. I know you want to."

She grinned at him and picked up her phone.

CHAPTER FOURTEEN

Daisy stood at the sales counter ringing up one of her favorite customers, Fiona Wilson. Fiona often bought chicken soup for the week along with anything else that suited her fancy. She'd seen tragedy in her family lately, and Daisy wanted to make life as easy for her as she could. She often told Fiona what she told her now. "If you ever need food delivered, just let me know. Foster will be glad to bring it over."

"I'm fine, Daisy, really I am. As long as I have your soup, a few scones, and other goodies, my doctor says I should keep doing what I'm doing. Walking to the tea garden is good for me. It gives me exercise."

Fiona was in her early seventies, diminutive and slender. Although she bought her clothes at the thrift shop, A Penny Saved, she always looked stylish and trendy. Today she was wearing black wool slacks, a pale blue pullover, and a striped infinity scarf. Her chin-length curly hair was clasped over her temple. She was smiling at Daisy now as if she'd been trying to get over the tragedy of the past six months and was succeeding.

Fiona leaned closer across the sales counter. "I hear you're getting married this summer. Have you set a date?"

The gossip train in Willow Creek ran fast and furious. Daisy couldn't stop it if she tried. "Yes, we're getting married this summer, but we don't know exactly when yet. We want to do it while Jazzi is still here."

"I heard Jazzi is majoring in social work. She'll make a great social worker. I mean, she's used to being with all these people in here when she serves. I remember when she was searching for her birth mother."

It seemed the whole town knew Daisy's business, and not only Daisy's but her family's, too. The truth was—even her customers seemed like family. "I remember that time, too. It was stressful, but I'm glad she found Portia and Portia has her. It's good when we add to our family, don't you think?"

Fiona nodded. "I don't have much family left," she said sadly. "But do you know what? I'm thinking of rescuing a senior dog. A little one. What do you think about that?"

"I think you'd make a terrific dog mom."

"Hopefully some time when Jonas is volunteering at Four Paws, I'll visit. I trust his judgment."

"I trust his judgment, too," Daisy said with amusement in her voice.

Fiona reached out and squeezed Daisy's hand. "You have a good man there. I hope you'll be happily married for a very long time."

Daisy handed Fiona her bag. "You take care now."

"I will."

Just as Fiona reached the door, Cade opened it. He held it for her as she passed through. Then he came into the tea garden, obviously looking for Daisy. His gaze found hers. She'd phoned him last night and asked him to stop in so they could catch up.

Cade Bankert was the real estate agent who had helped her find her barn property as well as the Victorian for the tea garden. They'd been high school classmates, and he'd taken her to their prom. Afterward, though, she'd left for college, and their lives had gone separate ways. She'd once thought they might have a romantic relationship, but that had fizzled out. Even their friendship had become unstable when she'd started dating Jonas.

She smiled at Cade, approached him, and motioned to the spillover tearoom. She noticed his burgundy suit fit finely over his broad shoulders. He had long legs, and she scurried to keep up as he went ahead of her. Cade's brown hair brushed to the side looked like it had a bit of gel on it. His brown eyes met hers as he sat at a table.

"Are you joining me for tea?" he asked.

She motioned to Cora Sue. "How about Earl Grey and some corn cake? I think you'll like it."

"I'm sure I will."

At one time, Cade had stopped in almost every day, but as she and Jonas had become closer, Cade had changed his habits. "How are the girls?" he asked. "I haven't seen them around lately."

She caught him up on what was happening with Jazzi and Vi. By that time, Cora Sue had brought the two cups of tea and the corn cake.

As Daisy reached for the pot of honey for her

tea, Cade's gaze targeted her engagement ring. "I hear a wedding is being planned. Congratulations."

Daisy remembered a conversation with Jazzi when her daughter had told her they needed all the friends that they could get. They shouldn't lose any. Daisy suddenly plunged in. "I'm sorry I haven't been in touch sooner. Will you come to the wedding?"

His eyes were kind. "I will if you invite me."

"Jonas and I will definitely invite you, and you can bring a plus one." As soon as she said that, she didn't know if she should have. She didn't know what was happening in Cade's personal life these days.

"Actually, I have been dating someone who opened a chocolate shop on Sage Street. Judith makes the most delicious chocolate confectionaries. Have you ever stopped in at Truffles?"

"I didn't know a new shop had opened there. No, I haven't stopped in, but I will." After they spoke about the chocolate shop a little more and what it had to offer, Daisy said, "I haven't been on Sage Street for a while. Vi works at Pirated Treasures, you know."

"Yes, I do. Otis claims he doesn't know what he'd do without her. I stop in there sometimes when I'm waiting for Judith to finish up with a customer, or at the end of the day. I'm glad to see that area of Willow Creek coming alive again. I think there's another shop that's going to go in there soon, handmade baskets, I believe."

After a pause when Cade ate his corn cake and they both sipped tea, Daisy asked, "How is the real estate market in Willow Creek?"

"There are more buyers than sellers, which is

good for me." He gave her a studying look. "I know you well, Daisy Swanson. Remember, I was your high school prom date. Why did you want to have tea with me today?"

She had to be honest with Cade. She always had been. "I did want to reconnect with you. Our friendship still means a lot to me."

"I guess I got bent out of shape when you and Jonas got close. I didn't expect it to last. But it has, and I hope you're happy."

"I am. But I did have another reason for asking you to come in today."

"And what was that?" he asked, leaning back with a smile.

"I understand that Titus Yoder is selling some of his property. Do you know anything about that? If you do, can you tell me?"

Cade sat up straighter. "Titus was related to Lydia Aldenkamp, right?"

"Yes, he was her brother-in-law."

"And Lydia was your friend, from what I hear."

"Yes, she was."

"So I suppose you're asking me about the Yoder property because it has something to do with Lydia's murder?"

"Not necessarily. I'd just like to know what's happening with it."

"From what I hear, Yoder talked to an independent realtor first—Jim Thornton. But then he thought he could get a better offer if he sold land with a member of *my* team. They've had several meetings. Is there something in particular you want to know?"

"Is he really selling off his property?"

"Yoder hasn't handled his land with the care it needs, and it's not supporting him. He's been old-fashioned about what he wanted to happen there. I think he's going to sell off either one tract or two for hobby farms."

"Have you gotten a feel for what kind of man Titus is?"

"I don't know if I can speak to that. He's definitely the silent type. When he and his wife are together, he seems very caring toward her."

"That was my impression, too," Daisy murmured.

"Do you think Titus had something to do with his sister-in-law's murder?"

Daisy was quick to say, "I don't want to give you that impression."

"But you're gathering information about all the possible people who could be involved, right?"

As soon as he asked, Cade held up his hands as if he were warding off her words. "Never mind. I'm not going to lecture you. I've learned before that doesn't work. And that it only comes between us. I know you have to do what you think is right, Daisy. I wish you good luck with that."

Cade was being kind, and she did want to rekindle their friendship. She hoped he could be friends with Jonas, too.

Plans had worked out for a few of Jonas's friends to arrive this weekend. Daisy and Jonas had readied the apartment over the garage so a couple in the group could be comfortable there and the men at Jonas's townhouse. Before preparing more, though, she and Jonas had decided to have dinner at The Farm Barn tonight to see how Neil and the restaurant were faring. However, it was easy to see that The Farm Barn was in trouble.

The parking lot only hosted five cars besides Jonas's SUV. As Daisy closed the car door, she noticed a black sedan and a man standing next to it. He was studying the restaurant. He was dressed in a brown rumpled suit. He was overweight, and his belly protruded over his belt. She wondered why he was standing there instead of proceeding inside. Maybe he was waiting for someone.

Half an hour later, inside the restaurant, she and Jonas sat at a table for four. Other tables were sparsely filled.

Jonas picked up a fried chicken thigh and said, "They left out all the spices." He poked at his side dish with very limp green beans and tiny bits of ham. "It looks as if they're skimping on the ham in the green beans, too. And they're cooking it too long. Even *I* know that."

Daisy finished a forkful of chicken pot pie and frowned. "The chicken broth is weak. I don't think the chef put any salt in it, and the dough's not boiled completely. I don't know what they're doing, but if they want to fail, this is the way to do it. Do you think the chef quit?"

"Who would take over if the chef quit?"

"Neil?" she asked, almost facetiously. "I don't see him anywhere around."

Again Daisy glanced around the dining room. She spotted April at a table of four. She was chatting with them, and they were all smiling. "That table seems happy with their food."

MURDER WITH EARL GREY TEA   213

"Or they're happy with April," Jonas said. "She's very personable. Maybe she makes the food seem good when it's not."

Watching April again, Daisy said, "She's one of the most adept servers. My guess is she recommended the dishes that she knew were passable."

"What? Like pork and sauerkraut?" Jonas asked, studying the table too.

"There's not much you can do to mess that up," Daisy commented.

Laying her hand on Jonas's, she said, "I think I'm going to go to the kitchen and just peek in at what's going on. Do you think that's too intrusive?"

"You managed a reception here. Neil asked you to do that. I don't think it's too intrusive, especially when you want to see what they're doing to Lydia's dream."

Daisy pushed her chair back. "Eat what you can. I'll be back soon."

"Unless they convince you to stay and cook," Jonas joked.

After Daisy made her way through the tables, she entered the outer area of the kitchen where the servers received their orders, supplies, and commands from the chef.

The chef, the same person she'd seen there before, looked harried. She waved to him. "Anything I can do to help?"

He just rolled his eyes. "Not unless you can make sure suppliers deliver. Neil expects me to be Lydia. I can't be, not and run everything at once. She was amazing. I'm not."

Daisy passed the walk-in refrigerator. Beside it was a pantry closet. The door was open, and a padlock hung from a latch on the door frame. If supplies were the problem . . .

But supplies didn't seem to be the problem. Neil was inside that closet, kissing a woman!

Well, he *had* been kissing a woman. Or a woman had been kissing him. Now he pushed the brunette away. "It's not going to happen," he said angrily. "I never should have had an affair with you in the first place. I was an idiot."

The woman looked to be in her early thirties. She was pretty, with a wide mouth covered in red lipstick, color in her cheeks, and smoky eye shadow on her lids. She was wearing a little black dress that molded to her body, and high-heeled black shoes. At Neil's words, she reared back and slapped him, her red acrylic nails glowing in the overhead closet light. Then she rushed out of the closet, practically knocking Daisy over.

Daisy righted herself and withdrew into the server's section, knowing that Neil was going to be embarrassed, maybe even more than embarrassed. He knew she'd witnessed that kiss.

The woman scurried out the back door of The Farm Barn and slammed it behind her.

April came up beside Daisy, her mouth agape. She said, "She didn't wear a coat in this weather. Maybe she intended to stay inside with Neil."

From April's assessment, Daisy didn't think this had been the first time the brunette had been around. "Do you know who she is?"

"I do. Her name is Mitzi Geitz."

"Has she been here before?"

"She's been here as a customer, once or twice back in the kitchen with Neil. Never when Lydia was here, though. I mean, she and Neil never acted too friendly when Lydia was around."

"I see," Daisy said, seeing all too clearly. If April knew about a connection between Mitzi and Neil, the police probably did, too. But Daisy would like a little more information. "Is she from Willow Creek?"

April nodded. "She works at the Rainbow Flamingo."

Daisy wondered how the clerk at a dress shop and Neil had met.

Someone in the kitchen dropped a serving tray. Fortunately, it was empty.

"Do you need any help organizing to serve the rest of the diners?" Daisy asked April.

"That would be great, Daisy. Even the tickets for the rest of the tables are getting mixed up. Servers aren't collecting the right meals. I'm recommending the pork and sauerkraut to everybody, because that's the best dish tonight."

"I'll do what I can to help. I imagine everybody's going to be glad when this service is over."

"You bet. I can't imagine The Farm Barn going on like this."

Daisy couldn't either. She returned to her table briefly to talk to Jonas about what had happened and what she was going to do to help.

"Are you going to speak with Neil?"

"Eventually."

"If this Mitzi slugged Neil, what else might she do to free him of his marriage?" Jonas asked.

Daisy didn't have the answer to that one . . . yet.

* * *

When Saturday arrived, Daisy had hoped that welcoming Jonas's friends into their home would be a relatively easy feat to accomplish. Now she wasn't so sure.

She'd been somewhat anxious about meeting his buddies, whom he hadn't had much contact with, especially over the past year that they'd been dating seriously. Yet she knew Jonas had a good read on people. If they were his friends, certainly she'd like them, too.

On the other hand . . .

Les Volmer was downright scary. Maybe it was his eagle-eyed gaze as he studied her . . . or maybe it was his heavy salty beard. His thick black and silver hair was a bit mussed, and the lines on his face looked as if they'd been etched there for years. As Les and Daisy shook hands, she felt the man's steel grip.

Jonas said, "Les does a lot of undercover work."

She didn't imagine either of the men was going to explain what that was. Narcotics, perhaps? Gang infiltration? She didn't think she wanted to know.

She'd dressed today in what she considered casual and appropriate fashion—dark purple jeans, geometrically swirled sweater with long sleeves, a crew neck, and violet and navy undertones. But as Les studied her, from her long blond hair and blue eyes to her short navy suede boots, she wasn't sure what she was wearing was appropriate. Why was that?

Apparently hoping he could crack the slight tension between her and Les, Jonas joked, "Les has a few years on me. He was one of my mentors on the force."

A mentor, Daisy thought. That meant Les might still want to look out for Jonas, including judging the woman he'd chosen to marry?

As if he sensed her thoughts, or even her uncertainty, Felix sidled up beside her and brushed his head against her knee.

When Jonas introduced Doug Newcamp, also a cop, he didn't extend his hand to Daisy. Actually, he looked uncomfortable. He was an ordinary-looking man. With his dark brown hair in an almost buzz cut, he looked to be about Jonas's age.

Jonas explained, "Doug and I became friends when our dads became partners."

"Jonas's dad was a stand-up guy," Doug said. "He and my dad took us on camping trips every summer."

Daisy's gaze went to Jonas. She saw in his eyes that he was reliving some of those trips. Soon after they were dating, he'd revealed his dad had been killed in the line of duty. That was one of the reasons Jonas had decided that as a cop, he never wanted to have kids. But his life had changed now, and so had hers.

Like Les, Doug also gave her a once-over in a cop assessing kind of way, as if he were wondering if she was good enough for Jonas. Or maybe that was her own insecurities rising up.

The couple whom Jonas had invited—Ray and Beverly Lafferty—appeared much more comfortable as they looked around the barn home, seemingly intrigued by it. During introductions, Beverly asked, "So this really was a barn at one time?"

"It was," Daisy answered. "I worked with an architect to make it into a home for me and my two girls."

"Ray and Beverly were my neighbors in Philly," Jonas explained. "Beverly is great at decorating like you are. She always wanted to come into my place and dress it up. But I told her it was a waste of time."

Ray checked out the wagon-wheel chandelier on the ceiling and the floor-to-ceiling fireplace in the dining area, as well as the kitchen with its knotty pine cabinets beyond. He gave a whistle. "Those renovations must have been extensive."

His wife gave him a nudge in the ribs and a chastising look.

Ray was trendier-looking than the other two men. His brown hair, thick on top and streaked with a bit of blond, was trimmed short on the sides. He looked as if he hadn't shaved around his mouth and along his chin, but that was fashionable now. His brown eyes were assessing her home.

Beverly explained, "Ray is a house appraiser, so don't mind anything he says. In fact, just ignore him."

They all laughed and seemed to know each other very well.

Beverly was pretty, around Daisy's age with chin-length sandy hair, green eyes, and a wide smile. Daisy felt a friendly vibe from her. Thinking it was time to cut the introductions and begin the get-to-know-you part of the weekend, Daisy asked, "Tea or coffee, anyone? I have some scones and—"

"I understand Jonas is going to show me and Doug to his townhouse. Maybe we should get settled in," Les suggested.

Did the man want time alone with Jonas to catch up?

Sensing that Les was being too abrupt for polite

friendship, Beverly said, "And Ray and I will be staying here?"

Jonas came over beside Daisy and laid his hand on her shoulder as if to say, *Don't mind Les*. She was trying not to. She leaned into Jonas slightly. He'd dressed in a casual outfit, too, with black jeans and a navy Henley shirt. She knew his bomber jacket, black leather, lay over on the deacon's bench, ready to go.

Turning to Beverly, Daisy smiled. "I thought you and your husband would appreciate some privacy. My daughter and her husband recently moved out of the garage apartment. It's furnished a bit sparsely right now. There is a bed and few pieces of furniture for the living area. It has a small kitchen and a full bath."

Ray responded, "That sounds perfect. We'd love having a honeymoon night on our own. Our kids are staying with my parents, and we don't get away much."

"It's ready for you," Daisy assured him.

"Daisy even stocked the refrigerator with bottles of water, fruit, and cheese," Jonas said.

"Just like a hotel," Ray joked.

Jonas gave Daisy's shoulder another squeeze of encouragement. "I'll take these guys to my town-house. Maybe one of them will want to buy it as an investment."

"Is it up for sale?" Les asked.

"Not yet. As soon as we set the wedding date, I'll put it on the market." Jonas gave Daisy a light re-strained kiss, tapped his leg for Felix to come with him, and then led Les and Doug out.

Today's temperature was in the fifties, and Daisy imagined her guests had left their outer clothes in their car. They had all come in Les's large SUV. She grabbed her cat-patterned long sweater from the deacon's bench where it had laid next to Jonas's jacket and shrugged into it. Five minutes later, she had shown Beverly and Ray to the apartment above the garage without much conversation on the walk over. She wasn't sure what she expected of them, and they obviously weren't sure what they expected of her. They were being polite, and she supposed that would go on until they had some real conversations.

As they mounted the stairs into the apartment, Daisy following the couple, Beverly exclaimed, "This is really nice. It must have been wonderful to have your daughter and her husband close."

"Oh, it was. And after the baby was born, it was extra nice. I loved coming over here to watch him and hold him and rock him to sleep."

"Our kids are preteens," Ray explained, moving into the kitchen area and having a look around there. There was a card table set up with two folding chairs. "They are just starting to make our lives miserable," he bemoaned. "I can't imagine the year ahead."

Daisy chuckled. "Girls or boys?"

"One of each," Beverly said. "Our son, who's twelve, stays to himself much too much, and our daughter—she's eleven going on seventeen—has no filter."

Daisy motioned to the sofa that had removable cushions on the seats and the backs. They were a pretty gray and blue floral pattern. "Jonas made the sofa. He moved it in from the store."

"For us?" Beverly asked.

"Not just for you. Eventually I'll rent the apartment."

Ray and Beverly sank down onto the sofa.

Daisy said, "I'll let you get settled. We're going to have a buffet at the house this evening at five. Vi and Foster will be there, as well as my daughter Jazzi, so you can meet them. And Zeke Willet is going to join us."

Ray and Beverly exchanged a look.

Daisy didn't know if that was about Vi and Foster or about Zeke. Better to find out. "Do you have a question?"

"I'm surprised Zeke will be there," Beverly said.

Jonas had left Philadelphia on tense terms with Zeke Willet. Daisy realized that Jonas might not have caught his friends up on the state of affairs with him and Zeke now. Still, this was Jonas's story to tell.

Daisy did say, however, "Jonas and Zeke realized their friendship was a lot stronger than anything that happened in the past." Facing the stairway, she turned back to them. "I almost forgot to say there's a bottle of wine in the fridge, too. I hope you enjoy it."

She left the apartment, wondering where in the world the night was headed.

CHAPTER FIFTEEN

Daisy's dining-area table looked ready for company. The round oak pedestal table had a distressed wood finish. She had added two supplemental boards to the center of the table, and it was now a long oval. There would be ten of them with Vi and Foster, Jazzi, and Zeke. It would be a little tight around the table, but it should work.

She was going to serve food family-style. After Jonas had started a fire in the fireplace, she'd covered the table with a seafoam-colored cloth. She'd taken her white Ironstone plates from the hutch and used those on the table. The rose-patterned silverware had been a gift from her mother-in-law when Daisy and Ryan had married.

Yes, she'd tried hard tonight to make this dinner special, and she hoped it would be for Jonas and his friends.

Beverly and Ray had arrived first and kept up a pleasant conversation with Daisy and Jazzi, as they'd admired Felix and caught a glimpse of

Marjoram and Pepper before the felines vanished upstairs.

Les and Doug trailed in with Jonas while Jazzi was setting out the appetizers on the island. Daisy had made small chicken croquettes, breaded and deep-fried until golden brown. Triangle-shaped shrimp salad and cucumber sandwiches were placed on a crystal dish. Puff pastry filled with bacon and cheese would also be tasty tidbits. Jazzi had arranged a sampling of area cheeses on another platter, with a basket of crackers nearby and dipping sauces like mustard and pepper jam.

As Daisy rearranged the plates, Jazzi leaned close to her and said, "I think you went overboard, Mom."

"Your gram says you can never have too much to eat."

"I suppose that's true," Jazzi agreed, looking over the spread again.

Jonas came up beside Daisy and put his hand on her waist. Felix had followed him into the kitchen. "Is everything ready?"

At that moment, Foster and Vi arrived. Daisy said, "Do you want to introduce them to everybody and offer our guests appetizers? Zeke texted me he might be a few minutes late. I'm going to put the casseroles and platters on the table. We can eat as soon as Foster and Vi take off their coats."

After Vi and Foster were introduced to Jonas's friends, Vi waved to her mom, shed her coat, and then came over to see if she needed help. "We decided to let Aunt Iris babysit Sammy so we could join in adult conversation tonight. What can we do?"

Although she'd miss seeing Sammy, she knew she'd probably be too distracted with readying food and serving it to spend much time with him. "Let's see if we can get the food onto the table without it growing cold. Most things should have a lid, and that will help."

Vi's eyes grew big as the pork loin roast Daisy had already sliced filled a platter. To accompany it, she'd created a cider sauce made from apple cider, maple syrup, and bacon drippings. She'd also made boiled chicken pot pie the day before and now lifted the crock from her slow cooker and put that on the table. A pot roast, a veggie medley, coleslaw, and pickled cucumbers made up the rest of the offerings on the table.

Daisy gave a signal to Jonas, and he clapped his hands. "Okay, everybody. Let's eat. Find a seat."

It only took about five minutes for the aromas to call everybody to the table. Felix settled in under the table by Jonas's foot. They were passing around the platters and scooping spoonfuls of pot pie onto their plates when the doorbell rang.

Jazzi, sitting beside Daisy, said, "I'll get it, Mom."

Seconds later, Zeke walked in.

Everyone at the table went quiet. Daisy knew this moment might be awkward, but she was going to erase it as soon as she could. "Hi, Zeke. Come on in. We have a chair for you."

As Jazzi hung up Zeke's coat, he came to the table, looking a little uncertain himself. He greeted Les and Doug with a handshake and nodded to Ray.

Sitting across from Daisy, he asked, "Have you been cooking for weeks?"

"No, just the last three days," Jazzi said.

Daisy elbowed her daughter. Zeke laughed. It was a good sound that seemed to break the tension a bit.

Beverly's gaze went from Zeke at one end of the table to Jonas at the other. Beverly murmured to Zeke, "Daisy said you and Jonas are friends again. Is that true?"

"It is. Daisy wouldn't tell you anything that isn't true."

Beverly's gaze shot to Daisy. "So *you* two are friends?"

"We are now," Daisy said with a smile. "Not so much when Zeke first arrived."

"I think there's a story to hear there," Beverly said.

Daisy thought it was fortunate then that Vi asked Beverly a question and the conversation circled in a different direction. Beverly began talking about her children, and Vi told her about mothering Sammy and the adjustment in moving to a new house.

"We're getting used to it," Vi said. "We have more space. There's a loft Foster uses for his web-designing business."

And so it went. Daisy had almost relaxed until it was time for dessert. The apple dumplings had been warming in the oven while they ate.

At the other end of the table, Jonas raised his brows at Daisy, and she nodded. "Time for dessert, everybody. I have apple dumplings and whoopie pies. You can take your pick or have some of both."

Jonas rose from his chair. "I'll pull them out of the oven if you get the rum sauce."

Doug asked, "Are you turning domestic, Groft?"

"I'm not sure what you mean by domestic." His gaze found Daisy's. "We help each other."

Daisy liked that answer.

The two of them arranged the apple dumplings on separate platters, one for each end of the table. The whoopie pies would go on the green depression-glass serving dish in the middle. Jazzi and Vi had volunteered to be in charge of tea and coffee. After everyone was seated again, Ray said to Daisy, "These are delicious. Did you make the apple dumplings yourself?"

"I did. It's my Aunt Iris's recipe. I used to make them with her when I was a little girl. The rum sauce is my addition."

Ray laughed. "Good addition. And you sell the whoopie pies at your tea garden?"

"We do," she said. "Along with scones, tarts, cookies, coffee cake, and anything we come up with that we think our customers will like. We usually have a special every week."

Vi interjected, "And there's usually a special on a particular tea every month. This month, it's Earl Grey tea. That's what we're having tonight. I worked at the tea garden, and so did Jazzi. So we're pretty well versed on everything Mom does. Foster still works there in between his college classes."

"Really?" Doug asked, looking at Foster in a different way. "You like serving women tea?"

Not much bent Foster out of shape. Now, however, his brow creased, as if he were thinking about the best way to answer. "The tea garden has men customers as well as women customers. I don't just serve tea. I mix teas, too. Daisy has taught me how to do that. I also know how to brew. But I do like mingling with the customers. It's good for my public relations skills, whatever career I decide to take up. Daisy took a chance on me because I knew my teas."

"Hmm," Doug said, as if he were thinking of it in a whole different way.

Les hadn't said much, at least not much that Daisy had heard. Now he looked Daisy's way. "I heard you not only run a tea garden, but you're a *wannabe* detective."

Daisy had wondered if this subject would come up. Trying to treat it lightly, she responded, "I'm not sure how you would hear that. I didn't think Willow Creek news was popular in Philadelphia."

Instead of dropping the subject or backing down, Les shrugged. "Oh, we see all kinds of things at the station. All police work is news. When an amateur gets her name in the newspaper and is considered a detective, that's something we take notice of."

Jonas targeted his friend with a frown. "Daisy is an intelligent woman who has deductive skills and the ability to listen well."

Daisy didn't want this to develop into a *thing*. She wanted to disappear into the woodwork.

Les jibed, "Hey, Zeke, maybe she's after *your* job."

On the same page as Jonas, Zeke replied, "Daisy has supplied important pieces of evidence, and she has emotional intelligence most guys can't understand."

"Emotional intelligence?" Les asked with a

quirk of his brow, as if that wasn't something he considered important in police work.

Without putting her hand to her cheek, Daisy knew her face was probably red. She could even feel the heat in her neck. She didn't know what to say or how to tamp down this subject and move on to something else.

Before she could figure out the best way to divert the conversation, Jazzi spoke up. "Emotional intelligence means my mom can sense an underlying cause. She has helped solve eight murder investigations. Though Zeke and Detective Rappaport protect her and try to keep her away from their cases, somehow her listening skills provide them with clues."

When she was met with perplexed looks from Jonas's friends, Jazzi went on, "My mom has Amish friends who help her provide a link to their community. The Amish really don't want anything to do with the police, but they'll talk with my mom."

Silence met Jazzi's pronouncement, though Jonas gave her a very proud look.

Daisy simply asked, "More tea or coffee, anyone?"

Beverly answered quickly. "I'll take another cup of tea. I want you to tell me about the tea garden, this place where you hear all the gossip."

The evening passed pleasantly after that. There seemed to have been some barrier crossed into friendship. Daisy found Beverly and her husband easy to talk to as they asked questions about the tea garden.

"Sometimes I feel like a confidant and a counselor," Daisy admitted. "Some of my customers have been coming in since the tea garden opened. I know about their lives, and word about mine gets around. Not much is secret in Willow Creek."

"What's the age bracket of your customers?" Ray asked, obviously a statistician at heart.

"We have all ages, though few teenagers. But even they stop in once in a while after school for cookies. Chocolate chip is a good takeaway, and of course, whoopie pies."

He grinned. "I can understand that."

"Young professionals might stop in before work, and moms after they take their kids to school. I've got to admit, I have more women customers than men, but men appreciate tea, too," Daisy assured him.

A short time later, Vi and Jazzi cleared the table, and Foster loaded the dishwasher.

Les came over to Daisy as she gave Felix a treat for being such a good boy, as he'd lain under the table during dinner. "Jonas was telling me he got to know you better during your first murder investigation."

Since she and Les were alone by the stairway, she decided to share a bit. "That's true," she admitted. "My aunt's boyfriend was killed out in back of the tea garden. Soon after, I had reporters all over the place and couldn't even enter the tea garden. Jonas helped with that. He's a great security guard. He had a friend help him, too."

"That's Jonas," Les said with a smile.

Daisy wasn't sure how much Les knew about her history with Jonas. "What really helped us get to know each other was when Jonas helped my daughter find her birth mother. Jazzi is adopted and went on a search on her own on Internet sites. But she couldn't make progress. After she told me about it, I enlisted Jonas's help. He found Jazzi's biological mother."

"Well," Les said, obviously surprised. "That would bring two people closer together."

"Jazzi, too," Daisy admitted. "She trusts Jonas. That was a good basis for their relationship."

"I imagine so," Les said with a nod. "Is her birth mother in her life now, if you don't mind me asking?"

"She is. It was hard at first," Daisy confessed. "And it still is at times. But I realized if I didn't let Portia into Jazzi's life, Jazzi could pull away from me. It really was the best thing to do."

After a heartbeat of silence, Les said, "Jonas was right about you."

"In what way?" Daisy joked.

"He told me that some people only see your blond hair and blue eyes and pretty smile. They think that's all there is to you. But he learned there was so much more right away. I can believe that. I'm a cop. I'm told civilians should stay far away from our investigations, and I always believed that. I think I still do. But I can understand your skills in getting people to talk to you when they won't talk to the police. That could be a help. I imagine it has been. From the bits and pieces I've picked up from Jonas, your latest case involves a friend who was murdered?" His gaze was sympathetic.

"Yes, my friend was murdered. I found her, and

that affected me deeply. Still, I'm not making much headway narrowing down suspects. I don't know if the detectives are. They're not sharing much."

"I understand that," Les said with a nod. "Maybe this time they'll get to the killer before *you* do."

Daisy certainly hoped that was true.

On Monday morning, as Daisy stood on the property designated for the homeless shelter, the March wind buffeting her, she thought about the weekend and Jonas's friends. Sunday morning, when they'd left after brunch, they'd wished her and Jonas happiness as they planned their wedding. Daisy knew cops could have a hard shell. But Doug's and Les's had cracked a bit.

Turning her attention to the groundbreaking ceremony, she'd supposed this event for New Beginnings was supposed to be festive. Daisy had hoped that more of the residents of Willow Creek would have turned out. But it *was* a colder day.

Most the shop owners were here. The president of the chamber of commerce had encouraged them to attend. Daisy had catered the last event on this property, and it hadn't ended in the best of ways. Nevertheless, today everyone was peaceful. A huge green ribbon stretched between two stakes became the centerpiece of the event. The mayor, together with the chamber of commerce president, would be cutting that ribbon with a huge pair of scissors.

Gavin Cranshaw held a shovel that was a symbolic gesture to show that the homeless shelter was indeed in its beginning stages. A loudspeaker system had been set up for the mayor to make a few remarks. He stood at the podium in his suit and tie while more residents gathered. Daisy was glad to see them arrive.

The mayor's suit coat flapped as he made his remarks. He spoke about what New Beginnings would mean to the community, the jobs it would give residents, as well as the publicity that could reach far and wide about Willow Creek being a caring community.

Jonas linked his arm into Daisy's. "I hope this project goes off without a hitch. The fundraising efforts have paid off. I think they have most of the funds they need for construction. Gavin says the faster they can build New Beginnings, the more they'll stay on budget. He doesn't want supply prices to go up."

"He told me he'll have two crews on this, so the work should be done quickly. I'm hoping Gavin's reputation and the work he does spreads around the area," Daisy said.

"I know Nola is pleased with the house he built for her. She has some prestige around here, and I know he's won a few jobs because of her."

Daisy recognized the town council members, who were milling about a table that had been set up with refreshments. Pastries To Go would be providing hot chocolate and croissants after the speeches and ribbon cutting. The wind blew a stack of napkins off the table. Nan Conroy, who had painted the sign with Jonas, ran to catch them, picking up the scattered napkins and stacking them back on the table. While the Mayor droned on about the history of Willow Creek and its tourist trade, passersby stopped to listen. Daisy glimpsed a tourist bus down the street. Its passengers had exited and were coming their way. Daisy hoped Pastries To Go had enough croissants to go around.

As another gust of breeze whipped by them, Jonas asked Daisy, "Are you warm enough?"

She'd worn her fleece jacket and was glad she had. She leaned into Jonas's shoulder. "I'm fine. Did you notice some of The Farm Barn staff are here?"

Jonas looked in the direction Daisy was scanning. "That's Jake Starsky over there, isn't it? With one of the servers? They look like they're more than friends."

Jake had his arm around a pretty redhead. Daisy thought her name was Stacy. Their heads were bent together, and he was whispering something in her ear. However, in the next moment, Daisy noticed Jake take out his phone. He looked as if he were either reading or sending a text. Her gaze canvassing the rest of the crowd, Daisy noticed April. She was also studying her phone. She looked upset.

Was Jake using his phone and April looking at hers connected? Maybe. Maybe not. Many people in the crowd were also checking their phones if they were bored or needing to be in touch with work. They sipped hot chocolate and handled their phones like pros. She imagined everyone tried to stay in touch with the world that way. Daisy preferred to people-watch and hold Jonas's hand, feeling their connection, being glad for their community, hoping the sun would rise on New Beginnings.

An hour later, after the residents attending the groundbreaking event dispersed, Daisy found she had an unexpected gathering in her spillover tearoom. While wind beat against the building, sun glowed through the diamond-cut front windows.

Daisy loved the spillover tearoom and the afternoon tea service, which included multiple courses and a real love of tea. Her servers had quickly materialized to handle service for the mayor, the chamber president, and other shop owners, who had come along for a short meeting. Daisy and her crew served Earl Grey tea with lemon, honey, sugar, or milk. Cora Sue brought out lemon curd in cut crystal nappies to accompany the cinnamon scones.

Betty Furhman, chamber president, had whispered to her when they'd come in, "The town council will cover refreshments today. Is that okay with you?"

Daisy had smiled at her. "I'll give them a discount." The town council and the chamber of commerce often worked together, and that was nice to see.

Heidi Korn from the Rainbow Flamingo, Keith Rebert from Pirated Treasures, and Rachel from Quilts and Notions ordered the potato and leek soup. Daisy served corn cake with a compound butter to accompany it.

Gavin had let the group converse for a while before he stood and spoke to the members who had gathered. He said, "Not many plans have been made for outside landscaping at the homeless shelter, because we didn't know how funds would stretch. But I'd like to propose something that might not need to come from our construction budget."

Daniel Copeland, who was assistant manager of the bank, said acerbically, "That would be novel that it's not going to raise the construction budget."

Piper Wagner, who was the owner of Wheels, a bike shop, said, "Let's hear it, Mr. Cranshaw."

"There are residents of Willow Creek who wanted to get involved in this project but couldn't afford to donate to the fundraising efforts with the shelter. I'm proposing a project that could involve the community even more. In fact, if we broaden it, it would be a foundation to fund the job counseling program. The town council will have to vote on the idea, of course."

Heidi Korn said, "We're on pins and needles. Tell us what it is."

Gavin proceeded, eager to share his idea. "I'm proposing a brick courtyard with benches. Any resident of Willow Creek could purchase a brick in memory of a loved one. Before we set them, a mason could personalize the bricks. I've already checked with a few. The benches would require a higher donation. I'm certainly open to more ideas about it. My son Foster offered to write up the proposal for us and present it to the town council."

Foster, who was serving today, smiled and waved at everybody. "I'll be glad to do it. All you have to do is give me your ideas. You can either give them to my dad or text or email them to me at the tea garden. I'd be glad to put it all together."

Daisy was proud of Foster and the way he'd taken on the responsibilities of fatherhood. She could see he'd also be involved in the community, and that was good for the whole family. It would create a sense of "giving back" for Sammy.

Nan Conroy had joined the group at the tea garden. Now she stood, crossed to Daisy, and pulled her aside. "I wanted you to know I have the clothespin dolls ready for the tea. You'll have to come over and see them sometime, and make sure they're exactly what you want."

"How about this evening?" Daisy asked.

"That would be good. I also wanted to tell you that I think Neil found a buyer for The Farm Barn."

"Really? Will the new owner keep it intact?"

"I'm not sure about that yet, but I have heard the new owner might not want any reminders of what happened to Lydia. The family-type atmosphere will be gone. He already has a restaurant in York, and I think he'll model it after that one. He'll serve cuisine a step up from the family-style meals."

"What does that mean exactly?"

"I think it means he'll serve whatever's the most economical for him—not free-range chicken, not grass-fed beef, not homemade desserts. He'll count on the suppliers he already knows. He'll utilize a salad bar that can also convert to a buffet at times."

A totally different look, Daisy thought, totally different service, totally different food.

"Do you know if he's going to keep on the servers who are there now?"

"That depends. I think he's interviewing. He'll keep who he likes and let go who he doesn't."

Daisy's thoughts went to April. Would she be hired to stay? "I'm hoping Neil didn't lose money on the deal."

"There's some concern over bookkeeping over the years, but I'm sure they'll iron that out."

Daisy had to wonder just what those concerns were.

CHAPTER SIXTEEN

Daisy worked in the kitchen at the tea garden alongside Tessa the next day, feeling the need to put her hands into dough, to make cookies, to bake anything that would give someone pleasure. The corn cake was easy, and she didn't have to keep her mind on what she was doing. She could just do it by rote.

Daisy kept busy that morning going from one task to another, helping where she could, stopping in her office to work on bookwork. It was mid-morning when Cora Sue rapped on her door and poked her head into her office.

"Someone would like to see you in the tea-room."

"Someone I know?" Daisy asked with a smile.

"Oh, yes. It's Cade Bankert. He asked if you were busy."

"Not too busy for him. Tell him I'll be right out."

"Do you want a cup of tea?"

"Sure. Give me the Earl Grey with a little bit of honey."

Daisy had no sooner washed up and gone to sit with Cade when Cora Sue brought her cup of tea and set it in front of her at the table.

Cade had an amused expression on his face when he said, "You seem happy to see me."

"I am. I'm glad you decided to stop in." She motioned to the blueberry coffeecake on his plate and his cup of tea. "Are you enjoying it?"

"I am. I've missed this place, Daisy. I plan to stop in more often."

"Good."

"I do have a purpose today, though. Are you still gathering info about Lydia?"

Was she gathering info about Lydia and all the suspects? Was she wading into investigation territory again? Yes, she was. "I am. Anything that could help us solve the murder, anyway."

Cade looked thoughtful as he squeezed his slice of lemon into his tea, set the slice on the side of the saucer, and wiped off his fingers. "I spoke with the agent who's dealing with the Yoders."

"I hope this isn't proprietorial information," Daisy said. "I don't want you to get into trouble."

"No problem with this. The deal's going through. There will be public records."

"So the sale is going to happen quickly?"

"Oh, yes. I think Titus Yoder wants the money as soon as he can get it. They're closing in about a week."

"That is fast. I suppose if they need the funds to run the farm, that's why they want to seal the deal."

"Titus and Leah came into the office to sign a few papers. I overheard something that intrigued me."

"Something you can share?"

"I don't see why not. Again, it's going to be public knowledge. Leah said they were going to raise more chickens. She made the comment that at least hers are going to be really free-range, unlike the man who sells to The Farm Barn."

Daisy was taken by surprise with that remark. The Farm Barn advertised their fried chicken was cooked with free-range chickens.

"Do you think The Farm Barn has been lying about using free-range chickens?"

"I have no idea," Cade said seriously, picking up his fork and slicing off a piece of the blueberry coffeecake. The blueberries were plump and fragrant. "I thought that might be an avenue you wanted to pursue."

Did she? She supposed it wouldn't do any harm to talk to Neil about it.

On her drive to The Farm Barn later that afternoon—another temporary server had been free to come in and cover for her—she considered the fact that Neil was a suspect. Did she think he could have murdered Lydia? She didn't, but that didn't mean her instincts were right. She'd been wrong before.

She couldn't let this go. She had more than one question for Neil. She didn't suppose the detectives had asked him about free-range chickens. If anything came of it, she'd certainly tell them what she'd learned. That's what she'd promised Zeke.

She thought about calling first to make sure Neil was at The Farm Barn. But then she decided she didn't want to give him a heads-up. She wanted him to be surprised by her questions; then maybe he'd answer truthfully.

Was that supposing he hadn't answered truthfully before?

When she parked at The Farm Barn, she saw Neil's vehicle, and she gave a sigh of relief. He was here.

After she parked, she went to the back door. She found it open, and she peeked inside. It seemed that no one was around. She called, "Neil, are you here?"

He appeared from his office, looking tired and rumpled. He was wearing a dress shirt, but it was open at the collar and didn't look as if it had been pressed. With it he wore khakis and a pair of loafers, no socks. She hoped he was doing a better job of looking after Frannie than he was looking after himself.

"Can we talk for a few minutes?" she asked, coming inside.

He motioned to her to enter. "Sure, come on in. We can talk in my office. Have you found anything that would clear me?"

"I wish I could say I have, but I haven't. I do have more questions for you, though."

He pointed to the chair across from his desk. "Sit and ask. I'd rather talk to you about it than the police."

"I want you to tell me about your chickens."

Neil looked perplexed. "I don't raise chickens."

"No, but you use a lot of them, and your fried chicken is supposed to be from free-range chickens, right?"

Neil looked frustrated as he pushed around a few papers on his desk and picked up a pen. "Yes, they're supposed to be. We had been using the same supplier, Holloback Chickens, since we opened The Farm Barn."

"Had been?"

"I stopped two weeks ago."

"Can you tell me why?"

He laid both of his hands on the desk, and they curved into fists. "Lydia was noticing something different about them in the past six months, in the taste and in the size."

Daisy had a feeling that Lydia wouldn't let that go. "Did she do something about it?"

"She did. She found out Holloback is no longer raising free-range chickens, and most probably, he was feeding them hormones to increase their weight. They had a rousing argument."

"Holloback was as angry as Lydia was?"

"She said he was. She said his face got all red, and his balding head got all red, and she thought he was going to burst a gasket. We buy a lot of chickens."

"Was Holloback the man you had an altercation with at the restaurant?"

Neil's face colored. He clicked his pen on and off. "Yes, it was. That's when he found out I was using another supplier."

Neil's phone rang. It was on his desk, and when he looked down to see who the caller was, his face suddenly went devoid of color. "It's the police," he said in a husky voice to Daisy. "I better take this."

"Should I leave?"

He shook his head, picked up his phone, and answered the call. After a short conversation, Neil ended the call and put down the phone again. "They want me to come down to the station another time, as if they haven't asked enough questions."

Daisy could see how upset he was. "If I can help clear you, I will. Not only for your sake, but for Frannie's. You both deserve to know what happened to Lydia. So that leads me to my next question."

He looked dejected when he asked, "What's that?"

"Tell me about the woman that I saw kissing you."

Neil had looked deflated and dejected before, but now he looked absolutely devastated. He ran his hand down over his face and then stared at her. "I had an affair, but it was over a long time ago. Lydia and I worked hard at repairing our marriage. Mitzi started showing up again after Lydia was killed. She wants to start all over. She thinks that now that I'm free, I'll want to pick up where we left off. I don't."

"Are you sure?" Daisy asked. "Have you given her hope in any way?"

"I haven't. When I split with her, I told her we were through. I can only think about Frannie and what she needs."

"Yet this Mitzi still came by and kissed you."

"That was supposed to convince me otherwise."

"Do you think Mitzi is volatile?"

"She has mood swings, but . . . what are you thinking?"

"Would she consider killing Lydia so she could have you?"

Neil looked stunned. Then he admitted, "It's possible."

Was it possible that Mitzi had killed Lydia? Run her down in a cold-blooded way? Or was Neil just trying to throw someone else under the proverbial bus to save his own hide?

Daisy was driving out of The Farm Barn parking lot when Jonas called her.

"Can I convince you to leave work early and take a drive with me?"

"I left work early. I met with Neil, and I'm heading home."

"Good. I'll meet you there. I have a surprise for you."

And so it happened that half an hour later, she was sitting beside Jonas in his SUV, Felix haltered in the back seat as they headed deep into Lancaster County.

"Is this a surprise I'm going to like?"

"I hope so," Jonas said, with one of those crooked smiles that always melted her heart.

She couldn't wait to see Jonas's surprise, but she had the previous part of her day on her mind, too.

"Cade came into the tea garden for tea," she said.

Jonas gave her a sideways look. "Friendly visit?"

"Yes, it was. I think we're back on friendship terms."

"I'm glad he's dating someone else," Jonas said, giving her another sideways glance.

"You can't be jealous," she teased.

He reached over and patted her hand. "No, I'm not jealous. But I do consider him a former suitor. I remember when we first got to know each other, you were considering dating him. In fact, you did."

"If you can consider two dinners dating," she said easily.

"He was your prom date, and those first loves hang on."

"He was my prom date when I didn't know what I wanted in a man. And when I dated him, that spark just wasn't there."

Jonas spared her a glance, then turned back to the road. "You mean the spark *we* have?"

"Exactly."

"I guess you recognize it because you felt it before with Ryan."

Daisy and Jonas had talked about her husband many times. She'd revealed the ups and downs in her marriage. "I was impulsively and deeply in love with Ryan, but I had the dreams of a young girl then. I was starry-eyed. I thought a husband and a family and moving away from home was all I needed to grow into an adult."

"And was it?"

"In part. But I think I really grew up and faced reality when we learned Ryan had cancer. Dreams pop like soap bubbles. The future can't be planned like noting dates on the calendar for upcoming events. I think Jazzi and Vi learned to appreciate every moment as unique, without tagging on a future to it. Maybe that's why Vi decided to get married. Maybe it's why Jazzi decided to search for her birth mother. They didn't want to rely on the future. They wanted to experience *now*."

"Do you think that helped them with their grief?"

"I do. They're making life meaningful each day. I hope Jazzi continues to do that when she's at college. Not *carpe diem*, for goodness sakes, but just appreciating each day."

"So how do you think our spark is different?"

"I think our spark is like a slow flame that built and grew. Now we have a fire going. It's going to keep us warm."

Jonas laughed. "I appreciate the metaphor," he said. "Life experience does change your perception. You and your daughters have brought light into *my* world."

Felix gave a little woof.

"I think he agrees," Jonas said.

"He knows chasing his ball is the be-all and the end-all of happiness," Daisy said.

"We should all be so lucky," Jonas agreed.

While they drove, Daisy conveyed to Jonas what Cade had said about the Yoders and chickens. "The sale of their land can prop up Leah and Titus for a while, I imagine."

"What are you thinking about doing next?" Jonas asked.

"How do you know I'm going to do anything next?"

He chuckled. "I know you, Daisy. I'm sure you have something in mind."

She did . . . possibly paying a visit to the chicken supplier who could have been defrauding Lydia.

She and Jonas fell into companionable silence

until Jonas turned onto a gravel driveway that led to a large lot. The lot was filled with outdoor structures—many of cedar, some of them white. There were benches, tables and chairs, small sheds, and chicken houses.

"Why are we here?" Daisy asked. "It doesn't look as if anybody's around."

"No, nobody's around, but I know the wood turner who built these. I want to show you something. Come on."

Felix was out of the car almost as fast as Jonas could undo his halter. He romped for a bit, sniffing, nosing around the legs of a table . . . and around the chicken house.

"No chickens in there," Jonas said.

Felix barked as if he knew that.

Taking Daisy's hand, Jonas led her toward the back of the structures. "I want to show you this one."

They rounded a large shed, and Daisy gazed at a structure that made her smile. "It's a gazebo." Jonas knew she liked those.

"Yes, it is. I want you to imagine it with a little more decoration on the eaves, columns that are a little wider, and a floor with only one step leading up to it."

Daisy looked at Jonas rather than the gazebo. "I can imagine that."

"Good, because I want to make us one. I'd like to make it white instead of cedar. I'd like us to use it for our wedding."

"Our wedding," she murmured reverently.

Jonas took both of her hands now and gazed into her eyes. "I was thinking, why don't we have the whole wedding in your backyard and the reception there, too?"

When Daisy had thought about a marriage to Jonas, she hadn't envisioned particulars. "Tell me what you're thinking."

He interlaced his fingers with hers. "I thought we could invite Reverend Kemp to do the ceremony, and we could do it in a gazebo in our backyard. That way, whenever we stare at the gazebo out the window, we'd remember we took our vows there. Every day, we'd remember that we committed to each other. I thought it might be a strengthening of everything we have, and everything we dream we're going to be."

Daisy considered what he was proposing. "I think it's a lovely idea. But wouldn't it be so much work?"

"That depends if you let me delegate the work. Can't you imagine tiki torches around the patio with the buffet there? If we start in the evening, maybe around seven, even if it's hot, it will be cooling down. We could have some of those fairy lights around the tents. Imagine it, Daisy. It would be uniquely ours—the ceremony, the reception, our friends and family gathered there."

As she gazed into Jonas's eyes, she could suddenly envision it all.

"I promise, I have a crew of men who can set up the tents and the chairs and the tables. I already talked to Sarah Jane, and she would cater the reception."

"But we don't even have a date," Daisy said, laughing, feeling Jonas's joy, more and more sure of his idea as he'd expressed a description of it.

"That's the next thing we have to do, and then we can start planning."

She was ready to start planning. The first thing on her list was to search for a wedding gown. She wrapped her arms around Jonas's neck and said, "Yes. Your vision is perfect. Let's make it happen."

CHAPTER SEVENTEEN

The following morning, Daisy and Jonas went for another drive. Iris had assured her the staff could handle customers this morning without her. Daisy knew that wouldn't be true for long, with the month of April just around the corner.

Because Jonas and Daisy were driving farther than the outskirts of Willow Creek, Felix was in a crate in the back of Jonas's SUV.

"He's not happy," Daisy said as they drove through the country, fields wide and expansive, the sky blue and cloudless.

"He will be when we let him out," Jonas joked.

"You're too practical. I heard his whine. I know it's for his safety, but I wish *he* knew that."

"You treat Felix like a person, you know that, don't you?" There was amusement in Jonas's voice and acceptance of the practice.

"Of course, I do. He's intuitive and intelligent."

"Like your cats?"

"Maybe a little more than Marjoram and Pepper."

Jonas laughed. "He'll be glad to know you think so."

She turned around and spoke to Felix over the seat. "Don't mind him, Felix. We know you're smarter than some humans, don't we?"

Felix looked her way and gave her a yip. Then he went back to lying morosely with his head on his paws.

"How much farther?" she asked.

"About five or ten minutes. Holloback's property is on the edge of Gap."

"You said his office wasn't on the same property as the chicken production business."

"That's right," Jonas said, "though I'm not sure why. Maybe he has other businesses besides chickens and the office is kind of a central coordinating point."

"*Does* he have other businesses?" Daisy asked.

"What? Do you think I Googled him or something?" Jonas's expression was the picture of innocence.

"I'm sure you did."

He shrugged. "I couldn't find another business listed in his name, but he owns property throughout the county."

"For what purpose?"

"That I'm not sure about. He's not a developer, but from what I could tell from public records, he buys parcels of land and then sells them at an increased price. It's sort of like a house flipper, only with acreage instead of houses."

"Interesting," Daisy said, but she wasn't sure how it was interesting or if it had anything else to do with Lydia.

The driveway to the office building was paved,

and there was a small parking lot with room for about fifteen cars. Two were parked there now—a silver pickup truck and a yellow sedan. The sign on the building simply said HOLLOBACK with no indication of what type of business was housed there.

It was about ten a.m. Jonas and Daisy had left their businesses to go on this errand, because they knew that time would be better to catch Holloback at his office. Even then they might simply find staff there.

Striding up to the door beside Jonas, Daisy suddenly stopped. "What are we doing?"

"We're checking into a clue that detectives might not," he answered reasonably.

"This just feels so weird, inquiring about chickens."

A small smile played over Jonas's lips. "Daisy, you can always reverse course, you know that. Do you want to?"

She didn't often reverse course, not when she had a gut feeling about what was going on. Why did she think these chickens had something to do with Lydia's death? She was about to find out.

"Let's do this. He might not even be here. That would be a sign."

Jonas placed his hand in the small of Daisy's back that was both comforting and encouraging. "Come on."

The door was plate glass. The hours were painted on it in white paint. Daisy put her hand on the knob and turned it.

Once inside, they found a small office with two desks. At one desk sat a dark-haired woman who looked to be in her forties. Her hair was cut short and tight to her face. She wore black-rimmed glasses and looked very efficient. At least her glasses looked professional.

She stood when Daisy and Jonas walked in. Daisy could see the woman's stone-washed jeans had slits in the sides and knees. Her sweatshirt read simply HOLLOBACK. She wore hot-pink lipstick, and her nails were painted the same pink.

"Can I help you?" she asked, even though there was a man sitting at the other desk in the same sweatshirt and jeans, his red hair in disarray and thinning, his chin stubble leaning into a partially developed beard. Daisy knew he was the man she had seen at The Farm Barn door.

"We're here to talk to Mr. Holloback," Daisy said firmly, not brooking any excuses.

The woman glanced over at the man at the other desk. "He's busy right now."

"We're busy, too," Jonas said, "and we'd like some answers."

At this, the man's face turned a little red, and he stood, his big burly shoulders blocking the light from the window. "Yeah, I'm Holloback. What do you want?"

"I'd like to know about your business dealings with Lydia Aldenkamp," Daisy said.

The man scowled at them. "Get out. I don't have to talk about that."

Even though Daisy was tempted to back down, Jonas didn't. He took a step forward instead of back. "If you don't answer our questions, I'm sure somebody else is going to come along to ask the same ones, or maybe even more important ones."

"I don't know what you're talking about," the man mumbled, still glaring at them in an imposing way. "Get out," he said again.

"I'm friends with the two detectives on the case, Morris Rappaport and Zeke Willet. I'm sure they'll be around tomorrow if you don't want to talk to me today," Jonas suggested calmly.

The mention of the two detectives seemed to change the man's stance an iota. His arms became less rigid, and he shook his head. "I don't want to talk to them."

Daisy said in a gentler voice, "Then tell us about your dealings with Lydia. What was going on?"

"Don't think you can sweet-talk me," he said, checking out her blond hair and slim frame. "You're probably like the Aldenkamp women. You want what you want when you want it."

"Does that sum up your business dealings with Lydia?" Jonas asked nonchalantly.

The man seemed to refill himself with a full steam of anger again. "Lydia Aldenkamp threatened to ruin my business by spreading the word that my chickens were an inferior quality. She came sneaking around, wanting to see my processing plant. It wasn't no business of hers."

"She bought from you," Daisy said. "I would think that it was her business to know where her money was going."

He took a few steps toward them again. "Get out of here, or I'll call the police myself. I don't have to answer your questions, and I don't have to answer theirs."

His receptionist had skirted to the door and opened it, as if to say, *You'd better go now, or the lid's going to blow off this place.*

Jonas exchanged a look with Daisy that meant, *Let's get out of here.*

The two of them left the office without a back-wards look.

The door slammed behind them.

Daisy said to Jonas, "I think we should talk to Zeke."

Daisy considered the Willow Creek police station to belong to another era. Yes, it had an electronic front door, but the inside was another matter. A dispatcher sat near the front door, and her desk had seen many years of use. The dispatcher, Marjorie Beck, had short brown hair. She wore headphones and typed on the computer keyboard. The reception area was separated from the space farther back in the room by a wooden fence. The swinging door in the middle reminded Daisy of an old Western. Inside that gate, there were six desks with computers. Right now, officers occupied two of the desks.

The dispatcher recognized Jonas and Daisy right away. After all, they'd been here many times before.

"Rappaport or Willet?" she asked.

Daisy smiled. "Today let's talk to whoever's here."

"You're in luck. Willet just came in. Give us a minute, and I'll buzz him."

Bart Cosner, who was standing at one of the desks, waved to them. "I hope you're here to help, not hinder."

"Don't we always help?" Daisy asked with an ingenuousness that made them all smile.

About to take seats on two of the three chairs in

the waiting area in case Zeke was busy, they stopped
when they saw him emerge from the back hallway.
Today Zeke was dressed in khakis and a tan T-shirt.
Daisy imagined a sports jacket lay wrinkled in his
office. He'd been assigned that office after the last
murder investigation by Chief of Police Shultz. He
now considered Zeke a viable member of the team,
just as he did Rappaport.

Bart opened the gate for them into the officer's
area.

Zeke preceded them down a short hall. "You
two might as well have badges," he said instead of a
hello.

"Do you really want to deputize us?" Jonas
joked.

Zeke shook his head and rubbed his stubbled
chin. "No. Bad idea. Come on in. Not much room
in here, but it's better than a closet."

The office was similar to Detective Rappaport's,
only a bit smaller. There was a file cabinet, a beat-
up wooden desk that took up half the room, and a
set of bookshelves that were stuffed with books
and file folders.

Zeke motioned around the office. "Welcome to
my abode. If I could put a sofa in here where I
could catch a few Zs when I'm here all night, I
would. Not quite roomy enough."

Daisy eyed the space. "Maybe with a smaller
desk, you could fit in one of those modern reclin-
ers that doesn't go back too far."

"You are always full of ideas," Zeke said with a
smile. "I'll think about it."

A folding chair was set up in front of his desk
and one alongside it. "Have a seat, though I don't
have much time to spend on trivia."

"Trivia?" Daisy asked, almost insulted. "Do I ever bring you inconsequential information?"

He exhaled heavily. "No, I suppose not. Go ahead and take a seat. Let's get to it."

Daisy really wasn't insulted. She knew Zeke was like this when he was working on a case. He had to be. Time was valuable. Already too much had passed. Clues didn't only get washed away as each day went by. They also got buried.

Jonas nodded to Daisy so she could take the lead.

"Where are you with the case?" she asked.

Zeke shook his head. "You know I can't talk about it. I can take your information, but I can't give any out. Chief Shultz's orders."

She decided to get under his skin a bit. "Look, I know you've settled on Neil as the main person of interest."

Zeke's face was impassive.

"Tell me one thing. Do you have any evidence to tie him to Lydia's murder?"

Zeke still kept silent.

"How about a damaged truck? Maybe somebody saw him near the property that morning. Anything?"

Zeke remained silent.

Daisy dove in. "Have you ever heard of a man named Cletus Holloback?"

"And who is he?" Zeke asked.

"He supplied chickens to The Farm Barn," Jonas said. "We visited him because there was some question about the birds he was supplying. It didn't take much to make him irate."

"He's big and burly and nasty," Daisy said. "He told us Lydia had threatened to ruin his business by spreading the word his chickens were inferior. I swear when he was talking to us about it, he looked like he could throttle anyone. He got riled up really quickly, and we didn't even egg him on."

Zeke pulled a notepad in front of him and picked up a pen. "Where can I find him?"

Jonas gave Zeke the man's address. Then he said, "His production factory is elsewhere. We just went to his office."

Zeke looked down at the address and sighed. "You asked me about Neil Aldenkamp. I'll tell you this. He had plenty of motive."

"If you're talking about his affair," Daisy shot back, "maybe you don't have all the facts about that."

"How do you know about his affair?" Zeke asked. Then he shook his head. "Never mind. I know you've been working with him."

"More than one person has mentioned the affair to me," Daisy told him. "Neil told me himself, and he said he and Lydia were getting their marriage back on track."

"Of course, he'd say that," Zeke said. "He doesn't want to be a suspect."

"It could be true," Daisy protested. "Have you looked at his ex-girlfriend, Mitzi Geitz? She seems pretty intent on restarting her relationship with Neil. She won't let him alone, especially since Lydia died."

"Daisy, why do you think I'm spending my nights here?" Zeke asked seriously.

"Because you're working on the case," she replied easily.

"Exactly. That means I'm looking at everyone who had *anything* to do with Lydia Aldenkamp."

* * *

That evening, Daisy, Iris, and Glorie decided to have an evening out and visit Adele Gunnarson, Felix's original dog mom. After Daisy picked up Iris and Glorie, she headed to Whispering Willows Assisted Living Facility. It was about two miles outside of Willow Creek. Willow tree branches swayed in the wind all over the property, the back of which stretched to Willow Creek. Daisy had brought Felix along, because Adele was always glad to see him, and he was always glad to see her. He sat beside Glorie on the back seat, his head on her lap.

When Daisy visited Adele, she always brought a basket of baked goods. Iris had packed it this time, and Daisy wasn't exactly sure what was inside, but all of it would be treats to have with tea. As they went inside the facility, Daisy noticed again how welcoming the lobby was. At the desk, they all signed in. Daisy always included Felix.

They soon stood at the door to Adele's suite. It had one bedroom and a kitchen, and Adele seemed happy here. The wreath on the door was a spring variety of forsythia and daisies.

Daisy knocked, and after a minute or so, Adele came to the door. She always reminded Daisy of the iconic Betty White with her snowy hair and curly bangs that she usually brushed to the right. It seemed a bit puffier tonight . . . wispier. Two bobby pins held her hair back over her left ear.

Adele said, "Welcome. Come on in. Hi there, Felix." She stooped to pet his head. "I just had a shower after chair yoga, and I'm a bit discombobulated." Dimples appeared on either side of her mouth as she grinned. "I have to find my glasses, or I won't even be able to see you."

Adele usually wore something flowered. To-night it was a calf-length dress with a ruffle around the bottom and around the three-quarter sleeves. The material was patterned with big pink roses. On her feet, she wore pink canvas shoes.

As she led them into the suite, she said, "I see you brought a basket of goodies again. I put the kettle on for tea."

She took the basket from Daisy and went over to the gray-and-black-tweed throw rug that lay across the vinyl plank floor, settled it on the low coffee table, swiveled around, and went to the dark sage laminated counter. She picked up her glasses on their turquoise chain.

After she slipped the chain over her head, she pointed to the chairs. "Take a seat, everybody . . . while I get the tea."

"Do you need help?" Iris asked.

"You could carry the tray to the coffee table. I'm brewing orange pekoe tonight. Jonas brought me a supply."

All of the appliances in the kitchen were white and matched the small, round, white table with its two chairs. The tray with its flowered teacups and saucers sat there. Iris brought it over to the coffee table while Adele poured water into a Wedgwood blue-patterned teapot.

Felix had followed her out to the kitchen, and he sat at her feet, looking up at her. "Hey, boy. I know what you want," she said. "While I'm brewing the tea, I might be able to find you a treat. Jonas keeps me supplied with those biscuits you like."

She took two from a ceramic jar on the counter that had painted dog faces all over it. Two dog bowls with Felix's name on them sat on a mat on the floor. Adele was always ready for his visits. The one held water, and in the other, she settled the two biscuits. Felix gave her a *woof* in thank you and then chomped them down.

"How are all of you ladies tonight?" Adele asked. She targeted her attention to Glorie. "How's your arthritis? With spring coming, I know we have a change in weather."

Glorie lifted one of the glitzy canes that her granddaughter Brielle had bought her. "As long as I have this with me, I'm fine. Brielle and Nola insist I use a walker when I go outside, but sometimes I sneak out without it." Giving the laser-sharp beam of her eyes to the ladies around her, she was daring them to scold her.

Daisy stepped into the breach. "As long as you're careful."

"You know how that is, Daisy. Even when I'm trying to be careful, I can miss steps. It's just the way it is at my age. Though I am jealous of Adele here, who can do chair yoga."

"If you feel up to it," Adele said, "there are videos that will guide you through it. It's no fun to do alone, though. I'll admit that. Maybe I can come visit you sometime, and we can do it together."

"That would be lovely," Glorie said, obviously meaning it.

A few minutes later, Adele brought the teapot to the coffee table and sat on the sofa that was covered in a sunflower print. Iris had chosen the pale green fabric easy chair, and Glorie sat in its mate on the other side of the coffee table. Felix had wiggled his body in between Adele and Daisy on the sofa.

They dug into the basket of treats, which included chocolate whoopie pies, oatmeal-raisin cookies, and corn cake. Each took their favorites and munched in between sips of tea.

"When Jonas dropped off Felix's supply of biscuits, he mentioned that you were handling a wedding reception at The Farm Barn," Adele said.

"I was surprised it went as well as it did," Daisy confessed. "After all, I don't know all the servers that well or the chef, but they all seemed to work together like a good machine."

"Maybe that was your leadership," Adele said. "My son took me there for dinner with his fiancée a few weeks ago. An embarrassing experience happened that evening."

"What was that?" Iris asked, giving Daisy a sideways glance.

Adele wiped a bit of the cream from the whoopie pie from the corner of her lip. Then she wiped her fingertip on her napkin and smiled. "I'm like a kid when I'm eating these."

She returned to their conversation. "A good-looking young man got into a kerfuffle with a fragile-looking waitress."

"Can you describe her?" Daisy asked.

"She had blond curly hair. She was very pretty. She wore a hair net, but you could see the curls peeking out here and there. She was pale. She just seemed anxious to me."

To Daisy, that description described April to a T. "Can you describe the man?"

"My guess was he was in his twenties. I can't always tell with young people these days. You know that musical *Grease*? Danny Zuko, slicked-back hair and all that. Though this young man had some stubble on his chin. I don't really get the point of that."

The man Adele was describing was Jake.

"What happened?" Iris asked before Daisy could.

"I was eating my fried chicken when a tray and dishes crashed all over the floor. When I looked, that young man was hovering over the girl. My son said he had put his hand on her shoulder, and she dropped the tray. It was quite a mess to clean up— fried chicken, mashed potatoes, coleslaw, even green beans all over the place. I suppose he startled her."

Was that it? Had Jake startled April? Or was there more to it than that?

As Adele motioned to the basket of goodies again, she said, "Come on, girls, you all have to have another treat so I can, too."

Daisy accepted an oatmeal-raisin cookie from Iris and took a bite. Was that kerfuffle at The Farm Barn an accident . . . or something else?

CHAPTER EIGHTEEN

The next day, Daisy continued to think about The Farm Barn and Lydia's murder. It was difficult to think about anything else as she served tea and mingled with customers. However, after she'd finished at the tea garden for the day, Daisy, along with Tessa, headed north to the Rainbow Flamingo.

As they walked, Tessa asked Daisy, "Why are you meeting Jonas at Four Paws after we pick up the aprons?"

"He just said he wanted to show me something."

"Maybe he wants you to volunteer with him."

"That's possible," Daisy said absently, thinking about what she wanted to accomplish at the Rainbow Flamingo.

"I'm glad Heidi called that the aprons were finished," Tessa said. "I was getting worried."

"I knew they'd have them finished. They're dependable."

"Is there a reason you wanted to wait until after

the tea garden closed to go fetch them?" Tessa asked.

"I'd like your opinion on the finished product," Daisy said honestly.

"Maybe you would, but I have a feeling there's something else going on, too. What is it?"

Daisy and Tessa had known each other since school. They'd been best friends then, and they were now. Tessa understood her moods and her motives.

"When Heidi called, I just happened to ask when Mitzi would be working there. She said she had a shift today from four to nine."

"Are you going to question her about Neil and her affair?" Tessa's voice held surprise, but she knew Daisy would do it if it helped her figure out who killed Lydia.

"I'd rather not do it directly," Daisy said. "I'm hoping maybe we can engage her in conversation and see what turns up."

"You think if Neil is the main focus on her mind, she'll let something slip?"

"Some women like to talk and maybe even boast about their love affairs. If she and Neil broke up, she might need to vent. We can be there to nudge and listen, right?"

"I think you've learned too many of Jonas's detective skills," Tessa muttered.

"Zeke and Morris would be insulted if they heard you say that. They think they've taught me about detecting."

"I think you've taught *them* a thing or two," Tessa said admiringly. "You've taught them they need to listen more."

"Maybe. But they've got the clout that counts."

Tessa laughed. "That's one way to put it."

The image of a rainbow flamingo painted on the plate glass window was at least six feet tall. In its beak it held a sign that said OPEN. When Daisy opened the door to enter, a loud bell dinged.

Since Heidi Korn had bought the business, she'd put in a new security system. Once a clerk there, she'd learned the ins and outs from the ground up. She'd changed some of the styles they had on sale, keeping more with contemporary trends. Daisy always liked to look around. This evening, though, they were intent on picking up the aprons. However, for Daisy to engage Mitzi, she was thinking of looking for a dress for a date with Jonas. It would be a good excuse to hold a conversation with the clerk.

After greetings all around with Heidi, Daisy noticed Mitzi hanging new dresses on a rack. For now, she and Tessa followed Heidi to the back room where the alterations were done.

Greta took the aprons from a shelf. Holding the first one in front of her, she said, "This is the Alice apron." It was a blue apron trimmed in a white ruffle. She took a baby blue bow that was attached to a headband from its pocket. "And here's the headpiece that goes with it," she said.

"That's absolutely adorable," Daisy said.

Tessa chimed in. "Cora Sue mentioned she might wear a blond wig. Can you imagine?"

"Since she's the hostess and not handling food, that would work," Daisy agreed.

"You'll look adorable in the outfit, too," Tessa said. "The perfect Alice."

Daisy laughed. "I don't know about that, but I might have to find a pair of Mary Janes to go with the apron." After Daisy examined everything the seamstress had done, she said, "These are perfect. I have temporary help that day, and these will fit whoever comes."

Greta showed them the vests she'd fashioned for the men, and Daisy approved those, too. She said to the seamstress, "Should I settle up with you or with Heidi?"

"Heidi will have the bill of sale in the computer. You can settle up with her."

"That's good, because I want to look around for a dress, something a little more elegant than casual."

"I'll package it all up," Greta said, "and bring it out to the counter. You go ahead out and look."

While Tessa wandered here and there around the shop, Daisy went directly to the better dresses in the back. Mitzi came to her immediately. "Are you looking for something special?" she asked.

"I am. My fiancé and I are going to a dinner theater, and I need something a little more special than what I have in my closet."

"Let's see," Mitzi said, looking over Daisy's figure, her hair, and her clogs.

"I'm sure we have something that would suit. Do you want black?"

"No," Daisy said. "I'd rather have something colorful."

Mitzi quickly determined Daisy's size and went to that section of the rack. "How about red?" she asked. Then she pulled out a dress that had glitter and spangles from the neck to the very short hem.

"It's pretty," Daisy said. "But I don't think it's quite my style."

"What do you think your style is?" Mitzi asked.

"Something classic, yet . . ."

Mitzi filled in, "Demure?"

Daisy laughed. "I suppose you could say so, though I do like to attract my fiancé."

Mitzi's eyes targeted Daisy's hand, and she saw the engagement ring. "How long have you been engaged?"

Daisy thought a little personal information might encourage Mitzi to open up, too. "We were engaged in the fall, and I think we're going marry in July. I'm so excited." And she was.

Mitzi's face fell. She said, "Well, I hope it happens for you. Men are so unpredictable."

"How so?" Daisy prompted.

"One minute they can be so into you and want a future, and the next minute they're gone." She threw up her hands, as if that action explained it all.

"Did that happen to you?" Daisy asked.

Mitzi looked around the store and saw that Tessa was across the way and no one else was nearby. "It did." Tears came to the woman's eyes.

"I'm so sorry," Daisy commiserated, and she was. Any breakup was difficult. "Have you broken up recently?" Daisy probed, shuffling through the dresses so she didn't seem too interested.

Mitzi pulled out a lilac confection with a sweetheart neckline, capped sleeves, another short hem. "A few months now," she said, sighing. "I met him at a convenience store. We both stopped for coffee every morning. We got to talking, and then . . . you know what happens."

Daisy wasn't sure she did. "A convenience store romance," she said conversationally, hoping that would prompt Mitzi to go on.

It did.

"I'm not giving up, though," Mitzi said. "If I let enough time pass, I'm sure we're going to reunite."

Daisy wondered exactly what Mitzi was prepared to do to make that reunion happen.

Daisy drove up to Four Paws Animal Shelter and parked in the parking lot. The building had once been an old schoolhouse and had been collapsing. Noah and Serena Langston had managed to buy it from the town for a mere pittance. The shelter had been created because a brother and sister had had a dream. Noah and Serena had taken care of farm animals on their mom and dad's farm. They'd also taken in strays and found them homes. Noah had become a veterinarian and Serena had earned a business degree so they could partner in the shelter. Their former lives had given them seed funds for the nonprofit, no-kill shelter that now relied on donations and fundraising.

Daisy walked up to the front porch. The black door was decorated with four huge white pawprints. The building, probably once a white clapboard, was now covered with red vinyl siding, and a cupola sat on the gabled roof. Daisy knew Jonas and Felix were probably near the dog runs. Felix often came along with Jonas. He was a calming source for the shelter dogs.

She stepped up to the butcher-block counter in the reception area where Serena Langston sat. Serena stood immediately when she saw Daisy and came around the desk to give her a hug. Serena was in her thirties and very pretty. Her dark brown hair was usually arranged in a distinctive braided corona around her head. Her companion, a black standard poodle, sat beside her and now came around to Daisy, too, brushed against her leg, and looked up at her with hopeful eyes.

"I know what you want," Daisy said. "You want a hug, too." She stooped down and gave the poodle all manner of petting.

"Bellamy likes to see you come because she knows she's going to get attention."

"I thought she might be frolicking with Felix."

"Felix is out back with Jonas. He's looking at something special. He probably wants to show it to you."

Now Daisy was extremely curious. "I'll go find out what it is." She went through the glass-paned door and down the hall past the Plexiglas separated rooms where dogs looked up at her. She'd like to take them all home.

One of the volunteers motioned her out the back door. Smiling at Daisy, she said, "Jonas and Felix are out there."

Daisy found her way through the back door and saw Jonas away from the dog runs at an old shed that was obviously being refurbished. It now had red siding like the main building. A few workers were attaching a new roof.

"What's this?" Daisy asked.

Felix practically galloped over to her, ran around her, then sat waiting for her to acknowledge him.

She laughed, crouched down, and gave him a good petting session.

"How about me?" Jonas asked.

Standing, she went over to him, wrapped her arms around his neck, and gave him a sound kiss.

"Now that's the kind of greeting I like," he said. He motioned to the smaller building. "What do you think?"

"I'll know what to think when I know what it is," she joked.

He motioned to the large plate glass window that had been inserted in one side. "That's a viewing window for whoever's inside to look outside at the birds and the leaves and the trees and anybody coming and going."

The birds and the leaves and the trees, she thought. "Really? It's going to be a shelter for cats?"

"It is. I told Serena you would be excited."

"Oh, I am. I know she's been wanting to add a feline room."

"The fundraising this past year has been good. I know it seems a bit odd, but with the fundraising for the homeless shelter, it seems people wanted to make sure pets had homes, too. Apparently they've been donating to both."

"I suppose there will be cat trees inside?"

"You can help pick them out. Serena hasn't decided exactly how the inside will be arranged yet. She and Noah are consulting on the best way to

treat cats that have just arrived and keep them separate from others who have been here longer. But
I'm sure they'll figure it out. How was your day?"

"Tessa and I went to the Rainbow Flamingo to
pick up the aprons for the Alice in Wonderland
Tea. You should see them. They're so cute. The kids
will love them when they see our servers dressed
up as the characters, mostly Alice. Somehow we'll
dress Foster as the White Rabbit."

Jonas chuckled. "I'm sure he'll like that."

"I also talked with Mitzi Geitz."

"Uh-oh. How did that go?" Jonas asked.

"It didn't take much to get her to spill her feelings. She seemed heartbroken over her breakup
with Neil. She told me she met him at a convenience store where they both stopped for coffee.
She didn't mention him by name, but I knew
that's who she was talking about."

"Is she a suspect?" Jonas asked.

"I don't know if the police consider her a suspect, but *I* certainly do. She's convinced if she lets
some time pass, they're going to reunite. I'm concerned about what she might have done or what
she might do to make that happen."

"Are you going to talk to Zeke or Morris?"

She looked down at Felix, then over at the cat
shelter, debating exactly what she was going to do.
"I'm not sure. I'm sure Neil's ex-girlfriend is going
to be on their list. Maybe the next time I talk to
them, I'll mention it."

"They're keeping everything bottled up this
time, probably because you were Lydia's friend.
They think that might skewer your perceptions."

"You bet they do. I'm determined to find out who murdered her if they don't."

Jonas said to Daisy, "I've finished everything I had to do here. Are you ready to go home?"

"I sure am. It's been a long day. Takeout from Sarah Jane's? I can call Jazzi and see what she wants."

"That sounds good. I think this is meatloaf special night."

Daisy shook her head. That was one of Jonas's favorite meals from Sarah Jane's. She was partial to the chicken croquette special night.

They went through the large building again so Jonas could tell everyone he was leaving. Serena was talking to someone at the desk, and she gave them a wave as they exited from the front door.

When Daisy caught sight of her blue Dodge Journey, she gasped. "It looks like I have a flat tire."

Jonas and Felix started toward the vehicle's back left tire. He stooped down to examine it. "You certainly do have a flat tire, and it looks to me like it was sliced."

Daisy had gone around the other side of the car, and she stopped when she saw what was there. "My car's been keyed." There was a long, ragged line along the driver's side that had ruined the paint.

Jonas came around to her to examine it for himself. "I don't like this, Daisy."

"Nan Conroy told me this had happened to Lydia. She had a tire slashed and her car was keyed."

"We're calling Zeke," Jonas said, taking out his cell phone.

Daisy imagined dinner was going to be held up tonight.

Last night, Jonas called Zeke. The detective had met Daisy and Jonas at Four Paws and listened to their story. However, Daisy could see that Zeke wasn't convinced the same person had hurt her car who had damaged Lydia's. At least, that was the impression he'd given.

When Daisy had gotten home, however, she'd called Tara Morelli and left a message. She needed a session with her, and there was no point putting it off. Fortunately Tara had returned her call and said she had a cancellation today.

So at 1:10 on Saturday, Daisy was sitting in Tara Morelli's office with Lancelot on her lap.

It had taken Daisy a few minutes to get comfortable and decide what she wanted to say. Tara wasn't rushing her. Rather, she let Lancelot work his magic. He did that with anyone who liked cats.

Daisy petted the yellow tabby's stripes down his back, and he rolled over a little so she'd have better access. Finally she looked up at Tara.

Tara was sitting at her preferred chair with a legal pad on her lap and a pen in her hand. When Daisy had asked Tara in her first session why she still used a legal pad instead of an electronic tablet, Tara had replied, "I think the legal pad relaxes my clients more. They are around electronics all too much as it is. It seems to work, so I stick with it."

Daisy liked that attitude. She liked Tara. The counselor had helped Jazzi so much, so Daisy trusted her. Finally she looked into the counselor's brown eyes and confessed, "I think I'm becoming involved in solving this murder case, too. What is *wrong* with me?"

"Why do you assume something's wrong with you?" Tara asked in that quiet calm voice she had.

"Because most women don't have people around them who get murdered. Most women aren't friends with two detectives, and have a fiancé who is a former detective. There must be something about me that attracts . . ." She waved her hand in the air, and Lancelot looked up at it. "This stuff."

Daisy's outburst didn't seem to unsettle Tara or Lancelot. He started purring as her hand went to the ruff around his neck, and she slipped her fingers into his silky fur, more for her comfort than his.

"Maybe you're asking the wrong questions," Tara said reasonably.

"What questions *should* I be asking?" Daisy was curious about this.

"Why do you care so much?" Tara asked, her pen not making any notes, her expression placid.

"I feel I need to help."

"Why?"

Daisy took a minute to think about that as she listened to Lancelot's purrs. Something about a cat's purrs was always so soothing for her. As her thoughts flitted around, she finally settled on one of the reasons why. "Maybe my caring has something to do with the way I grew up."

"How so?"

Tara was always full of more questions than answers. But that's what counselors did, Daisy knew.

They led you on that inner journey so you could find your own answers.

"My best friend before middle school was an Amish girl. Her name is Rachel. We're still friends. I went to church with all my family most weeks, but as we discussed before, my mother was kind of cold with me. My sister always had her places to go and things to do. My dad and my mom always worked so hard, first getting the nursery off the ground, and then making it a success."

Tara cocked her head. "I'm not sure I see the connection between that and going to church."

Daisy sat up a little straighter and thought about the best way to explain. "Rachel's family seemed different from ours, more than in the obvious ways. Her family pretty much did everything together from morning till night—chores, work, even school. She and her siblings were in the same one-room schoolhouse. They had church every other week, and those services were long. I went along with Rachel a few times. On their off church weeks, they visited other friends and family. It was all part of this big circle where everything was connected."

"You didn't feel you had that big circle at home?"

"Not really. I mean, I was loved. Don't get me wrong. My Aunt Iris and my dad made up the slack from my mom caring more about Camellia than she did for me. Now I understand all that. I understand her postpartum depression. I understand why there was always a wedge between us until recently. But as a child, I really did love playing on Rachel's farm with her and her siblings. I loved collecting eggs, pulling weeds from the garden, even digging up potatoes in the fall. There was something so basic about their family and the way they lived, the way they cared about each other and everything, the way they lived day to day. That made an impression on me."

"Let's drop back into your thoughts a bit. You said you knew you were loved. Did you know your mother loved you?"

Daisy wanted to answer, *Of course, she did.* The truth was harder to admit. "No, I didn't always know she loved me. Even when she said the words, I don't know if I believed it. I didn't see it. I didn't feel it. Do you know what I mean?"

"Would you say your gut instincts drive what you say and do?"

"As an adult, I'm sure they do. When I was younger, I kept quiet more than I was assertive. It was just an easier way of getting along."

"So when you didn't say what you thought, what happened?"

"I'm not sure what you mean."

"If you didn't say what you felt, where did those feelings go?"

"I don't know. I guess I turned them into something else. I would spend the day with Rachel, and we'd bake blueberry pies with her mother and her grandmother. My Aunt Iris would take me on a road trip somewhere, to a corn maze or to a farm to play with goats or to simply have tea with her and make cookies to go with it. My best friend Tessa and I were close in middle school and high school. She had a difficult home life, and I wanted her to know our friendship meant a lot to me. In high school we went to cooking classes. The course was labeled Recipes from Around the World. After that, we'd make up recipes and bake them or cook them together."

"For the people you loved."

"Sure, or anyone who needed something sweet, or something to warm them up."

"Do you see where I'm headed with this, Daisy?" Tara asked.

Lancelot stretched his paw over Daisy's knee and tapped it on her leg as if that might help her think about Tara's question.

"When you felt lonely or scared or unloved, my guess is you did something to make others feel better," Tara pointed out.

Daisy considered what Tara had said. "So you think I tried to give to others so they'd give love back?"

"It's more important what *you* think, not what *I* think."

"I don't want to think my whole life was transactional."

"I don't think that's it at all. Why are you petting Lancelot?"

"Because he likes it and he needs it."

"And because he does, what do you get back?"

"Affection and a comforting feeling that I'm doing something good for him."

"Exactly. I think that's the way you see the world. If you do something to help, it makes the whole world better."

"That might be a lofty way of looking at it," Daisy said in a wry tone. "But I'm not sure my helping to solve murders is as noble as that."

"When you know someone involved in one of these cases, you want to help. That's been your history up until now, right?"

"Yes, and that's the problem. Sometimes I wish I could just stand back and let the detectives do it."

"If you did that, that wouldn't be owning your place in the world. That would be stuffing those feelings again, and as an adult, you don't want to do that."

What Tara said made sense. It was a lot to think about.

CHAPTER NINETEEN

Daisy thought about her discussion with Tara throughout the weekend. On Sunday after church, she told Jonas about it.

"So what do you want to do next?" he'd asked. "Drop the search for clues . . . or pursue them?"

She'd told him what she wanted to do next.

So after the tea garden closed on Monday, she'd met him at Woods, and they drove to Eli Lapp's buggy shop.

When Daisy and Jonas spotted the building they'd been looking for, Jonas said to Daisy, "It looks as if Eli is doing well. Good for him."

Daisy gazed at the two white buildings that appeared to be side-by-side garages. A sign stood on a post between them: LAPP'S BUGGY SHOP.

A few buggy wheels lay sideways at the edge of an open hangar door at the one building. Daisy could see two buggies inside that looked older and must be there for buggy repair.

Jonas pointed to a long side of the building.

There sat two new-looking gray-bonneted buggies, and one that looked as if it had seen wear and tear.

"Is that Miriam Yoder in there?" Jonas asked.

Daisy knew Miriam was Eli's fiancée. She sat at the sewing machine back in the corner of the building with supplies around her. She was sewing and hadn't seen them.

Miriam was a beautiful young woman in her teens. Her light brown hair was pulled back in a bun, and a heart-shaped *kapp* sat on her head. She was wearing a hunter-green dress with her apron.

"Eli and Miriam are supposed to marry in the fall," Daisy reminded Jonas.

"I know. Eli has to put in time with preparation and studies for the bishop to approve their marriage."

Daisy had gotten to know Eli when he'd become a suspect in a murder investigation. He'd been born into the Amish community but then had left during *rumspringa*. Even so, last year he'd decided he still embraced the tenets of his faith. He still believed in the deep values, and he'd fallen in love with an Amish girl. He was recommitting himself to the Amish faith and community.

Miriam's foot on the treadle stopped when she looked up to see Jonas and Daisy.

Daisy waved and said, "We don't want to bother you."

"No bother. I was just sewing the covering for one of the buggy seats."

Most of the buggies in Lancaster County had gray bonnets, but many other aspects of the buggy could vary. New customized buggies could run about sixty-two hundred dollars. There were options regarding upholstery, lighting, and the style of the dashboard. Some had back windows; others enabled passengers to enter through a sliding door. Some used roll-up curtains. Buggy wheels could be metal or rubber. Besides the traditional carriage, young Amish boys often had courting buggies, two-seaters. A date often consisted of a boy asking a girl to drive home after a Sunday evening singing. Amish children sometimes drove pony carts, which were sort of a training buggy. Buggies were an integral part of the Amish community and signaled a slower-paced life. They reminded fellow travelers not to be in a rush. They took the Amish off the grid, so to speak, to a time that was more peaceful, wholesome, and less complicated.

Miriam stood and gave them another smile. "Eli and Titus are in the other building," she said, motioning next door. "They're scheduling work for the week and ordering parts they can't fix."

"It sounds as if Eli is busy," Jonas said, giving Daisy a sideways look, because they hadn't known for sure that Titus would be there.

"So Titus Yoder is working here?" Jonas asked.

"Ya, started last week. Eli is wonderful busy, and he needed help."

Jonas and Daisy had come here to ask Eli about rumors on the Amish grapevine concerning Titus, Leah, and Lydia. Maybe even Neil. Titus being here could hamper their questioning. Nevertheless, on the other side of it, maybe he could have something to add.

"I heard Titus and Leah sold off a parcel of their land," Jonas said.

"'Tis so," Miriam agreed. She lowered her voice. "Titus doesn't like to talk about it."

"I imagine it's not something he wanted to do," Daisy added.

"He is terrible sad," Miriam said, looking sad herself. "But we have to do what we must, ain't so?"

"You and your family are doing well?" Daisy asked.

"Oh, yes. Wonderful *gut*. We're so excited about the wedding. You're getting married this summer, ain't so?"

"That's right," Jonas confirmed, wrapping his arm around Daisy's shoulders. "So we can imagine your excitement."

"I'm going to work here with Eli until babies come. By then, if business is *gut*, we can look for a place of our own instead of living with my parents."

"Would you consider building on their property?" Jonas asked.

Daisy knew that was the way of many Amish families. The men work the farms together, and the women could help each other with childcare.

"Maybe so," Miriam said with a nod and eyes that were shining with dreams for the future.

After Daisy and Jonas finished their conversation with Miriam, they left the building fashioned for repairs and crossed to the building beside it to the office. Jonas opened the creaky door with partial plate glass, and they stepped inside. This building was much smaller than the other. It housed an L-shaped counter with a computer. Titus Yoder sat at a table and chair, studying papers before him. Shelves lined the side wall with many cubicles. They all contained parts of some sort. The only ones that Daisy recognized were the reflectors that were attached to the back of buggies.

When Eli looked up from his stance at the counter, his face broke into a wide smile. "Jonas," he said, "are you here to order a buggy?"

Jonas laughed. Before Eli's life had turned around, he had helped Jonas at Woods. Jonas turned to Daisy. "I don't know, Eli. You'll have to ask Daisy if we're ready to turn my SUV in for a buggy."

She laughed, too. "Not quite yet. But you never know, do you?"

Eli said, "No, you don't. I never would have expected last year at this time I would be running a buggy shop and be engaged."

"All is going well then?" Daisy asked.

"It is for me," Eli said. Then he turned to Titus.

Titus pushed back his chair, stood, and came to the counter. "Did you come to question me about Lydia? I hear you are doing that with many people."

"We didn't know you were working here, Titus," Jonas said honestly. "Actually I was going to ask Eli if he knew what you were doing with your land. I heard you were selling."

"Not all of it," he said, looking down at his hands and then folding them together on the counter.

"Farming is taking its toll?" Daisy asked gently.

He shook his head and pressed his lips together.

Daisy knew this man didn't expound on his emotions or his life. She hoped he could give her details about Lydia's life that no one else could. It was a bonus finding him here. Anything he said wouldn't just be hearsay. It would be the truth.

Jonas seemed to understand what Daisy wanted to do. He moved closer to Eli and said, "Why don't you show me all the options I could get on a new buggy."

"Seriously?" Eli asked him.

"A courting buggy could be fun. Sammy would love it."

"And the horse?" Eli asked with a quirk of his brow.

"I'm thinking maybe Rachel Fisher might have a place to board one on her farm."

"Are you serious?" Eli asked.

Jonas leaned close to Eli and whispered something in his ear. Daisy had no idea what that was. Eli took a look at her and then grinned. He moved farther down along the desk and took out a paper from a drawer. He put it in front of Jonas and began explaining the options.

That gave her the opportunity to speak with Titus alone. He looked increasingly uncomfortable until Daisy asked, "How is Leah?"

The man shook his head as if he didn't have words for how his wife was.

"I know how hard her twin's death had to be. At least I can imagine it. I have a sister, and I know how I would feel if something happened to her, especially in this way."

Titus nodded and admitted with uncertainty, "I don't know what to do for her. What can I do so she's not so sad?"

"Grief is like one big storm that has to pass, and then even when it does, little storms assault you whenever you least expect it. It's something everyone just has to wade through." Daisy could see that this man actually hurt for his wife. He might not show emotion much, but he obviously loved her.

Daisy couldn't believe he would do anything to hurt Lydia or Leah.

"Does anything help relieve her grief? Anything at all?" Daisy asked.

"Only being with Frannie. That's all she wants to do is spend time with her. And since Neil seems overwhelmed with everything, he lets her."

"I know the police have probably asked you this, but do you know of anyone, anyone at all, who would want to hurt Lydia?"

She could see in Titus's eyes that he had an answer for her, but she also knew this Amish man wouldn't gossip. "Can you tell me if Lydia and Neil were actually trying to mend their marriage?"

Titus's eyes grew wide, as if he hadn't expected her to know they'd had problems, or that there had been an affair.

"I can tell you true they were fixing it. I cannot say what happened with Neil, but he does love Frannie, and he did love Lydia. They wanted to hold onto their vows for their little girl so she could grow up with two parents."

Daisy pushed a little. "Is there anyone who might want that not to happen?"

Titus looked torn by what he thought he should do and whatever might help Daisy. "That woman, Mitzi Geitz."

"I spoke with her. She seems to think she and Neil can get back together now that Lydia is gone."

Titus's scowl was dark and ominous. "I hope that doesn't happen. I think she was the only one who might want to hurt Lydia."

* * *

Daisy was standing at the sales counter at the tea garden the following morning when April Jennings came in. Daisy had just sold three more tickets for the Alice in Wonderland Tea this coming weekend. They were almost full up. She was looking forward to the day with the kids, the parents, the storybook quality, and Ned's music that always made it more festive. For this tea, the pseudo-costumes and big placards would help make the day even more special. The kids would love it all.

April looked so pretty today without her server's net over her curly blond hair and her uniform. She was dressed as if she wanted to make a good impression—a short red peacoat with a black scarf around the collar and black slacks. Her boots were suede and a little worn, but she still looked as if she might be going on a date.

After greetings, she asked Daisy, "Can I talk to you in private?"

Daisy glanced around the tearoom. All the tables were covered. She spotted Foster on his way to the kitchen, and she asked, "Can you cover the sales counter for a little while?"

"Sure," he said with grin. "I'll be here for another half hour yet."

Daisy motioned April to follow her to her office. Once there, she asked, "Would you like a cup of tea?"

April bowed her head. "I don't want to take up too much of your time."

"A cup of tea won't take up that much of my time." She kept an electric teapot in her office, and she quickly brewed two cups of tea. She used teabags in here for convenience. After she opened a wooden box on her desk that held an assortment of flavors, April chose one and dipped it into her cup.

"Sugar or honey?" Daisy asked. She had packets of both.

"No, this is fine. Thank you."

Daisy set out two teabag holders. April sat on the other side of her desk, and she sat on her side. "So what did you want to talk to me about?"

April had opened the top two buttons of her jacket. Daisy could see that she was wearing a white blouse underneath.

"I came to ask you again if you have any positions open here."

When Daisy didn't answer right away, April rushed on, "You might have heard, business at The Farm Barn isn't good, and my tips are terrible. Rumor has it that Mr. Aldenkamp sold the restaurant. It's been okay up 'til now with my bills, but I don't want to get behind, and I don't want to lose my apartment. I don't know where I'd go."

Daisy was about to put together a response when she heard a buzzing coming from April's pocket. April's face pinkened and she said, "That's my phone. I'll let it go to voicemail."

Daisy appreciated that April was considerate of their meeting. The phone had hardly stopped buzzing when now there was a ping. She looked at April questioningly, suspecting what it was—probably a text message.

In a low voice, April said, "I'm sorry. I don't have to look at it."

Daisy smiled, knowing how her daughters used their phones for everything. She said, "Go ahead. I don't mind."

April took her phone from her pocket and checked it. The young woman's face went white.

"What's wrong, April?" Daisy could see that something was.

April vehemently shook her head. "It's nothing important."

But Daisy could easily see that the text had affected April in some way. She thought about her staff, what she knew about them, and upcoming plans. She considered April again, and she made a decision. "All I have to offer you right now is a part-time position. One of my part-time servers is moving with her family to North Carolina."

April's face looked hopeful but a little disappointed, too.

Daisy went on. "However, I might have full-time employment for you if you work out as a temporary server. My son-in-law will be graduating and is hoping for full-time employment in his field. I don't think that will be a problem with his major in business management and the fact that he's tech savvy. So if he does find employment, then I'll have a full-time position open in May. How does that sound to you?"

"It sounds wonderful, Mrs. Swanson. I'll do my best to learn everything you need me to learn. I want that full-time position. I'm on my own. I don't have any family."

April didn't explain further, and Daisy remembered that the young woman's family was deceased. In order to be of more assistance to April, she asked, "Are you working at The Farm Barn on Saturday?"

April shook her head. "My hours were cut. I work on Sunday."

"How do you feel about serving at my Alice in Wonderland Tea on Saturday?"

April's face broke into a wide smile. "I'd love it." Although April looked relieved, a trace of her earlier upset remained. Daisy wondered what had caused it. She might never know.

The call from Iris came in at nine p.m. that evening. Daisy, Jonas, and Jazzi were in the kitchen, around the island, making a late-evening snack of nachos dripping with cheese sauce. Daisy had whipped up the cheese sauce, and Jonas was brewing tea. Daisy would miss these times with the three of them, when Jazzi was taking a break from schoolwork to spend some time with her and Jonas. They all had finally agreed on a movie that they wanted to stream.

The tuba sound from Daisy's phone was loud even amidst their chatter and laughter. She picked it up from the counter, saw Iris's picture, and answered it.

"Hi, Iris. If you come over, we'll share cheese nachos and tea with you." Her voice was teasing. She liked to hear from her aunt. Even though they worked together at the tea garden, they didn't have that much time to chat there.

"I think you might want to come over here," Iris said, her voice serious.

Daisy was on alert immediately. "What's going on?"

Since her aunt had broken up with the man she was dating, Iris and Daisy had spent many evenings after work having long chats. Maybe this was one of those evenings. Maybe Iris was trying to make a decision whether she should date Morris or Marshall exclusively.

"A box came for you. It's strange."

"I'm going to put you on speaker. Jonas is right here beside me," Daisy told her aunt. "Why do you say it's strange? What's inside?"

"First of all, it didn't have a return address," Iris said.

"Do you know if a service delivered it, or was it delivered by the post office?" Jonas wanted to know.

"I didn't see a delivery truck or anything like that," Iris said. "I didn't even hear a vehicle. I just came to the front door to look out, which I often do before bed . . . before locking down the house for the night. And there it was on my porch."

"So what's inside?" Jonas asked.

"I'd rather you see it," Iris said, a tremor in her voice.

"We'll be right over," Jonas told her.

When Iris opened her door to Daisy and Jonas a short time later, she looked worried. "I probably shouldn't have opened it," she said sorrowfully. "My fingerprints are probably all over it."

"The police can always do an elimination of your fingerprints," Jonas told her as Iris led them into her living room. An open cardboard box sat on her coffee table.

Iris pointed to the inside of the box. "That's our missing yellow teacup, isn't it?"

Without touching it, Daisy examined the yellow teacup with the red floral pattern. It was easy to see that the bowl of the cup had been broken in half. "Yes, that's the one that Tamlyn told me was stolen, or had disappeared, however you want to look at it."

"A stolen teacup?" Jonas asked. "Tamlyn would notice that?"

"It's one of our Varages, France vintage ones," Daisy said. "I have a teapot and three other cups in that pattern. We use it for service, and it's a particular favorite."

"And is that a cutting board?" Jonas asked, looking at the other item inside the box.

It was indeed a small rectangular cutting board. It had a daisy etched on its surface. It was one of those decorative items that Daisy had placed on a shelf along with teacups that were available to buy.

"What happened to it?" Iris wanted to know, pointing to the corner that was now ragged and dark brown.

Jonas examined it without picking it up. "It looks as if someone damaged that corner by using a hammer on it or something like that, and then they burned it."

"Burned it?" Iris asked, her voice high.

Jonas leaned closer to it and smelled it. "Yes. I don't think an accelerant was used. Whoever did it probably held the corner of it over a fire. That would be my guess."

"What does this mean?" Iris asked.

"I don't need a police detective to tell me what it means. Someone is sending us a warning. But why send it to Iris and not me?" Daisy asked.

Jonas was quick to reply, again thinking like the detective he used to be. "If someone tried to deliver it to our house at night, he or she would have seen the security lights blaze on, and they'd guess there are cameras. It would be easy to guess that at Iris's house, there isn't anything but a porch light."

"It would be easy for anyone to steal the teacup and cutting board at our busiest times," Iris surmised. "When tourist buses arrive, we're all concentrating on service."

"It would also be easy for the perpetrator to pay someone to lift them, maybe saying it's a practical joke," Jonas pointed out.

"So it's a warning," Iris repeated in a low murmur, as if she didn't want to consider that.

"It is," Jonas maintained, then studied Daisy. "The question is—what are you going to do about it?"

CHAPTER TWENTY

The past few weeks had led up to today. At least, that's what Daisy's staff thought. The Alice in Wonderland Tea was about to begin. Cora Sue was standing at the door, taking tickets. Foster, who'd put on hold anything else he'd had going on today, looking indeed like the White Rabbit in a black vest, white shirt, and bunny ears, was seating their guests. Ned, wearing a black vest, white shirt, a black bow tie, and a top hat resembling the Mad Hatter's, was strumming his guitar in the spillover tearoom. He was mostly playing childhood ditties and anything else that seemed to go with the occasion.

Children were *ooh*ing and *aah*ing over the large cardboard figures—the Queen of Hearts, a large cat with a wide grin, and a huge daisy. The staff distributed the Alice et al. clothespin dolls, and the kids were trading them and dancing their dolls across the tables. The servers in their fancy aprons smiled as if they were in a fairy tale.

Daisy dashed to the kitchen to take a last look

around at the food before it was served. Since kids loved peanut butter, Daisy had sent emails to all the parents so they knew exactly what would be served. She decided to make Amish church peanut butter spread today. She spread it on triangles of oat bread. It was only one of the servings, but she knew the kids would like it. The staff had mixed sugar and molasses and water, boiled it, and let it cool. Then they'd added peanut butter and marshmallow and stirred until it was well mixed. Other selections included a cinnamon cream cheese spread on raisin bread, a miniature version of grilled cheese, and egg salad triangles. Mini scones on tiered trays were both chocolate chip and cranberry. She'd also had to serve tartlets, of course, since they were part of the Alice in Wonderland feast. These were cherry. Tessa and Eva had decorated sugar cookies with Alice in Wonderland symbols like Alice, the pocket watch, a trumpet, a fan, flowers, and small hedgehogs. Daisy suspected they would be a big hit. She certainly hoped so.

Iris fluttered into the kitchen as Daisy was looking over everything. She looked flustered.

"What's wrong?" Daisy asked, hoping there wasn't a glitch that she hadn't expected. You never knew at one of these teas what could happen. Parents and kids could be unpredictable.

"Did you know both Marshall and Morris bought tickets for the tea?"

Daisy had to smile, even though she was preoccupied by all that was going on around her. "It doesn't surprise me. They want to stay in your orbit. Morris might also be here to check on us." Daisy had turned over the box with the teacup and cutting board to him.

"My orbit?" Iris was frustrated and glowed red. "I don't need them cluttering up my workday."

Daisy had to chuckle at that. "I'm sure they don't see it that way. They want to remind you that they're here."

"Well, I hope they like children. Foster set Morris over at a table where there was a mom and two daughters. Marshall is sitting at a table with a son and his mom, as well as grandparents with their grandchildren."

"This could be your chance to see how they interact with kids," Daisy pointed out.

Iris looked thoughtful. "I suppose that's important with Sammy around a lot."

Daisy knew her Aunt Iris liked to babysit for Sammy whenever she had the chance. Her aunt and her mom vied for the responsibility.

"I think everything in here is ready to go," Daisy assured her.

Eva called from across the kitchen. "It sure is, including the herbal red tea. I hope everybody's ready to pour."

Red tea without caffeine was made by a certain supplier that Daisy could trust. She knew it would be all right to serve to the children . . . or they could have apple juice. This day had taken a lot of planning and care. They'd sold all the tickets, and she hoped everyone would be pleased.

Iris said, "Foster seated Neil Aldenkamp and his daughter Frannie in the main tearoom. Is that what you wanted?"

"It doesn't matter. I just hope they have a good time. Frannie needs something to put a smile on her face, and I suppose Neil does, too."

The volume of chatter in both tearooms was rising. Daisy knew it would subside again when everyone started sipping and eating. Once everyone was served, Ned would start an interactive program with the kids and music.

After Daisy entered the main tearoom to check on service, Ned came in with his guitar. To keep his audience calm and entertained before service, he started a song that he'd made up himself. *There was a young girl named Alice. She and her sister were reading by a stream. Alice fell asleep, and her adventure began with a dream.*

Ned was quite good at storytelling as well as music. For the children who hadn't read Alice in Wonderland, he told the saga of a girl who had unusual adventures, including meeting a White Rabbit, a Mad Hatter, a Queen of Hearts, and a Cheshire Cat. Children looked intrigued, and their parents seemed satisfied that their kids were enjoying themselves. At least most of the parents looked satisfied. Neil was scowling at Daisy. She didn't run from conflict, so she decided she'd better take care of this now.

Sidling up to his table, she could see Frannie was listening to Ned. Neil said in a low voice to Daisy, "Did you do this on purpose?"

"Do *what* on purpose?"

"Ask me here with Detective Rappaport close by."

Daisy glanced to the section where Foster had seated Morris. He was looking their way.

"I certainly did *not.*"

"I can tell he's just waiting to question me again."

"Neil, that would be impossible here with the

music and the kids. I'm sure he wouldn't separate you from Frannie. Morris is here because he's interested in dating my Aunt Iris."

"Honestly?" Neil asked, looking perplexed.

Daisy wasn't one to give out her aunt's personal information, but today Neil seemed to need some reassurance.

"Do you see that gentleman on the other side of the room who's glaring at Detective Rappaport?"

Neil glanced that way. "That's Marshall Thompson. I consulted with him when the police called me in."

"Yes, that's Marshall. He and the detective are vying for my aunt's affection. They're only here today because they don't want Aunt Iris to forget about them."

Neil's shoulders lowered, and he seemed to relax. "That's interesting." He heaved a sigh. "Maybe I can slip down a rabbit hole with Frannie and not worry today."

"I hope so," Daisy said, and she meant it.

As with all specialty tea days, Daisy felt as if she were being pulled in all directions as food was served and tea was poured. That was the essence of a day like this, and she truly enjoyed it. Jonas stopped in while everyone was munching on the sandwich course. He'd helped her set up for the tea. He pointed to her office, and she nodded. She could take a few minutes with Jonas to catch her breath.

When they met in there, Jonas wrapped his arms around her and gave her a brief but exciting kiss. "That's something to keep you going," he teased.

"And here I thought you stopped in for Amish

church spread." She knew Jonas liked the peanut butter treat as much as any child.

He grinned. "I wouldn't mind if you had an extra sandwich or two."

She shook her head at him. "I'll bring any extra home."

"I don't know," he said, looking toward the tearoom. "That looks like a hungry bunch. You might not have any left."

"Did you stop by to see Morris and Marshall vie for Aunt Iris's attention?"

"I knew they were both coming. They'd better behave themselves, or Iris will take them to task. I wanted to see how you were faring and make sure there weren't any disasters."

"Not at one of my teas," she said with mock horror.

"You look cute as Alice. The ruffled apron and hairband becomes you."

She curtsied. "Thank you, kind sir."

Suddenly Foster was at her office door, looking stricken. "Daisy, you're needed out here."

"What's wrong?" Jonas asked before Daisy could.

"There's a man out here who insists on coming in. I don't know what to do about him."

Both Daisy and Jonas followed Foster out through the main tearoom to the front door. Daisy stepped outside but left the door open a crack so Jonas could hear. She recognized the man, who had a balding head, wire-rimmed glasses, and a sturdy frame. He was wearing an ill-fitting brown suit. He was the man she'd spotted in The Farm Barn's parking lot the last evening she and Jonas ate supper there.

"Can I help you?" she asked in a firm voice.

"This is a public establishment, isn't it? I need to come in to talk to one of your guests."

"Do you have a ticket?"

"No, I don't."

She didn't like the looks of him, and she didn't know whom he wanted to talk to, but she didn't care. "I'm sorry, sir, the tea garden is full. We have to adhere to the fire marshal's guidelines." Children's voices and the music from inside soared out the open door.

"You've got quite a party going on in there. Are you sure you can't handle one more person?"

"Not one more," Daisy assured him, following her gut.

"That's a shame. So I guess you're just going to have to give a message to Neil Aldenkamp for me." Since she'd seen him outside The Farm Barn, his request wasn't a total surprise. Still, Daisy's heart took a dive.

Suddenly the expression on the man's face changed from bully-determined to fearful. He was looking over Daisy's shoulder through the door. Did he see Jonas?

She glanced through the glass and spied Morris Rappaport standing there, glaring out. Before Morris could come through the door, the man took off running down the street. Morris jogged after him, his cell phone in his hand, as though he were calling for backup.

Jonas came outside to stand beside Daisy.

"Why did Morris go after him?" Daisy asked.

"Apparently, he's a bookie that Morris has been wanting to question. Neil owes him money."

* * *

On Sunday evening, Daisy was experiencing a rare few moments alone in her house. Essentially alone. Marjoram was sitting on an island chair, watching her. Pepper had climbed to the top of the refrigerator and was bathing there. Puttering around the kitchen in a pink pullover sweater, jeans, and fluffy bedroom slippers, Daisy experimented with a new recipe for rhubarb muffins. May would be rhubarb season in Pennsylvania, and the muffins would be a great special for the month. It felt like a long time until May, but it was only a month away.

As she chopped rhubarb, she smiled, remembering the Alice in Wonderland Tea, which had been a deliciously successful event. The children and parents had enjoyed themselves, and Ned said he'd had a good time, too. He helped them raffle off the cardboard cutouts. The kids who won them were so excited. The clothespin dolls had also been a big hit. One mom had stopped to tell Daisy the event had been well worth the money for a ticket. She certainly would come to more of Daisy's specialty teas when she held them.

The brief occurrence with the man at the door and Morris running after him was less of a spectacle than she'd been afraid it had been. There had been so much noise in the tearoom and the spillover tearoom that day that most guests weren't even aware of what had happened. Earlier this evening, Morris had called her. He'd caught the guy who was a bookie. If Neil owed money to him, had that been another reason the detectives suspected Neil? Were they close to charging him with his wife's murder?

Daisy pictured Frannie, a little girl who looked like a cherub and who had no idea what her mom or dad had been involved in that had caused this horrific event in their lives.

As Daisy swirled batter for the muffins in her stand mixer, her cell phone played its tuba sound. Since the phone was charging on the counter, she considered letting it go to voicemail. However, she thought about Jonas and Jazzi. Jonas had spent so much time helping her set up for the Alice in Wonderland Tea, and he had a few orders for islands that he had to finish. He was in his workshop tonight at the store. Jazzi and Mark had gone bowling with friends. Vi, Foster, and Sammy should be enjoying an evening in their new house. But any one of them could need something.

She switched off the mixer and picked up her phone.

It was April's number. Her new hire had helped serve expertly yesterday at the tea. She'd told Daisy that today she was working an event at The Farm Barn.

Even though Daisy had put her phone to her ear, when she answered, she could hardly hear April's voice. The young woman was whispering.

"April, I can't hear you," she said, wondering what this was all about.

"Jake is coming after me. He locked me in the pantry closet until everybody left."

April's voice was hoarse. Why?

"What do you mean Jake locked you in the pantry closet? Was he playing a prank?" That room was practically a cubbyhole, with boxes from floor to ceiling. Daisy remembered there was a padlock hanging on a latch on the door frame. A padlock.

It never seemed to be fastened, but now maybe it *was.*

Before Daisy could ask any more questions or even decide what she was going to do, April went on with a sob in her voice. "Jake says he's going to lock me in the walk-in refrigeration unit until I agree to take him back. We dated for a while," she explained breathlessly.

April was crying now, and Daisy knew exactly what she was going to do. Marjoram and Pepper must have heard the concern in her voice because they both sat at attention. The tortoiseshell meowed loudly.

Daisy left the mixer where it was, kicked off her slippers, and went to find her trainers at the door.

Still holding her cell phone to her ear, she reassured April, "Honey, hold on. I'm calling for help, and I'll be there as soon as I can." She glanced at the two cats as she grabbed her cat-patterned sweater coat and set the security alarm on her way out.

She ran to her garage. As she climbed in her car, she called Jonas. "I need your help. April is locked in a storage room at The Farm Barn. I think Jake murdered Lydia."

"Jake?" Jonas asked, as if he'd been miles away in work and it took him a second or two to recalibrate.

Daisy rushed on. "I might be putting two and two together and getting five, but I don't think so. Call Zeke, and I'll leave a message for Morris."

"You should wait for me, Daisy," Jonas said, as if knowing she was already on her way. Daisy pressed the remote for the garage door. Backing out, she simply said to Jonas, "Meet me there."

He didn't say anything else, because they both needed to call the detectives right *now*.

Daisy didn't know what to expect when she arrived at The Farm Barn's parking lot. On the way over, all she could think about was April, Jake, and Lydia, and what had gone on among the three of them. She could guess as she looked back over her history with them all, and facts finally lined up in a possible pattern.

The first fact was that Jake hadn't been working at The Farm Barn at the time of Lydia's death. Why? Daisy doubted now that he'd really been on vacation. Because he hadn't been around, everyone had considered he'd had nothing to do with Lydia's murder.

Fact two. April had told Daisy that she'd stayed with Lydia now and then. Why? Daisy had thought maybe April had been sick at those times . . . or lonely. Neil hadn't mentioned anything out of the ordinary. Maybe because of his own personal problems, he hadn't noticed what might have been obvious to someone else. Lydia had cared for April since she had no family of her own. Possibly there was a lot more to it. Something sinister.

Fact three. Jake, himself. His charm. His attention to April that April didn't seem to want. Daisy had noticed April trying to avoid Jake whenever she could. According to Adele, April had dropped a serving tray when Jake had touched her. When April had been in Daisy's office, she received a call she'd ignored and a text message that had drained color from her face.

Daisy came to a jerky stop and could see the inside lights from The Farm Barn shining into the dark night. The parking lot light was still on, as was the light over the back door. Whatever happened between Jake and April must have happened after everyone had left. She could only guess.

Right now, it would be better if Daisy could sneak up on Jake. She went to the front door, hoping it was still open. It wasn't. She pulled it back and forth. With the little bit it would move, she hoped she could set off the security alarm. She hoped the police were already on their way, but the alarm could startle Jake. The alarm didn't go off.

Should she wait for Jonas? What if Jake had already hurt April? What if April was in the refrigerator? It was hard for Daisy to believe that Jake would do that to her. But it was also hard to believe Jake might have run down Lydia in cold blood.

That thought urged her past good sense. It urged her past Jonas's warnings. Would Zeke or Morris even come?

Daisy rushed around to the back door, and opened it a crack. She could hear Jake yelling even from here! Could he really have locked April in the refrigeration unit? Jake didn't seem to hear Daisy as she slipped quietly inside. She needed to observe the lay of the land, so to speak. His voice became clearer as she closed distance between them. She spotted him standing near the closed door of the refrigeration unit, yelling at the top of his lungs, "You love me. I know you do."

Could he even hear April through that thick door?

In range now, Daisy could see Jake was holding a butcher knife in his hand. Was that how he'd forced April into the refrigeration unit?

From the side, Daisy could see that Jake's face had an angry flush. There was spittle on his lips. His eyebrows drew together, and his hair was wild, as if he'd run his hand through it repeatedly. His face was contorted in rage or maybe misplaced passion for whatever he felt for April. He definitely looked like a wild man . . . a man with nothing left to lose.

She had to get April out of there. Hypothermia could set in. The temperature inside the refrigerator was forty or below. The Farm Barn tried to regulate the temperature at thirty-six degrees for optimal food safety, yet to keep the food unfrozen.

Silently, Daisy laid her purse on the side counter, knowing it wouldn't do her any good. Perhaps she should merely talk to Jake . . . reason with him. She'd left that message for Morris, and if Jonas had reached Zeke. . . . Her goal was to switch Jake's attention away from April. If she could do that, she might be able to slip toward that refrigerator handle and open it. Panic made breathing difficult and lodged in her chest. Her palms were sweaty.

She reassured herself. All she had to do was hold Jake off, lead him to talk, maybe get through to whatever feelings he had for April . . . and wait for Jonas and the police.

She cleared her tightened throat and asked clearly, "What are you doing, Jake?"

He swung around, then leapt toward her, his knife poised to slash. Had he hurt April already?

Daisy grabbed for a nearby serving cart, her best

defense. She wheeled it in front of her and it served as a barrier between her and Jake.

"What are you doing here?" he snarled, taking hold of the cart with one hand and trying to force it away from her.

Jake might be stronger than she was, but he had one hand to use. She had two. Without giving him a second advantage, she shoved the cart into him . . . with all of her strength. He fell back, lost his balance, and landed on the floor. He was truly filled with rage now, and jumped up before Daisy could reach the refrigerator door.

"Did you hurt April?" she called to him.

The question rolled off of him, and he moved too quickly for her to turn the handle on the door. Again, she was defending herself with the wheeled shiny silver cart, keeping it between them. He lurched forward, the knife catching the arm of her sweater coat and ripping it. It hadn't hurt her. At least, she didn't think it had.

"Jake," she yelled at him in her best mother's voice. After all, he was hardly out of his teens. "Why do you want to do this? Why do you want to hurt someone you *love?*"

The word *love* seemed to descend on him like a brick. "She doesn't love me back," he railed. "Why do people always come to her rescue? Lydia did the same thing. Why couldn't she have stayed out of it?"

He was talking now. At least, he was making some sense. "I don't understand," Daisy said softly. "Explain it to me." She was hoping that since she was a woman about fifteen years past his age, he'd look at her as a mother figure . . . or a big sister . . . or something.

"I never meant to hurt April, ever," he defended himself. "But she did things."

"What things?" Daisy asked, trying to slow her heart rate, attempting to insert calm she didn't feel into her voice.

From the corner of her eye, she thought she caught a flash of light outside the kitchen window.

"She wanted to go out with friends without me. She didn't want me to text her."

Calling on her knowledge of abused women she'd learned over the years, Daisy asked, "How many times a day did you phone or text her, Jake?"

"Apparently not enough," he insisted like a stubborn child. "Every time April got a bruise or fell down, she'd go calling Lydia. She'd tell Lydia she was lonely and stay there overnight."

"How did April get bruised or fall down, Jake?"

He bit his lower lip like a child who'd been caught in wrongdoing. "I pushed her a little."

"Is that all you did?" Daisy probed.

The knife in his hand bobbed. A new surge of adrenaline seemed to fill him as he shouted at her, "That's none of your business. Just like it wasn't any of Lydia's business. She was constantly meddling, so I had to get rid of her." He lunged forward again, trying to move that cart out of the way.

However, Daisy was stronger than she looked. After all, she adeptly handled heavy trays and serving carts of her own. She held her own, securing it between them.

"You women are all the same," Jake spat. "All pretty and friendly, and then when a man wants to touch you, you say 'Oh, no.'" His voice went high like a child. "You can't touch me now unless you prove you're worthy."

Jake's anger gave him the adrenalin rush he needed. Even with the knife in his hand, he managed to wrench the serving cart from Daisy. But she grabbed onto the tray that was set into the top of the cart.

Because of the situation she'd found herself in with murder investigations, Daisy had taught herself some self-defense moves, and Jonas had shown her others. Jake's knife slashed at her again. She swiveled, holding the tray as a shield. The knife hit the metal instead of hurting her. Although Jake lunged again, she evaded him, and kicked out with all the force she could muster at his knee. She hit her target.

With Jake's loud cry, the knife went flying, and he crumbled on the floor, holding his leg and crying like a baby.

In the next instant, Jonas came barreling in like a white streak of outrage. He charged into Jake to make sure he was disarmed and harmless.

"Zeke's right behind me," Jonas called to Daisy as he pulled Jake's arms behind his back and wouldn't let him move.

Zeke *was* right behind Jonas. He ran inside with two patrol officers. Assessing the scene before them, they took over.

Free to move away from Jake, Jonas hurried to Daisy and spotted the slash on the arm of her sweater. He took her by the shoulders and into his arms. "Did he hurt you?"

"No, he just caught my sweater. We have to let April out of the refrigerator."

Daisy could tell Jonas reluctantly let her go. She could feel him take a deep breath. Taking one of her own, she gave him a hard hug. Then she rushed toward the refrigerator door, unlatching it.

April was sitting on the floor, her arms wrapped around herself as she shivered. Her teeth were chattering. Daisy went to the young woman and crouched down beside her, wrapping her arms around her. "You're okay now, honey. You're okay."

As Jonas helped April to her feet, Daisy shrugged out of her sweater and wrapped it around April as they led her out of the refrigerator. Someone found a chair for April to sit on as Daisy rubbed the girl's arms.

Zeke said to them, "The paramedics will be here in a minute."

April's lips were blue-tinged. "I always knew he could hurt me worse than he had. I always knew." She was sobbing now.

"You don't have to talk," Daisy said. "Let's get you warmed up."

But April seemed to need to expel words she'd most likely kept secret before. "The last time before I left, he hurt me bad," April said. "He punched me in the ribs. Lydia took me in and fired him. She told me when I felt better, she wanted me to press charges. But I was afraid to. I didn't know he was the one who hurt Lydia. Honest, I didn't. I would have told somebody. After Lydia died, he came back to work and I was afraid to say Lydia had fired him. I never could have believed he'd hurt Lydia. He just told me tonight that he killed her."

Jonas had crouched down next to April, too. "Had Lydia told anyone she'd fired him?"

"No, I asked her not to. If he couldn't get a job

somewhere else, he'd be that much more mad at me. I was so afraid."

The paramedics came rushing in. Zeke directed them to April first, even though Jake was groaning in a heap on the floor.

"You don't have to be afraid anymore," Daisy told her. "Not anymore."

The paramedics took April into their care. Jonas took Daisy into his. He circled his arms around her, holding her so tight, she knew she was never going to fall. Desperately, he kissed her with the fear, love, and passion he'd been feeling. She kissed him back, holding on, vowing never to let him go.

EPILOGUE

The welcome sign above the stairway at Daisy's garage apartment had been Jazzi's idea. Daisy looked over the family and friends milling about as they ate chicken salad or ham sandwiches, munched on carrots, broccoli, and cucumbers with a dip, and enjoyed chocolate-chip cookies and snickerdoodles as well as small slices of shoo-fly pie from the dessert table. In the cozy kitchen, Daisy pulled more cans of soda from the refrigerator and set them on the counter.

April came to her, her face shining, her eyes glistening with unshed tears. She was in jeans and a red sweater. She looked happier than Daisy had ever seen her. The reason for that was obvious. She felt safe, and she now had a place to live.

"I don't know how to thank you," she said to Daisy, obviously filled with emotion. "I thought your family might resent me staying here. I promise I'll pay as much rent as I can."

Daisy laid her hand on April's shoulder. "I told

you, you're not to worry about that right now. The apartment was vacant. You're going to be my care-taker for as long as necessary."

Jazzi joined them. She must have overheard part of the conversation. "Mom needs someone to look after her since Vi and Foster and Sammy moved out. Now you can take some of the pressure off of me."

They all laughed.

"Your daughters made me feel more than wel-come," April assured Daisy.

In the past two weeks since Jake had tried to harm April and Daisy, much had happened. That night after the police had done their preliminary questioning, Daisy had brought April home with her. The young woman had been traumatized and needed comfort, warmth, and compassion. She blamed herself for what had happened.

Over and over again, Daisy and Jonas had told her it was not her fault. It had been clear to see that Jake had been obsessed with her.

That night, April had related how she and Jake had started dating. He was handsome, flattering, and could be charming. April had never had a se-rious relationship. When her parents had died, she'd crawled into a shell and had simply tried to survive. Jake had taken advantage of her vulnera-bility. He'd become more and more possessive and controlling. One night he had pushed April, and she had a bump on her head. April had called Lydia, not sure what else to do. Afraid to stay with Jake, she'd told Lydia she'd fallen. Lydia had in-vited her to stay overnight, and Neil hadn't known why April was there. After that first incident, Jake was so repentant . . . so sorry. He'd said it would never happen again. It hadn't, for a couple of months.

One day, April had told Jake she was looking into community college courses. She wanted to do more than work at The Farm Barn. He tried to convince her otherwise. In an argument, he'd pushed her into a wall and hurt her. Again she'd stayed with Lydia for a few days. She'd told Lydia she was feeling lonely. This time April had been more wary of Jake. This time she'd avoided his calls. He confronted her at The Farm Barn in the parking lot after everyone had left, everyone except Lydia. She'd intervened, telling him if he didn't leave, she'd call the police. And she'd fired him. That had been a week before he'd murdered her with his truck.

April had told Daisy it was her fault because she hadn't let Lydia call the police. She hadn't wanted more trouble. She hadn't wanted even more of Jake's wrath. Apparently, that anger had built inside of him until it had exploded at Lydia.

After Lydia died, he'd pretended he hadn't been fired. He'd tried to ingratiate himself into April's good graces. He'd tried to comfort her and commiserate about Lydia's death. April hadn't suspected he'd been the one to hurt her friend. She should have, she'd told the detectives over and over again. She *should* have. She was wearing tons of guilt on her shoulders. Daisy hoped to alleviate some of that.

When Vi came over to join them now, Sammy

was in her arms. She and April had bonded and didn't have any trouble finding conversations to explore. Vi had been encouraging April to start online classes to see what she was interested in. Daisy knew April needed time to recover and find out exactly who she wanted to be. Sammy, who had been around April as Daisy had helped her move in, reached out to the young woman with a happy grin on his face, chubby arms extended. April gladly took him and jiggled him a bit, making him giggle.

Daisy knew that children and pets were often the best healing medicine. Felix, who was sitting between Zeke and Jonas on the sofa, had made friends with April, too, when April had stayed with Daisy. Pepper and Marjoram had been the first to offer her comfort, Pepper settling in her lap as if she were an old lost friend.

Suddenly, Daisy's mom and dad came up the steps from the garage. They said hello as they entered the apartment, Daisy's dad holding a lamp. It was pretty, one Daisy had seen in her mom's spare bedroom. It had a cut-glass base and a white shade. Her Aunt Iris was behind them, holding a big box.

Daisy's parents came to the kitchen area with the lamp.

"Here's something we thought you could use," Rose said. "This place was practically empty when you moved in. This will make it a little homier."

April said, "I can use that in the bedroom. Thank you so much."

Iris set the box down on the table. "This is something for you to keep no matter where you go."

With questions in her eyes, April raised the lid on the box. Inside rested an afghan in the colors of the sunset. "I just finished it this morning," Iris confessed. "That's why we're a little late."

April took it from the box and let it unfold. "It's beautiful. I don't deserve this." Tears that had been floating in her eyes started dripping down her cheeks.

Iris wrapped her arms around April. "You *do* deserve it. Everyone deserves to be loved. Wrap yourself in it any time you want and know that you are."

Zeke was beckoning to Daisy, and she extricated herself from the group, knowing that April was in good hands. Zeke was just finishing a snickerdoodle. "Good cookies," he said.

"He's just trying to butter you up so you join the police force," Jonas commented.

"I'll bet," Daisy returned wryly.

"We were right behind you," Zeke said. "We had to eliminate other suspects. I suppose by now you know most of what we know."

"For example . . ." Daisy prompted.

"Did you know the Yoders were in so much debt that Leah had gone to Lydia to ask for a loan?"

"I suspected something was going on between them, but I didn't know what."

Zeke added, "Lydia told Leah she couldn't give it to her. That was the issue between them. Our investigation revealed not only was The Farm Barn going under, but Lydia's husband Neil had embezzled money from the business. But you know that, since charges were already filed."

Daisy was sorry about that, but Neil had broken

the law. Daisy had been glad to learn that while Neil went through his legal woes, Leah and Titus would be taking care of Frannie and would become temporary guardians if they had to. Neil hadn't protested, because he knew that's what Lydia would have wanted.

"I hear Jake finally confessed," Daisy said.

"Sure," Zeke assured her. "We were zeroing in on him by the time you confronted him. We followed the line of evidence. By the time we looked into him, he'd had his truck fixed. On a second look, however, his neighbor told us he'd seen a dented bumper. We finally tracked down the body shop where he'd had it repaired. But we had to get a warrant or two. The body shop still had the old bumper. The crime lab was still analyzing it the night you rescued April."

Zeke shook his head. "I'll never understand the criminal mind. Or men who are threatened by women. Jake didn't like Lydia bossing him . . . or you either. That was another reason why he keyed your car and slit your tire. He's a manipulator who couldn't control his impulses. Jake's reason for killing Lydia was simple. She was in his way. His convoluted reasoning told him if she was dead, April would come back to him."

"I suppose he knew Lydia hiked every morning?"

"Yes, he did. We had our eyes on him because he had an assault charge against him when he was in high school. Now he faces first-degree murder charges and simple aggravated assault charges, as well as reckless endangerment."

Then Zeke said, "We shouldn't have spent so much time looking into Neil and Mitzi Geitz. And you should have waited for backup."

Daisy had known that scolding would be coming eventually. "I know I should have. But would you want to be locked in a refrigerator any longer than you had to be?"

Zeke ran his hand through his hair. "You were just lucky that the self-defense moves Jonas taught you worked."

Trying to lighten the atmosphere, Jonas added, "She's also lucky she wheels trays and food carts and knows how to handle them."

With a roll of his eyes that Daisy was sure he'd learned from Detective Rappaport, Zeke rose to his feet. "I've got to be going." He looked around the apartment. "April has thanked me for my help about a thousand times. You like to fix broken wings, don't you?" he asked Daisy.

"I fixed yours," she jibed.

"You started the healing," he said to her seriously. He looked at Jonas, and they bumped fists. On the way out, Zeke waved.

"He's right, you know," Jonas murmured close to her ear. "You fix broken wings. You helped heal *me*."

She wrapped her arm around Jonas's waist, feeling the taut strength beneath. "And you've helped me find a future and love again. I love you, Jonas Groft."

"I love you, Daisy Swanson."

Daisy's mother approached them with a wide smile. "So, are you ever going to tell us about your wedding plans?"

Jonas and Daisy nodded at each other. Daisy

said, "We're getting married on July twenty-ninth in our backyard."

"The reception?" Aunt Iris asked, coming over to join them.

"Same place," Daisy assured her.

After Rose and Iris exchanged a look, Rose said, "We'll fill your yard with flowers and lights and food and lots of love."

Daisy had no doubt that they would.

ORIGINAL RECIPES

Apple Cider Pork Loin

2 cups apple cider
1 cup white wine
2½-pound pork tenderloin
½ teaspoon salt
¼ teaspoon black pepper
2 tablespoons olive oil plus one tablespoon
   to grease the slow cooker
2 tablespoons butter
1 cup chopped onion
2 cloves grated garlic

Grease slow cooker with olive oil. Heat cider and white wine in slow cooker before adding the other ingredients.

Sprinkle salt and pepper over the pork loin. Braise the pork loin on all sides in the olive oil and melted butter. Add onion and sauté. Add the garlic and cook for about one minute. Transfer all to the slow cooker with the cider wine mixture. Cook on low for 6 hours or until pork is tender and falling apart.

Serve with cider sauce (below) spooned over the meat.

Cider Sauce

1 cup chopped onions
4 tablespoons bacon drippings
2 tablespoons flour
½ teaspoon salt
⅛ teaspoon pepper
1¾ cup apple cider
¼ cup maple syrup
1½ tablespoons apple cider vinegar

Sauté the onion in the bacon drippings. Stir in flour, salt, and pepper until smooth. Add cider, maple syrup, and vinegar. Bring to a boil for two minutes, stirring constantly until slightly thickened.

Spoon over the sliced pork loin to serve.

Cabbage Walnut Salad

4½ cups cabbage, sliced thin

3 Jazz or Envy apples (I also use Granny
   Smith apples but prefer Jazz or Envy for
   color)

1 cup chopped walnuts

1 cup Ocean Spray Craisins (Dried cranberries)

½ cup plain Greek yogurt (I use Greek
   yogurt because it is thicker)

1¼ cup ranch dressing

Mix cabbage, walnuts, and Craisins. In a bowl,
whisk together Greek yogurt and ranch dressing.
Add cubed apples to cabbage mixture. Pour dressing over all and mix well. Store in refrigerator at
least one hour before serving.

Serves about 12.

Corn Cake

1 cup all-purpose flour
⅓ cup sugar
1 teaspoon baking powder
¼ teaspoon salt
1 large egg
½ cup milk
¼ cup melted butter
1 cup canned corn or cooked frozen corn,
    drained

In a bowl, stir flour, sugar, baking powder, and salt until mixed. Beat the egg with a fork. Whisk the beaten egg with the milk. Add to the dry mixture. Stir by hand. The batter will be a little lumpy. Add melted butter and mix well. The batter should look smoother. Stir in the corn until mixed well through the batter.

Pour batter into a greased and floured 8x8-inch square pan. Bake at 350 degrees for 30 minutes or until cake is golden brown and a toothpick comes out clean. Cut into squares and serve warm or cold. Refrigerate leftovers.

Makes 9 servings.

Visit our website at
KensingtonBooks.com
to sign up for our newsletters, read
more from your favorite authors, see
books by series, view reading group
guides, and more!

Become a Part of Our
Between the Chapters Book Club
Community and Join the Conversation